S0-AGA-189

Under a Prophet's Moon

R. T. Ray

R.T. Ray

Under a Prophet's Moon

This is a work of fiction. Names, characters and places are the product of the author's imagination, or are used fictionally. Any resemblance to any persons living or dead is entirely coincidental.

All rights reserved, including the right to reproduce any portion of this book, to include any form of electronic or mechanical means without the permission of the author.

Copyright © 2012 Raymond T. Ray

All rights reserved.

ISBN: 9780615854991

PRESS

Linthicum, Maryland

R.T. Ray

DR. BRIAN K. DRAGAN

physician and friend

Chapter One
Late August - 1912
The Royal Blue, en route to Baltimore

The engineer leaned into the wind roaring past the cab window. Only the heavy set of goggles protected his eyes from the cinder-laden wind. Withdrawing his watch he cocked an ear, timing the pounding of the locomotive's massive eighty-inch drive wheels against the steel rails. He scowled. A glance at the steam indicator only deepened his sour mood. He leaned forward, tapped a gloved finger against the steam indicator's glass window. The scowl deepened.

"You're going to break that damn glass if you're not mindful, H B."

The engineer, a grizzly old veteran, looked across to the young fireman. As usual Hank, his fireman of six months, was preoccupied putting a match to a half-smoked stogie. Hands cupped around the match flame, failed to hide the crooked grin hanging on the fireman's cinder-smudged face.

"Bah!" the engineer retorted. He spat a generous helping of tobacco juice into the strategically placed coffee can. With the back of his hand he wiped the thin line of spittle oozing from the corner of his mouth. He glared; first at the young fireman, then back at the gauge.

"Can you blame me now?" Without waiting for a response he growled, "This here's a passenger train for God's sake! Not some grimy old coal drag. Damn them loggerheads in Baltimore. Don't they know anything about railroading?"

The reference was to the change of orders, consigning a flatcar to *his* train. A highly unusual move – consigning a flatcar to a passenger train – even more unusual when one considered the train was The Royal Blue, the B&O's premier passenger train. The flatcar's cargo consisted of a lone, rectangular-shaped packing crate. Securely lashed and covered by heavy canvas, it had been added over the engineer's objection during the stop at the Point of Rocks Station.

"This old girl's a thoroughbred," the engineer boasted, his gaze sweeping across the array of levers, valves and gauges. "A Pacific. Fast too, but dammit she's not made to pull heavy loads. Certainly not on this grade." His eye returned to the speed indicator gauge. "How am I expected to keep to a schedule under these conditions? Just you tell me that."

Hank's reply was lost in the clanking of the firebox doors, as they swung open to accept another offering of coal.

The locomotive was racing skyward, past mixed stands of oak and pinery, toward the summit at Grinder's Ridge. Still, it would be a long ascent with several sweeping curves, further draining the engine of its rapidly dwindling water supply. Already the engine's twin water gauges hovered perilously near the empty mark. A short length of pipe in hand, the fireman gave a precautionary rap against the tender's iron plating. He received a hollow thud in reply.

"Better pull off when we reach Grinder's Ridge," he yelled over the roar of the engine, "else we'll not make it to Relay."

"Good God Almighty!" the engineer cursed. "What else can go wrong?"

Grinder's Ridge was a stark, desolate way station consisting of a few outbuildings of rough-sawn planks and still fewer inhabitants. It owed its meager existence to the lone water tower; a giant wooden structure that served as the daily reward for thirsty, heavily laden freights, once they had crested the torturous grade. Sleek passenger trains, such as The Royal Blue, routinely ignored the mountaintop way station, preferring instead the village of Relay, which lay a scant twelve miles beyond. There the train crews could top off at their leisure, while waiting for eastbound passengers to board.

"Sheer incompetence!" the engineer growled. He snapped the cover of the pocket watch closed, and returned it to the breast pocket of his bib overalls. "By God, that's what it is. Sheer incompetence!"

Hank fought to hold his tongue. If anything, H B was a stickler for keeping to a schedule, and was known for his fiery outbursts should things not go exactly to his liking. This wasn't the time to remind him that it had been his decision not to take on water at Point of Rocks, not the added drag of the flatcar, that resulted in the nearly depleted water tank.

"No sense getting all riled up, H B. This old girl has pulled you through tougher runs than this. We'll make up the time when we get on the flats."

"You're right there," the engineer conceded. His voice softened somewhat, but still the scowl refused to completely fade. "But, what I'd like to know is, what's so all-fired important that we had to take on that damn flatcar in the first place. That's freight! Not fitting for a passenger run. It's undignified, I tell you. What if another crew sees us toting that thing about? Why I'd be the laughing stock of the entire eastern division, that's what I'd be. I'd like to know who's responsible for this. I'd tell them a thing or two." He rechecked his watch. "Damnation! We're still a good seven minutes behind schedule."

Hank removed his cap, wiped his sweaty brow with the back of his arm. "If it's blame you're looking to lay on, you can squarely place it on them highbrows in the club car. Surely it's their fault."

The engineer's ears pricked. "Highbrows?" This was the first he had heard of this. "What are you talking about? What highbrows?"

"Why, the Wright brothers, of course. Haven't you heard? The newspaper's been full of their exploits. That crate we're a-hauling belongs to them. The way I hear tell it, they've got some newfangled aeroplane packed inside."

"Bah!" the engineer sneered, dispensing another well-aimed stream of tobacco juice into the coffee can. "Don't you believe it. Probably nothing more than some fancy furniture one of the company's directors shipped back from Europe."

"Maybe ... maybe not. But I'll tell you this," Hank jerked a thumb towards the rear of the train, "whatever is packed away in that crate, it's powerful. And it's all done up so secret-like to boot."

The engineer squinted, turning his brow into a mass of furrowed lines. "Secret-like? What in tarnation do you mean, all done up secret-like?"

"OK, maybe secret isn't the correct word. Secure is more like it. Dammit, H B, didn't you inspect that car at all before you signed? It's got priority shipment stenciled all over that damn tarp, and there's enough government seals to choke a mule."

"Government seals?" The engineer's voice took on an almost reverent tone. "Is that so?"

In his haste to leave Point of Rocks and regain the lost time, he had merely glanced at the new orders before affixing his signature. Any engineer worth his salt would point out, there hadn't been time enough to inspect the flatcar, not if he was expected to arrive in Baltimore on schedule. Now, with the Wright brothers aboard and a top-secret government cargo in tow, things were looking up. He inched the throttle back another notch, smiled. A high priority consignment, especially one laden down with government seals, might be turned to his advantage. Certainly it would silence any stigma of an ungainly flatcar being attached to his train, should the occasion arise.

"Yep," the fireman continued, "the way I hear tell it, the Wrights wouldn't have it any other way. Had the yardmaster at Point of Rocks uncouple the car off an eastbound freight, while they telegraphed Washington. You mark my words ... that's why that flatcar's coupled to your train ... it's not some company director's furniture we're a-pulling. This is all the Wright brothers doings."

"You think so, Hank?" The old engineer scratched the gray stubble at the tip of his chin. "Mmmmmmm, I don't know. Persuading someone to change a shipping order on the wing, that's not an easy chore. For one thing that would take moxie, or a powerful dose of persuasion on somebody's part."

"Depend on it," Hank replied. "Don't forget, it's the Wright brothers we're adealing with. That's the beauty of it. The Wrights get to ride in comfort, and still keep a eye on that precious crate of theirs at the same time. From the look of things, I'd say the Wright brothers and that fancy crate will be with us all the way to Union Station."

The scowl returned. "I've got no say in that. Orders are orders." The old engineer ran a thumb behind the strap of his overalls and gave a boastful tug. "But, as you rightly point out, this here's my train. As soon as we clear the last switch at Relay, there's a level stretch of mainline, running clean near to Baltimore. I'm going to turn the old girl loose." He motioned toward the firebox door. "You just keep that box well-stoked, and mind you, this time keep an eye on the steam gauge."

"This time? Me?"

"I'll not have it bantered about the east end that H. B. Twining can't keep to a schedule." The engineer turned, stuck his head out the cab window. "Get ready now," he called back, "we're coming up on Grinder's Ridge."

* * *

The task of replenishing the locomotive's supply of water was completed in short order. The engineer lost no time in releasing the Johnson bar and easing the throttle forward. The Royal Blue crept slowly back onto the mainline.

The remainder of the run was uneventful. As it approached the Patapsco River, the train slowed, hissed its way across the great stone viaduct and came to a halt in front of the train station in the village of Relay. Alerted by telegraph, a group of local dignitaries had assembled on the station's platform, accompanied by the hastily assembled members of town's brass band. Leading the delegation was Mayor Hightower, banker Foxworth, followed by John Willaby, editor of *The Sentinel*, the village newspaper.

Amid the sweltering heat of an August sun, barking dogs, and the blaring strains of a military march, Mayor Hightower stepped forward.

"Welcome gentlemen, welcome." He grasped the hand of each Wright brother as he descended the club car steps, giving it a vigorous shake. "Welcome to our fair village of Relay. I'm Mayor Cornelius P. Hightower."

"Why, thank you, Mayor," Orville Wright said. Removing his bowler, he waved, acknowledging the gathering crowd before turning back to face the mayor. "I'm sure I speak for my brother when I say, it is an honor to be in your most gracious village."

"The pleasure is entirely mine, gentlemen, I assure you." However, as he spoke a confused expression crept into the face of Mayor Hightower. He edged closer. "Mind you, Mr. Wright," he said, in a somewhat somber tone, "the townspeople will be a bit dispirited."

"Dispirited? Why is that?"

"Why, it's your aeroplane, of course. We were under the impression you would be escorting it personally to Washington. I ... er that is we, were looking forward to seeing it. Especially Mr. Willaby, of our village newspaper." He gestured toward John Willaby, who stood off to the side, accompanied by the town photographer, the latter burdened down by a rather large cumbersome camera, mounted on an unyielding tripod. Willaby, notebook at the ready, waved.

The mayor continued. "Mr. Willaby entertains high hopes of obtaining a front page accounting of your latest flight, perhaps a photograph of you posing next to your wondrous machine if that's agreeable."

"Always glad to accommodate the journalists, Mayor."

Mayor Hightower's eyes traveled to a group of small boys, who having ventured as close as they dared to the famous duo, stood nervously twitching about. He sighed.

"Then there are the children to consider." He reached out, and with a well-practiced politician's flare, ruffled the hair of the nearest boy, a scruffy, barefoot lad of ten years. "Like so many of our fine citizens, the lads were hoping you would bring your fabulous flying machine along."

Laying a reassuring hand on the Mayor's shoulder Orville Wright chuckled. "We *did* bring our flying machine, Mayor."

"You did?"

"Most certainly. It's right there," said Orville, giving a nod of his head towards the rear of the train, "lashed to that flatcar."

"Flatcar?" The confused expression etched in Mayor Hightower's features only deepened. "What flatcar?"

The brothers turned to follow the mayor's mystified gaze.

"Are you blind, Mayor? That flat-"

Mouth agape, Orville Wright's reply was frozen in mid-sentence. Unable to believe his eyes He stared at the vacant space once occupied by the flatcar.

He blinked in disbelief. The flatcar along with its valuable cargo had vanished.

Chapter Two
The Wednesday Night Club

News of the missing flatcar quickly spread throughout the village. It seemed only natural therefore that it would be the main topic of conversation at weekly gathering of The Wednesday Night Club. Although not a true club - at least not in the normal sense of the word - The Wednesday Night Club did, as its name implied meet every Wednesday night. It could more accurately be described as a loosely knit, social gathering of some of the town's more colorful citizens.

As usual, The Viaduct Hotel's dining room provided the setting. Missing from his usual position at the far end of the table was John Willaby. Willaby had excused himself, citing the urgent need to publish a special edition detailing the mysterious disappearance of the Wright Flyer. Also not in attendance was Sheriff Higgins, the town's peace officer. Although possessing no jurisdictional authority outside the village, Sheriff Higgins had nevertheless volunteered to ride out in the direction of Grinder's Ridge in hopes of locating the missing railroad car.

Their places were filled by the brothers Orville and Wilbur Wright. Colonel Musgrave, the club's self proclaimed leader, having spied the brothers entering the dining room, quickly rose and intercepted them.

He insisted they join the group and partake in the discussion. Being that it was the height of the dinner hour, and there wasn't another table to be had, the brothers readily acquiesced.

"May I introduce your dining companions?" Colonel Musgrave said, as the group went about the process of rearranging chairs to accommodate the new arrivals. "Foremost is our town's post mistress, the lovely Miss Victoria Byron."

Orville Wright gave a polite, courteous bow then took Victoria's outstretched hand. "A pleasure, Miss Byron," he said.

Across from Victoria sat an elderly priest in a timeworn cassock. Colonel Musgrave laid his hand on the priest's shoulder. "Next is Father Meguiar, Priest of St. Albans."

The elderly priest paused in his swirling of the dregs of a glass of Old Stoudt. He looked up. "Ah, a pleasure to be knowing ye, lads." His brow wrinkled. "Wright," he said, signaling for a refill, "that would be a fine old English name, would it not?"

The two brothers nodded in unison.

"Attended seminary school with a lad by the name of Wright," the priest continued, "though that was many years ago. Don't suppose there's much chance yourself being related?"

Orville Wright shook his head. "No, not likely, Father. We're dyed-in-the-wool Protestants. Been so for generations. However, our grandfather on our mother's side is a minister in the United Brethren Church, if that's any consolation."

Father Meguiar nodded and returned to his lager.

Colonel Musgrave turned next to Calder who was seated to the right of Victoria. "And lastly, gentlemen, may I present Ret. Inspector Calder Donahue. The Inspector's recently purchased the old Burrow's estate and currently enjoying the life of the landed gentry."

Calder rose and shook each brother's hand in turn. "It's an honor to meet you, gentlemen," he said. "Like many of my colleagues, I've followed the tales of your daring exploits in the newspapers. I must say they have kept us on the edge of our seats on more than one occasion."

"Inspector?" Orville Wright echoed. "A police inspector?" Assured that that was the case, he said, "Then surely providence has seen fit to intercede on our behalf. You are just the man we need."

"Inspector is a purely honorary title," Calder replied. "As the colonel so correctly pointed out, I've retired."

"A pity," Orville lamented. "For at the moment a good detective is what we require. Still, being familiar with the countryside, perhaps you might see fit to counsel us on how best to proceed with our dilemma."

"Very kind of you, Mr. Wright. But I'm sure the railroad has competent investigators at their disposal, and they will undoubtedly spare no expense to get to the bottom of this mystery."

"Poppycock!" Victoria said. She wigwagged a finger. "Don't you believe a word he says, gentlemen. In my estimation Inspector Donahue is the perfect solution to your dilemma."

Calder held up a hand in protest. "Now, now Victoria, I-"

"Oh, rot! Now you know it's true, only you are too modest to admit it. He may no longer be in active employment of the metropolitan police," she said, turning back to the two brothers, "but if it's a detective you need, Inspector Donahue is your man. Make no doubt about it. Why only last autumn he solved the most puzzling of cases." She looked to the old priest for conformation. "Isn't that so, Father?"

"Aye, child," Father Meguiar nodded, "that it is."

"Speaking of puzzlements," Colonel Musgrave interrupted. His comments were directed to the new arrivals who were now seated at the far end of the table. "What I consider a puzzlement is the state of the railroads. In this modern era we live in, I find it extraordinary singular that they could manage to misplace something as large as a railcar. Not to mention that marvelous flying machine of yours."

Orville Wright sighed in response. "A puzzlement? Indeed it is indeed that," he said. "As for the flatcar, I can't imagine what has become of it. As you have suggested, Mr.-"

"Colonel," Colonel Musgrave quickly corrected, wiping the tips of his great walrus mustache with the back of a large bony hand. "Colonel Rutherford H. Musgrave, at your service, sir."

Now it was true Colonel Musgrave had been a military man. In reality he had never risen above the honorable, but somewhat lowly rank of corporal. It was only a chance error in *The Sentinel* - a self-authored article chronicling his bravery in the War Between the States that elevated Musgrave to the lofty rank of colonel. Musgrave reveled in the newly acquired title and saw no need to revert to his former rank, and, in Relay villagers were permitted their little idiosyncrasies.

Orville Wright gave a nervous smile. "Yes. Well, as the inspector has suggested Colonel, the railroad authorities have been most attentive to our plight. It's their belief that the car had accidentally uncoupled. An unfortunate occurrence, but not unheard of. All the eastbound trains have been alerted. Speeds have been reduced, least they collide with the wayward car."

Colonel Musgrave's head bobbed in agreement. "Yes, yes. A wise precaution. Of course," he said, stroking the tips of his mustache in what could only be described as a boastful manner. "Under my command such transgressions would not have occurred. Posting of sentries and timely inspections would have prevented the loss of such a valuable piece of equipment." He leaned back, puffed contently on his cigar. "Don't you agree, Inspector?"

Command? Calder stifled a chuckle. He could not begin to envision what possible bizarre, chaotic circumstances would have to transpire that would place Musgrave in command of a passenger train. The man was full of himself. Still, Colonel Musgrave's dreams of self-grandeur were harmless enough and it served no useful purpose to argue the point. Calder merely gave a polite nod, smiled amiably. "Most assuredly not while under your capable watch, Colonel."

Musgrave, pleased with Calder's assessment, called for a fresh round of drinks.

It was midway through the meal when Orville Wright raised his glass. "A toast," he said. "To our hosts. Never, since our departure from our workshop in Dayton, have my brother and I experienced such pleasant company." He turned his glass to Victoria, "Or enjoyed the presence of such a rare beauty."

Victoria, her cheeks blushing a dusty pink, gave a polite smile in return. Her smile quickly dwindled however when she observed when a white robed figure, followed by several similarly dressed individuals, entered the dining room.

"That man," Orville asked, turning to follow Victoria's stare. "Who is he?"

"What man?" Father Meguiar said, surveying the crowded dining room.

"That fellow in the tattered robe," Orville said. "Earlier this afternoon he gave me the most awful glare when we passed in the hotel foyer. His stare chills the bone."

"Oh, him." Father Meguiar chuckled. "Pay him little mind, Mr. Wright. He's of no consequence."

"He seems vaguely familiar. I can't help feeling we've met before. What can you tell me about him?"

Father Meguiar shrugged. "Only a wee bit, Lad. Calls himself Brother Nathan. Messenger of the true Prophet."

"What church does he represent?"

"No church you'd know," said Higgins. "They call themselves Brothers of the Heavenly Clan. Set up a bunch of raggedy tents several days ago, in a field just out of town. Been whipping up his flock ever since."

Sensing the conversation shifting away from his control, Colonel Musgrave, as was his custom, thumped a large bony hand on the table. "This fellow, Brother Nathan, puts me in the mind of a fellow I once served with. From Pennsylvania I believe. Now if you were looking for a character, there was a character, a real fire and brimstone preacher if there ever was one. Why I recall one time-"

"Preacher?" Victoria gave a mock shudder. "Brother Nathan is no preacher. If you ask me, Prophet of Doom is a more fitting title. He gives me the willies, what with that unkempt hair of his and those sharp, penetrating eyes. I for one shall be only too pleased when we are rid of him and his flock." She turned to Orville. "Did you know, Mr. Wright, that he's telling everyone who will listen that that wonderful aeroplane of yours will bring on the end of civilization? He says bombs will rain down from the heavens like brimstone. That both sinner and non-sinner alike will suffer the wrath of an angry God."

"Armageddon will descend upon us, to use his exact words," said Father Meguiar. Having given up his quest for his ever-elusive pack of cigarettes, he took to looking longingly around the table.

Taking the hint, Calder slid his fresh tin of Turks across the table. "Bless ye, lad," the old priest said, seizing the tin and fingering out a cigarette.

Wilbur Wright, who had been sitting quietly, staring at the untouched plate before him, suddenly looked up. "Armageddon?" he said in a thin, rather weak voice. "That's a commonly held misconception. We've encountered such beliefs many times in our travels, haven't we, Orville?"

The younger Wright nodded in agreement.

"It's nonsense, of course," Wilbur continued with rising vengeance. "Our machine's role is purely that of observation, with a secondary mission of photographing. The machine's occupants are merely observers of the destruction occurring below them. They take no active part in the conflict."

The effort proved taxing and Wilbur broke into a coughing fit. With a trembling hand, he reached for the water goblet. After a few moments the coughing subsided and he was able to continue. "This drivel about dropping bombs on the civilian population is nothing more that a mare's nest. We'll never witness such dastardly deeds, even if we live a thousand lifetimes."

Signaling a passing waitress to refill his brother's glass, Orville said, "You'll have to forgive my brother, Father Meguiar. Wilbur's a hopeless romantic. He envisions pilots as gallant knights of the sky, instilled with a code of medieval chivalry too moral to permit such acts of barbarism to occur."

"What is your prediction, Mr. Wright?" It was Calder who spoke.

Orville did not respond immediately, but seemed to ponder the question. After a few moments of quiet deliberation, he spoke. "I must confess, Inspector, I'm the pragmatic member of the family. As much as I would like it to be other, one must simply face facts. I'm afraid someday our invention, no matter what our wishes are, will be turned into an instrument of destruction."

Wilbur lowered his glass to the table. "I'd beg to differ-"

"Now, now, Wilbur, it's true," Orville said, with a gentle dismissive wave of the hand. He turned back to Calder. "Granted, such acts are technically not feasible, at least not at this time. This is due primarily to the lack of lifting power of today's engines, not to some higher moral thinking. I fear it may not remain so for very long."

Calder reached for his drink. "I'm forced to agree with you, Mr. Wright. Newspaper accounts predict a great calamity is looming in Europe. Some say maybe even a great war is possible."

Orville nodded in somber accord. "An accurate assessment, Inspector. My brother and I just returned from an extensive aeronautical exhibition in several European capitols. Europe is in a state of turmoil. Brother Nathan's prediction may come to fruition. America would be wise to prepare itself for such eventualities."

Further conversation was prevented by the arrival of Sheriff Higgins. Orville, glancing over Calder's shoulder, was first to observe Higgins approaching their table. He quickly rose to greet him. "Did you find our missing flatcar, Sheriff?"

Higgins looked to the two brothers. He shrugged his shoulders. "The flatcar, yes. It was still sitting at Grinder's Ridge siding when I got there."

"Thank God," sighed Orville. He slumped back into his chair, visibly relieved. "Our machine is safe."

"Not quite, Mr. Wright."

Orville looked up. "But you said-"

"Oh, the flatcar is there all right, that much is true. However I'm afraid all that's left of your flying machine is a empty shipping crate. Your aeroplane is gone."

"Gone! You mean stolen?"

Higgins nodded.

"How can that be? Surely someone at the way station would have noticed anyone removing something as large as an aeroplane from its crate. Surely they would have intervened."

"Sadly," Higgins said, "that's not the case here. Grinder's Ridge is a way station. Except for the water tower, it's not much more than a collection of wooden huts strung alongside the railroad tracks. There are times, when there is no track maintenance underway; the place is all but deserted. Now, I spoke with the caretaker, old man Grimes. He's getting to be old bones, I'm afraid he wasn't of much help. He remembers the Royal Blue stopping to take on water all right, but that's about it."

Orville's brow twisted in confusion. "You mean he didn't notice the flatcar wasn't coupled to the train when it departed the station?"

"No. And in his defense there was no reason he should have. The Royal Blue is a passenger train. One doesn't normally expect to see a flatcar attached to a passenger train. Besides, the rear of the train held no interest for him. It was conversation with the fireman and engineer old man Grimes was interested in ... and they were up front tending to the engine's needs. They were new faces. Being in such a desolate place, the caretaker was intent on catching up on the latest gossip from the outside world. When the train pulled out, he was content to stand at trackside and wave. There was no reason to check the siding for abandoned cars. With the train's departure, it was back to chores and currying time for the station's two mules."

The color drained from Orville Wright's features. He sank slowly back in his chair. For the second time this day he was too stunned to continue.

Calder used the lull to draw Higgins aside. When they were out of earshot of the table, he asked, "Purely as a matter of interest, in your opinion, was this a crime of opportunity or was it a planned heist?"

There was no hesitation on Higgins's part. "It's got all the earmarks of a well-planned scheme, all right. I don't see how it could be other. Too remote of a location and too many people involved to be anything else."

"Remote? Yes," Calder concluded. "I cannot imagine a more suitable location."

Higgins scratched his head in bewilderment. "What gets me is how the thieves knew the flatcar would be attached to the Royal Blue in the first place."

Calder was forced to agree. "Good point. It's common knowledge freights regularly stop at Grinder's Ridge. On the other hand, a passenger train like the Royal Blue is a different matter. What is clear however is that someone has managed to pull off a most cunning act of thievery, and did so under the railroad's very own nose."

"What do the Wrights have to say about it, Inspector?"

"They've only just joined us. I haven't had the opportunity to question them fully on the matter. Now, what about this caretaker, Grimes. You spoke with him. What's your impression? Any possibility he may have been involved?"

Higgins shook his head. "I honestly don't think so, Inspector. Long in the tooth, seventy-five, if he's a day." Higgins tapped his temple, "And a bit substandard, if you know what I mean. He seemed genuinely surprised when I showed up, even more when he learned an empty flatcar was sitting abandoned on the siding."

They slowly began making their way back to rejoin the group.

"Your next step?" inquired Calder.

"Get some dinner." Higgins slowly arched his back, attempting to work out the stiffness from his muscles. "Must be getting old myself," he said. "Two hours on horseback has about done me in. I'll say this, whoever made off with the Wright's aeroplane, did me the courtesy of doing it outside my jurisdiction. My involvement in the matter is over. It's the railroad's and the government's worry from here on out."

R.T. Ray

Chapter Three
Old Dunham House
The following morning

Calder was in the library, attempting to bring some semblance of order to the massive volume of books accrued by his recent purchase of Old Dunham House. His task was interrupted by the arrival of the housekeeper, Mrs. Chaffinch.

Mrs. Chaffinch was a smallish woman, luminous skin, with gray hair drawn tightly back into a bun. Her cheeks, rosy pink with excitement bore a telltale smear of flour, for it was Tuesday and at Old Dunham House Tuesdays were normally reserved for the weekly baking. She gingerly placed a visiting card on the end table and stepped back. "Beg pardon Inspector but there's a gentleman, a very distinguished gentleman, at the door to see you."

Calder noting the uncharacteristic excitement mounting in the housekeeper's voice, looked up from his work. "Very well, Mrs. C. Am I permitted to know this very distinguished gentleman's name?"

Mrs. Chaffinch drew herself up to her full five foot two inch height. "Indeed sir," her voice bubbled over in awe struck disbelief. "It's none other than the famous flyer, Mr. Orville Wright, himself

Calder picked up the card. "Mr. Wright? Well, well. By all means show him in, Mrs. C, show him in.

21

We mustn't keep such a prominent visitor waiting at our doorstep."

"No, sir," Mrs. Chaffinch said as she turned toward the library doorway.

As she turned the knob on the library door, Calder called after her. "Oh, Mrs. C. Perhaps you might serve coffee, and if there are any left, some of those delicious crumpets of yours."

Mrs. Chaffinch nodded in approval. "The hired lads had a fine fling at them." She planted her hand on her hip in a mock gesture of disapproval, "but I've managed to set aside a wee portion for this afternoon's tea. Don't you fret none, sir it will only take a moment to prepare a proper tea." With that she turned and hurried out the door.

Calder set the book he was holding aside. He had not quite become accustomed to the ritual of afternoon tea, a simple meat sandwich and beer was more to his liking. Still, cooks of Mrs. C's caliber were hard to come by and he was slowly adapting to her continental ways. He rose and hastily began clearing the stack of books from the wingback chair in preparation of his guest's arrival.

Moments later Orville Wright was ushered into the library.

"Sorry to intrude uninvited, Inspector," he said, handing his hat to Mrs. Chaffinch.

"Not at all, Mr. Wright," replied Calder. "Welcome to my home."

"You are too kind, Inspector. I'll be brief and come right to the point. I wasn't quite forthright at last night's dinner, and I would like to set things right before my brother and I depart."

"Depart? So you have decided to return to Dayton, after all?"

"Oh, no, Inspector, not to Dayton. Wilbur and I have decided our only course is to continue our journey with all possible haste." He cast a glance at the long case clock. "We have reserved passage on the afternoon train to Washington."

"But surely, without your machine there is little need in continuing your journey."

"To the contrary, Inspector. A 25,000 dollar contract hinges on the ability of the company that can delivery of a heavier than air flying machine to the War Department. I intend to claim that contract!"

"Without your aeroplane I don't see how that would be possible."

Orville Wright paced about the room. "It won't be an easy task. This is an important contract, one The Wright Aeroplane Company can ill afford to forego. Above all else we must persuade the Ordinance Department to grant us additional time; time enough to recover our machine."

Calder gestured his guest toward the empty wingback. "I see. Your haste to get to Washington is understandable. Yet I'm puzzled, Mr. Wright. If time is of the essence, why didn't you catch the morning train? To linger in Relay merely to apologize for not being more forthright at last night's dinner? No, no, that is unacceptable. There is more to the tale, is there not?"

"Very perspective of you, Inspector," Oliver Wright replied settling into the chair. "You're quite correct, of course. There's no sense beating about the bush. The true purpose of my visit is to seek your professional assistance. I've come prepared to offer you a proposition."

"To find your aeroplane, no doubt."

"Yes, but it's more than the mere loss of the aeroplane that concerns me."

Conversation waned as Mrs. Chaffinch entered the room bearing a tray laden with delicate tea sandwiches, cakes and a silver carafe of coffee.

"Just set it on the table, Mrs. C. We'll serve ourselves."

Mrs. Chaffinch deposited the tray on the side table and after a smile in Orville Wright's direction, quietly exited the room.

As the door closed, Orville Wright turned to Calder. "As I had said, Inspector, I want to be frank and aboveboard. If there is to be any hope of soliciting your assistance in recovering our aeroplane, you must have a complete and accurate accounting."

Calder nodded in agreement. "That would be most helpful, Mr. Wright."

"I think I should start by saying the machine we were escorting wasn't a typical Wright Flyer."

"I gathered as much. The mode of shipping made that quite obvious."

Orville Wright chuckled, turned an empty palm. "The attachment of a flatcar to a passenger train? A bureaucratic decision, Inspector. The government bean counters seeking the most expedient method of transportation."

Calder nodded and Orville Wright continued. "Now, as to the aeroplane, it's a 1912 "EX" model with several innovations incorporated into its design." He reached for a crumpet. "By the way, "EX" stands for exhibition, not experimental. The airframe was derived from the 1910 Model R Baby Wright, a small, fast, single-seat aeroplane built for exhibition flying. We reduced the gap between the wings, thereby substantially reducing the amount of rigging wire. This, in turn, reduced drag and allowed speeds approaching 55 miles per hour with a standard thirty horsepower engine. In addition the wings have been lengthened providing more lift and better control."

He paused, allowing Calder time to appreciate the accomplishment. Accepting the offer of one of the tray's dainty sandwiches, he continued. "The most important modification is the rudimentary bomb release mechanism-"

"Bomb release? I should have thought your brother would be dead set against such a device be installed. He made his views well known on that subject last evening over dinner."

"Oh he is." Orville paused, gave a hopeless gesture. "It's no secret, The Wright Aeroplane Company has suffered a financial set back and no longer produces the same quality of aeroplanes it once did. To be quite frank, Inspector we're pinning our company's future on this highly modified "EX" model to regain stability and our company's lost reputation. That is the only reason Wilbur agreed to the modification. The device is similar to the one the French are reported to have developed. The government wants to evaluate it before the Hague Conference takes a stand against dropping explosives from aeroplanes."

"Should you be telling me these things, Mr. Wright?"

"Strictly speaking?" Orville Wright shrugged. "Perhaps not. It's not for public disclosure, but under the present circumstances, I see no harm in taking you, and if you so deem, Sheriff Higgins into your confidence. Being familiar with the countryside and its people, you two are my best hope in retrieving the machine."

Calder settled his cup to its saucer. "I appreciate your candor, Mr. Wright, but as I understand it, the aeroplane was being transported under government supervision and seal."

Wilbur Wright nodded. "Yes, that is so. Still, I don't see how that has a bearing on any private arrangement our company may enter in with you."

"The government may take a different view. The authorities have not only a national, but also a contractual investment in your aeroplane, and most importantly, more resources at their disposal than I could possibly muster. I suggest you leave it in their capable hands. I'm sure the authorities will be quite diligent in their investigation of the matter."

"Perhaps so, Inspector, but I'm a simple man, I prefer the more direct approach. I'd rather do business based on a handshake and a look into a man's eye, not on a signature on a fancy piece of paper. Now if it's a matter of money that concerns you." He reached into his jacket's inside pocket and removed his wallet. "The Wright Bros. Aeroplane Company is prepared to offer you a substantial retainer. We are an honorable company. Be assured you will be compensated for your labor as well as any and all expenses incurred."

Calder held up his hand. "It's not that. I find the theft of your aeroplane most intriguing. Money?" He looked around at his comfortable, well furnished surroundings. "You will find my fee will be quite small. No, if I accept your offer, Mr. Wright, it will be with the understanding that I will be able to move about with a free hand."

"You have my word on it, Inspector. Wilbur and I will be departing on the afternoon train, so we will pose no hindrance to your investigation. You are free to act on our behalf as you see fit."

Calder reached out and the two shook hands. "Then I accept your offer. Calder extracted a Turk cigarette from the tin and tapped it lightly against the side of the tin. "Now, down to business. Tell me about this machine of yours and the events leading up to its theft. Leave nothing aside, even the small detail may be of importance."

"I'll endeavor to do so, Inspector." Holding his cup for Calder to refresh, he began his tale. "It started several months ago. The Department of the Army issued a contract for a prototype of an aeroplane, a new type of machine they call a bomber. There is a 25,000 dollar contract awaiting the winner, but that is merely a start up contract with the promise of larger amounts to follow."

Taking the carafe, Calder refilled Orville's cup and then his own. "A goodly amount," he observed.

"That it is," agreed Orville. "Wilbur and I elected to ship our entry by railcar. We decided to personally oversee its shipment. As we were traveling by freight train there were only the barest of accommodations, we were forced to share quarters with the train's crew in the caboose." Removing a telegram from his jacket pocket and handing it to Calder, he said. Events altered when we reached Point of Rocks, Maryland. The stationmaster came rushing out of his office, telegraph in hand. The date of the aeroplane's demonstration had been moved ahead by a two full days, severally eliminating most, if not all the available assembly and flight-testing time. It seems Washington wanted the demonstration of the plane's performance to coincide with the conference of heads of state gathering at nearby Camp Meade."

Calder nodded, striking a match and putting it to the cigarette. He exhaled. "Go on," he urged.

"Not much more to add, Inspector. Except to say I now see I should have insisted we stick with our original plan. Oh, I'm not saying we wouldn't have ruffled the tail feathers of some Washington bureaucrats, but at least the machine wouldn't had been stolen."

Calder returned the telegraph. "Perhaps, Mr. Wright, but I don't see how that would have prevented the theft. The freight would have stopped at Grinder's Ridge to take on water just as the Royal Blue did."

"Ah, but that was the beauty of it, Inspector. The flatcar containing our machine was situated in front of the caboose. It was under constant observation. It would have been impossible for anyone to uncouple the flatcar or make off with the machine without our knowledge."

"I see your point," Calder said. "Very unfortunate that you chose not to stay with that arrangement."

"It wasn't by choice, Inspector."

"No?" Calder looked over the rim of his cup. "This mornings newspaper suggested you telegraphed Washington, demanding a more accommodating mode of transportation. One more suited for your station."

"Pure poppycock, Inspector. We were quite prepared to travel in the caboose, all the way to Washington if need be. I'll admit four grown men confined in a caboose are not ideal accommodations, but rustic accommodations are nothing new to either my brother of myself. We endured far worse accommodations during our flight experiments at Kitty Hawk. The train crew was amiable and we got along quite well. The attachment to the Royal Blue was at the government insistence. The railroad was forced to accept the government's demand to attach the flatcar to The Royal Blue."

Calder nodded. "I understand your problem, Mr. Wright. There is one other point. Couldn't you continue to follow your previous procedure, that is keep your machine under a watchful eye while it was coupled to the Royal Blue?"

"No. The last car of the Royal Blue was the observation car. It's a very fashionable gathering place and passengers often filled it to capacity. Even there the only place one could obtain an unobstructed view of the flatcar is from the car's observation platform." He smiled. "A popular rendezvous for young spooners, unfortunately they didn't take kindly to our constant intrusions."

Setting his cup aside, Calder settled back into the chair. "Where were you and your brother when the machine was stolen? Understand, I only ask this for clarification so that I can better comprehend the problem."

"Certainly, Inspector. No offense taken. Let's see... Grinder's Ridge, I believe we were in the dinning car. Yes, now that I think of it, I recall we were engaged in conversation with an elderly gentleman, a Mr. Delahaye. A delightful gentleman, he served as a balloonist during the war years. He shared intriguing accountings from some of his more harrowing adventures, tethered over the Union lines. Naturally he was fascinated by the principals of powered flight."

"This Mr. Delahaye sounds like a most amazing fellow."

"Oh, that he is, Inspector. Perhaps you should look him up. He's staying at the Viaduct Hotel." Orville Wright chuckled. "His tales were such that I'm afraid we lingered longer than we should have. The maître d was forced to render us a gentle reminder that there were other quests waiting to dine."

"So," said Calder in summation, "you were not·in a position to be able to witness the actual theft of your machine."

"Unfortunately no. But that was merely the beginning of our dilemma. You see, there is another problem more pressing than the theft of our machine." He paused, "My brother's health."

Calder nodded in agreement. "I understand. He did appear a little frail and out of sorts at dinner last night." This was an understatement, as the elder Wright seemed a rather sickly individual, merely a shadow of his more robust younger brother.

"You're being too kind, Inspector." Orville Wright produced a nervous smile. "I'm afraid it's more serious than that. You witnessed that coughing episode last evening?

Calder nodded.

"The lingering ravages of typhoid, I'm told. In Washington I hope to procure the latest medical treatment for my brother, perhaps gain admittance to the Weldor Sanatorium. I have it on good authority they employ only the most modern of treatments. So you can understand my desire to get there with all haste."

The case clock chimed eleven. Orville Wright rose. "It's getting late and I have a train to catch, Inspector. I'll detain you no further."

At the door the two men shook hands. "Advise me where I may contact you once you have obtained lodgings in Washington. Meanwhile, rest assured the sheriff and I will make every effort to locate your machine and return it to your care."

Orville nodded. "I will, Inspector. Until then I leave it in your capable hands."

Mrs. Chaffinch, hair freshly brushed and her cheeks cleansed of every trace of baking flour, stood off to the side; the renowned aviator's hat in her hand. Accepting his hat, Orville Wright did not fail to note the change.

"And now Mrs. Chaffinch, I must not take my leave without first complimenting you on your extraordinary baking skills. Never have I tasted such a delicacy as your crumpets. And those sandwiches..." He held three fingers to his lips in salute. "They were delightful!"

The pink hue in Mrs. Chaffinch's cheeks deepened.

Chapter Four
A Visit From An Angel
Construction site, alley, rear of the bank

It was well past midnight when Clem Simpson stumbled past the flickering flames of the kerosene fired road torches. He paused, steadying himself against an abandoned packing crate. "Damn rotgut," he grumbled. Like the rest of his body, his speech was hampered by the intoxicating effects of Big Apple wine, contained in the bottle in his hand.

His head reeled, his vision blurred as he slowly sank into the pile of excelsior spilling from the abandoned crate. Laying the bottle to the side, he struggled, attempting to extract the cloth sack of tobacco, along with a packet of cigarette papers, from his shirt pocket. He spilled half of the bag's precious contents unto the ground. Uttering a string of profanities he gave up, letting the bag slowly slip from his fingers.

Clem slumped backward. His last thoughts before Morpheus overtook him were; *If I only had fifty cent more, I could've had another bottle.* An alcohol induced smile appeared on his weathered face. *Or better still, the pleasures of the town whore.*

* * *

"I've seen the angels of death!" a wild-eyed Clem Simpson declared, stumbling through the jail's doorway. Regaining his balance, he managed to half-staggered, half-hobbled across the structure's wooden floor until he reached the nearest cell door. Promptly entering its cramped confines, he slammed the iron door securely closed behind him. Collapsing on the cell's metal-framed cot he cowered in fear.

Sheriff Higgins looked across the desk to Calder and then back toward Clem. "What in damnation is going on?" he bellowed.

Clem, shaking uncontrollably, did not answer, at least his answer made no sense to an astonished Grandville Higgins. "Oh sweet Jesus," he wailed. "Lord, you've got to help me, Sheriff. I've seen the angels of death, and they were a-coming for me."

"Nonsense!" Higgins roared. "Have you been dipping into that rotgut them Kale boys are running again? I've warned you about them."

Clem, his eyes wide as saucers, gave a violent shake of his head. "No sir! Only natural *Sneaky Pete*, store bought and paid for, same as always. Now, you've gotta save me, Sheriff. Send for Father Meguiar, he'll know what to do."

Placing his coffee cup on the desk, Calder eased himself out of his chair and crossed the room. "Angels of death, you say?"

"That's right, Inspector," Clem declared, turning his attention to Calder. "Just as sure as I'm looking at you now, they were the angels of death."

"Maybe you had better start at the beginning, Clem. When did this all happen?"

"Last night."

"Last night?" Calder looked at the wall clock; the hands were approaching the nine a.m. mark. "Why did you wait so long to report it, Clem?"

Clem lowered his eyes in shame. "I reckon I musta got scared and passed out."

"That's understandable," consoled Calder. "Go on, tell me how this all came about."

Seeing he had a receptive ear, Clem nodded. "Well, sir, it was like this. I was on my way back to the stable. You know, Mr. Oney. He lets me lay myself down in the hay, as long as I promise not to smoke."

Calder nodded. It was common knowledge; Clem had no fixed address. *On the wing* was the police department's term for it. Home was wherever Clem hung his hat, and lately that had been the town livery stable. In exchange for mucking out the stalls, Clem received the occasional meal and use of a pile of hay for a bed.

"I got so plumb tuckered out. Couldn't make it all the way to Oney's. So, I sat myself down to rest a bit."

"Where?"

"In the alleyway, rear of the bank. I musta had more than I thought, cause I fell asleep on a pile of excelsior."

"Yes," Calder urged. "Go on."

"Well, sir, sometime later, I don't know exactly how long, I heard a noise." His head flicked back and forth, "Maybe it wasn't noise, more like voices. I can't rightly say for sure. Anyways I opened a eye and there they were, as sure as you're standing in front of me now."

"There who was?" said the sheriff, crossing the floor to join Calder.

"The angels of death," Clem said, his voice showing signs of irritation. "Dang, Sheriff, ain't you been listening at all?"

"We're listening, Clem," Calder said. "Now tell me, what did these angels of yours look like?"

Accepting a cigarette from Calder, Clem puffed for a few moments while he considered. Finally, he spoke. "Couldn't rightly make out their faces. They were all done up in their pearly white robes and carrying the torch of truth. They were a-searching for me; as sure as I'm sitting here. Make no mistake, Inspector, they've come to carry me across the River

Jordan. I can feel it in my bones."

"How do you know that?"

"One, the one with a fiery halo, bent down, looked me straight in the eye and shown the light of truth in my face. He said they should take me with them. No," the other angel said. "Ain't got time. Leave him there, we'll come back for him later."

Clem drew his knees up under his chin. Despite the heat of the day he was shivering. He looked sheepish at Calder. "I don't mind admitting, Inspector, I was scared, plenty scared. Right down to the tip of my toes. I think I must have passed out then, for when I next woke it was daylight."

Calder turned to Higgins. "You still keep that bottle Doctor O'Keefe sent over in the desk."

The reference was to a large medical bottle that Doctor O'Keefe had affixed a prescription label in Clem's name, calling it Dr. O'Keefe's Medical Elixir, and dispatched it over to the jail.

The bottle contained no medication, no elixir, no wondrous compound or drug. What it did contain was pure, 100 proof Maryland rye whiskey. Higgins knew this of course, as the rye's fine aroma was unmistakable. He had often partaken of the very same whiskey at Dr. O'Keefe's weekly card game.

Higgins had often described it as *the smoothest sipping whiskey this side of the Alleghenies.*

"That's reserved for emergencies only," said Higgins.

"Well," Calder said looking at Clem's trembling hands and confused mutterings, "I think this qualifies as a medical emergency, don't you?"

Higgins reluctantly nodded and turning started for the desk.

In short order the whisky worked its magic and Clem with a fresh cigarette began to settle down. Higgins and Calder retreated to the far side of the room where they could talk freely without being overheard.

"What do you make of it, Higgins?"

Higgins, seated at his desk, leaned back, propped his feet on the opened drawer. "Given Clem's history, I'd dismiss it as another of his drunken episodes, only...."

"Exactly!" said Calder completing the sheriff's thoughts. "Only Clem did nearly the same thing last spring with that sighting of a dancing ghost out near the viaduct. And we know what happened then."

Higgins nodded. "What do you suggest we do?"

Calder looked to the now locked cell door. Clem, a rolled blanket serving as his pillow, lay contentedly snoring. "Wait a bit more to make sure Clem's sound asleep."

"Then?"

"Then, I think we should pay a visit to that alley and see what we can turn up. Maybe Clem's *Angels of Death* have left some indication to their intent."

* * *

A short time later Higgins and Calder made their way along the earthen alleyway in the rear of The Farmers and Mechanics Bank. A freshly dug slit trench dissected the alley's length. Nearby, on plank stretched between two kegs, sat a group of itinerant laborers sipping tepid coffee from mason jars, and eating soda bread coated with bacon dripping.

"Mind the trench, Higgins," Calder said, careful to avoid the iron stakes, rope and the occasional coal oil flare that ringed the narrow excavation. "It wouldn't do you to go tumbling in."

"Progress is upon us," replied Higgins. "Won't be long until all the stores along High Street will have electric lighting and indoor water closets."

Moments later the two peered down at the abandoned packing crate Clem had described. The wine bottle, now drained of its intoxicating spirits, lay discarded several feet away.

"Well," Higgins said, "at least Clem was right about spending the night in the packing crate." He probed the damp earth with the toe of his shoe, scattering a small mound of tobacco and the crumpled, damp remains of several cigarette papers. "Here's his spilled makings."

Kneeling, Calder, his keen eyes scoured the ground, searching for any trace of Clem's mysterious angels of death. After a few moments he rose. "Well, not much to go on here," he said. "The soil's been too heavily trampled by workers' boots to be of any practical use."

"A pity you can't call on that Brother Nathan," said Higgins. "Being a man of God, he might be able to tell us where these angels went. Maybe he could-"

Higgins's reply was interrupted by the rusty squeal of a protesting door hinge. He turned to find Brother Nathan, dressed in a freshly washed white robe, emerging from a nearby building. Gingerly threading his way around the mound of construction dirt, Brother Nathan crossed the narrow wooden plank spanning the trench line and ambled down the dirt pathway leading to the privy.

"Damn," Higgins cursed, as the wooden door of the privy slammed shut. "Spoke too soon. I'd forgotten Nathan's taken up temporary lease on the old carpentry shop. He oftentimes spends his nights in town. Guess a tent's not good enough for him."

Calder smiled. Turning his attention back to the inspection of the crate's interior, he remarked, "A strange man, this Brother Nathan." Reaching out, he removed a tiny swatch of white material snagged on the packing crate's rough edging. "He interests me," he said over his shoulder.

"You found something?" Higgins inquired.

"A bit of cloth. Probably nothing of importance," replied Calder, placing the shredded bit of cloth in his pocket.

"I see you've come to witness the abomination, Inspector."

Calder turned.

Brother Nathan, nature's call answered, had returned and was standing behind Higgins, securing the length of cord that held the robe to his gaunt frame.

Calder gave a nod of greeting. "Ah, good morning. It is Brother Nathan, isn't it?"

"That it is, sir. Brother Isaac Nathan, the Prophet's humble servant."

"What abomination are you referring to, Brother Nathan?"

Brother Nathan waved a hand in a sweeping arc. "Why look about you, Inspector. The laying in of electric and the piping for those cursed water closets, of course. As sure as we'll stand before the Prophet on Judgment Day, they are the devil's own instruments."

"Oh, come now. Surely you don't consider electric and water closets abominations. To most people they are a Godsend. Think what wonderment they will perform for the common man." He gestured toward the old carpentry shop with its freshly installed electrical wires clinging to its exterior wall. "It would appear you have no qualms about reaping its benefits."

"Bah!" retorted Brother Nathan. "Not my doing, Inspector. Those are not for my benefit; I much prefer to lead a simpler life. I tolerate none of this foolish extravagance." He wagged a thin, boney finger. "We must harken back to the old ways... to the old ways if we are to find true salvation. As for my presence here," his eyes strayed toward the group of idle workmen, "it is the Prophet's wish that I must dwell in town to eradicate the evil nest of vipers from its midst."

"I'd be threading lightly if I were you, Brother,"

a voice laced with a thick, Irish brogue called. "One of them vipers might take it upon himself to shimmy up under that fancy robe of yours. Then what would you be doing, I'd like to know?"

"Would be hard telling which were the snake and which were Brother Nathan."

Brother Nathan whirled. "Which one of you said that?"

The group of laborers, having made no effort to conceal their culpability, were happily snickering away.

"Brothers!" The morning air rang with Brother Nathan's thunderous voice. "Repent. Reject your slacking ways. Come, join the flock, seek salvation with the Prophet." He waved a bony finger at the group. "Else your souls will ever burn in the fires of damnation and brimstone."

Apparently accustomed to Brother Nathan's verbal retorts, one worker raised his morning drink in mocking salute. Another, a burly fellow with a rubicund complexion, began to recite a vulgar limerick, while the others roared with laughter.

Seeing his words were only urging the group to further mockery, Brother Nathan whirled and stalked off.

Chapter Five
High Street on a Sunday morning

"Good morning, Doctor O'Keefe."

Doctor O'Keefe, Relay's general practitioner, looked up from his morning paper. "Ah, and the top of the morning to you, Inspector." He folded the newspaper and tucked it neatly under his arm. "What brings you into the village so early this morn?"

The two men stood beneath the unfurled awning of The Farmers and Mechanics Bank. The bank, a stand alone building of native granite, occupied a prominent corner of the town square.

"I thought I would call upon the sheriff, perhaps pay a visit to The Scarlet Lady before the temperature becomes too unbearable." Noting the absence of the doctor's black medical bag, he added, "What, not out on your daily rounds?"

Doctor O'Keefe smiled with pure satisfaction. "The good Lord in his wisdom has seen fit to grant the fair citizens of Relay a reprieve from illness this fine day." He looked up at the clear blue August sky. "Barring some unseen tragedy, there will be no house calls today. Might I add, it's a gloriously fine day for a humble country physician to savor. Now what about yourself, Inspector? This case of Mr. Wright and his missing aeroplane, how is your investigation progressing?"

There wasn't much for Calder to report. The

sheriff and he had visited the station at Grinder's Ridge and spoke with its aging caretaker. Saying they had run into the proverbial stonewall could best sum up their visit. He shrugged. "It's progressing. There are one or two little interesting items to follow up."

The doctor tapped the folded newspaper. "Speaking of the Wrights, have you seen this morning's *Sentinel*? It contains a rather detailed accounting on the untimely passing of the elder brother. Typhoid." He sadly shook his head. "Not the most pleasant way to go, I fear."

"A bad ending indeed," Calder agreed. "Certainly not a death I would have chosen if given the chance."

"Nor I." Doctor O'Keefe accepted Calder's offer of a Turk cigarette. "But I suspect Mr. Wright had little say in the matter. Do convey my sincerest condolences to his brother at your next meeting."

"That I will, doctor."

The topic of conversation shifted and the two men continued to chat aimlessly for the next few moments. Then, a chance glance over Calder's shoulder caused Doctor O'Keefe's features to suddenly drain.

"Pardon me, Inspector," he said, "but I've just remembered an urgent house call I need to keep."

"House call? I thought you said there were no cases this morning."

Doctor O'Keefe did not answer. Still, it took no great skill to deduce something had garnered the good doctor's attention. Turning to follow the doctor's stare, Calder observed the plump form of Nora Battington, the town's chief purveyor of gossip, bearing down on them. With her oversized black pocketbook clutched tightly in one hand, and the other clamping the straw bonnet fast to her head, she weaved her way through the morning congregation spilling out of St. Barnabas Church into the morning sun.

"Damnation!" Calder swore.

"Doctor O'Keefe!" Nora's shrill voice called, as she skirted a group of elderly parishioners. "Yoo-hoo, Doctor O'Keefe."

Doctor O'Keefe hurriedly begged his leave. "Sorry to forsake you, Inspector, but I have no desire to get ensnared by that irritating female. Damn woman practically demands free medical advice for every ailment known to modern man, then has the gall to challenge it. That," he confessed, "I could almost tolerate. However, I suspect her true intent is to ply me for any dirty little medical tidbit on anyone she can."

He tipped his hat and hurried away, leaving a defenseless Calder to face an onrushing Nora Battington. Before Calder could react, Nora was upon him.

"Where is Doctor O'Keefe off to in such a hurry?" Nora said, watching the retreating figure disappear around the corner. "I did so want to consult with him. It's my lumbago, you know. Been acting up as of late."

"He mentioned something about an urgent house call, the case of the grippe I believe."

Nora stepped in front of Calder, effectively sealing off his own hastily conceived escape. "There's a lot of that going around," she said. "Why just last week my Robert was complaining of the grippe. Did I tell you about my Robert, Inspector? He's the assistant night manager at the Viaduct Hotel, you know. A healthy dose of honey, vinegar and castor oil soon set him right."

Hopelessly trapped, Calder was forced to listen to Nora's long-winded recital of the town's shortcomings, be they social or medical. She droned on and on. "Wasn't it a shame, the passing of that poor man, Mr. Wright. And from Typhoid too. I could have predicted that the moment I saw him stepping off the train. Why, it was as plain as the nose on one's face, wasn't it? Relay was indeed fortunate the dreaded disease had chosen to bypass it."

Unable to get a word in, Calder merely nodded.

"Still," Nora persisted, "there are problems enough in Relay." She gave a precautionary glance about. "Did the inspector know the Lockhart's eldest girl, Lisa, was with child?"

Calder didn't and he slowly shook his head.

Nora pursed her lips, her head bobbing in an all-knowing fashion. "Yes, sir, and nary a husband to be found. Such a pity, don't you think? And the parents," Nora huffed, laying a hand to the side her cheek. "Well, I never did think much of them, I can tell you that. No sir! Them and their newfound ways. Shameless, they're not sending that poor child away to a home to have the baby proper-like."

Nora took a deep breath. "Then there is the young widow Collins, and that mysterious ailment of hers. Doctor O'Keefe seems to make a good deal of house calls to her cottage, I've noticed."

Ah, thought Calder, now we're coming to it.

If Nora Battington detected the beginnings of a smile on Calder's lips, she gave no hint of it. "Oh Inspector, the tawdry rumors one hears!" Nora placed her hand on Calder's arm, rolled her eyes heavenward, "I can't begin to tell you. So shameful! Intemperance. Dipsomania some say. So wicked the way people are quick to repeat such rumors, don't you think, Inspector?"

Finally, in need of breath Nora paused, allowing Calder to respond. "I do, Mrs. Battington, I do indeed."

Nora nodded. "As you can well attest, Inspector, I would be the very last person to spread idle gossip about ... the very last. Still," she turned an empty palm, "no smoke without fire, I say." She kept a sharp eye on Calder to see if she was getting near the mark.

* * *

Several shops away Henry Wadsworth Longfellow, proprietor of The Scarlet Lady Pub, reached for a copy of his namesake's poem, *The Midnight Ride of Paul Revere*. As townsmen knew, and new patrons quickly learned, Longfellow kept a ready stash of the poems tucked away under the bar, and freely handed them out at the slightest provocation.

"With my compliments, gentlemen," he said, handing each new patron a gilded edge copy of the document.

"I do declare Mr. Longfellow," the first patron, a rotund individual with protuberant eyes, said. "Your establishment is certainly a most unusual place." His gaze swept over the polished wood paneling, the heavily timbered ceiling, and finally came to rest on the leaded glass windows with stained glass insets. "I never thought stopping for lunch in a saloon would result in my receiving such a splendid document."

Saloon!

The word cut a swath like a butcher's cleaver through Longfellow's soul. His nose titled upwards as if he had detected a bad odor. Saloon indeed! Since his arrival from England, and his subsequent purchase of The Scarlet Lady, he had strived to establish a literary haven in the town - in his estimation a quality that Relay sorely lacked.

"Well, gentlemen, if I do say so myself, there is a certain *Je ne-*"

Longfellow paused in his polishing of the bar. He turned an uneasy eye toward the massive fireplace, where Bounce, a scruffy Jack Russell terrier, laid blissfully dosing on the hearth's cool stones. Longfellow had intended to say, *je ne sais quoi* - a phrase he didn't quite know the meaning of, but one he had grown fond of using. However with Bounce near by, this would only serve to provoke yet another vicious attack on his already frayed trouser leg.

Bounce had appeared at The Scarlet Lady's doorstep one stormy winter night. Over Longfellow's objection, he claimed squatter's rights next to the warming flames of the massive stone fireplace and quickly settled in. An uneasy truce prevailed, broken only by Longfellow's usage of the phrase, *Je Ne Sais Quoi*. Bounce took bitter exception to this un-English phrase and the mere utterance of it sent the little Jack Russell nipping at Longfellow's pant leg. Thereafter a battle of wits ensued - a battle in which Longfellow, more often than not, found himself on the losing end.

"If you will excuse me a moment, gentlemen," Longfellow said. He crossed the room, retrieving the straw broom resting against the bar lift. A few well-aimed swipes of the broom, and Bounce was rudely rousted and ushered out the pub's back door.

With Bounce safely on the other side, and the latch bolt thrown, Longfellow returned to his customers.

"Now where were we, gentlemen?" he said. "Ah yes, we were discussing the finer points of my establishment." He fumbled in his shirt pocket, removed a pair of rimless spectacles, and looped the wire ends about his ears. He squinted, taking in his surroundings. "Surely you must agree gentlemen, there is an air, a certain *Je Ne Sais Quoi* about the place."

* * *

Outside, Bounce settled into a slow gait as he began the daily ritual of patrolling the alleyways. He poked his head under a pile of scrap wood, looking for the stray rat adventurous enough to sally forth in the daytime. Finding none he continued on. His route took him across High Street to the alley in the rear of The Farmers and Merchant Bank. There he paused long enough to leave his mark before continuing up the narrow, dirt alleyway separating the bank from the storefronts facing High Street. Midway up the passageway the little dog stopped, his head tilted sharply from side to side as he stared down at the damp earth. He growled. First, he pawed cautiously at the moist earth, and then quickly switched to a fit of frenzied digging. In a matter of seconds paws, snout and coat were covered in a layer of dirt. Pausing to survey his work, the terrier broke into a series of excited yapping.

Annoyed by the uproar, Nora Battington turned from her conversation with Calder. She scowled. "What's gotten into that fool dog? You'd think Mr. Longfellow wouldn't permit such a vile creature in his establishment."

Nora and Longfellow were as thick as thieves. Longfellow, in his continuing battle with the pub's regulars to change the pub's name from The Scarlet Lady to Longfellow's Pen, found a willing accomplice in Nora Battington. It was a beneficial arrangement, for in Longfellow, Nora found a ready source of tantalizing tidbits, gained in overheard conversations from lips loosened by too many pints of lager. These she quickly scooped up, altered or embellished, and then just as quickly pressed back into circulation.

Calder was quick to come to the little dog's defense. "Oh, Bounce isn't such a bad fellow," he said. "Keep in mind he is a Jack Russell, a born ratter if ever there was one."

Nora couldn't argue the point. "But-"

"But nothing," Calder replied with a nod of his head. "Bounce is merely doing what breeding and nature dictates, hunt rats. He probably detected some tunneling vermin."

"Well, be that as it may, Inspector. Still, I say something ought be done. Why only last week-"

Calder paid scant notice to Nora's continuing ramblings, preferring instead to keep an eye on Bounce's digging antics. Then, as if he had become aware he had an audience, Bounce stopped his digging. He looked to Calder. Retrieving a nearby stick, he seemingly ignored a mud puddle barring his pathway, merrily plowing his way through the muck and mire, and adding another layer of wet grime to his already soiled coat.

Reaching the alley entrance, Bounce deposited the stick at Calder's feet. He gave a quick, vigorous shake, ridding himself of most of the mud, then proceeded to dart and romp round the couple yapping wildly as he went. He finished by skidding to a halt in front of Calder. Sitting bolt upright, he pawed at the air, an act that usually resulted in an appreciative pat on the head or a tasty morsel gathered from a half-finished meal. He looked on expectantly.

"Oh you horrid little dog!" Nora screeched, as she attempted to brush away bits of spattered mud from her best Sunday frock.

Bounce paid little heed to the woman's yammering. Having gotten the attention of Calder, he meant to keep it. He yapped even louder. Then, true to his name, bounced like a coiled spring up into the arms of the man.

Calder smiled as he watched the scurrying form of Nora Battington retreating down the sidewalk. He didn't mind the splattering of mud, or for that matter, his now thoroughly soiled shirt. Indeed, it was a small price to pay to rid himself of Nora Battington.

"Good boy," he said, giving the little dog a playful rub of the ear and returning him to the sidewalk. "Good boy."

Chapter Six
The Reunion
The Viaduct Hotel - mid-afternoon

Colonel Musgrave sat at his favorite table, the one tucked under the veranda's eave, overlooking the Patapsco. He dipped his spoon into the bowl of terrapin soup, and raising it to his lips blew across the utensil to cool the steamy broth.

"Rutherford Musgrave? Do these old eyes deceive me? Could it be? Why you old bluecoat devil. By Jove, I do believe it is!"

Musgrave looked up from his soup to find an elderly gentleman, armed with a walking stick, hobbling in his direction. He lowered his spoon.

"Beg pardon, sir. Do I know you?"

"Know me, he says?" the old man said to no one in particular. "After the many of times we shared cold coffee over a meal of hardtack and day old beans? Do you know me?" He shook his head in dismay. "I'd say you most certainly do!"

Musgrave, his bushy eyebrows scrunched nearly to the point of touching, peered closer at the intruder. No, he didn't recognize the aged, weathered lined face, nor the labored voice, that he was sure of. What he did recognize was the gold star with its distinctive red, white and blue ribbon affixed to the man's coat lapel. He had seen his share of GAR medals. Had one himself! It was worn by veterans of the Grand Army of the Republic, in that great conflict some had taken to call the War Between the States.

"Rutherford, it's me, Albert," the old man said, thumping his chest with his free hand. "Albert Delahaye. Private Albert Delahaye. We served together in the Fifth. The Dandy Fifth, we used to call it. Now surely you remember the Dandy Fifth."

Ah yes, The Dandy Fifth, he did remember that. But Albert Delahaye? No, the name didn't sound familiar. Musgrave squinted hoping to get a better look.

Despite being supplemented by the walking cane, the old man reached out, grasping the back of a nearby chair to support his stooped, arthritic frame. "In my younger days I was known as Frenchy." He turned his face side to side, affording Musgrave a profile view. "A bit worse for wear, I'll admit, but surely now you hadn't forgotten your old comrade, Frenchy."

"Comrade? Frenchy? Well, I..."

"Summer of sixty-one," the old man prompted. "I was what you call the *observatuer* on the balloon, *Enterprise*. We were tethered out by the Thomas Viaduct, looking for rebel troop movement, or signs of sappers intent on undermining the viaduct's stone works." The old man raised the cane with a shaky motion. "That's why I have returned to Relay... to walk the old ramparts and recall the days of glory. And who do I find sitting at the hotel restaurant sipping turtle soup? None other than my old friend Rutherford Musgrave."

Musgrave's mind raced back through time, back to the war years. But try as he might he couldn't recall the incident, or the newcomer's face.

"The clerk at the front desk saw my medal," the old man continued. "Naturally we got to talking. He told me there was a Colonel Musgrave who also served in the Fifth. So, I thought to myself ... could it be old Corporal Musgrave he's speaking of? Colonel?" Delahaye chuckled. "I'll say this for you, Rutherford, you sure made short work of the rank ladder since I last saw you."

Musgrave's face reddened. "It's not my official rank, of course," he said, stumbling awkwardly over his words. "It's just that some of the villagers, they a ... they insist on calling me colonel." He turned an empty palm. "Now what's a fellow to do? Besides, there's no harm done. It's merely an honorary title, a patriotic gesture of sorts from the townspeople. This is a small village. I didn't want to offend anybody by refusing."

"Sure, sure, Rutherford," the old man said with a dismissive wave of the hand. "I quite understand. Say! Remember that time my balloon got hung up in that dang blasted sycamore tree, and those rebel sharpshooters had a field day using me for target practice? There I was, hung out like Monday's wash on the clothesline. You climbed up and pulled me from that wicker basket. Carried me all the way back to our line. As I recall you got a medal for bravery! Deservedly so I might add. Me?" Thumping the floor with his cane, Albert Delahaye rubbed his hip. "I'm still carrying one of Johnny Reb's mini balls as a souvenir."

Again Musgrave racked his memory, but to no avail. Surely one could remember an event as momentous as saving another man's life. He had been cited for bravery. Frenchy had his facts clear there. And them damn observation balloons were prone to snapping their lines, and landing where they weren't supposed to. Still, for the life of him, he couldn't recall saving Frenchy's life, or for that matter Frenchy himself ... not really.

True, there had been a lot of foreigners serving in order to get their citizenship papers ... mostly low class Irish, fresh off the boat with a brogue so thick you could barely understand a word they said. Now that he thought about it, there might have been a Frenchman or two serving in the regiment. But, he thought they went by their Christian names, André and... Damn, what was the other name? Certainly wasn't Frenchy. Oh well. The passing of the years does tend to cloud one's mind, and his recall had never been that good. Perhaps there had been one called Frenchy. The more he thought about it, the surer he became. After due deliberation he decided there must have been a Frenchy scattered among them.

"Of course I remember you, Frenchy," he said, pulling out a chair and motioning for his guest to join him. "It's just that it's been a long time." He tapped a finger against the side of his temple. "Mind you, I wouldn't want it to get around, but I'm not as fast as I used to be."

"That could be said of us all," chuckled Delahaye. Easing himself down into the chair, he eyed Musgrave's nearly depleted glass. "Let me buy an old comrade a drink." He signaled to a passing waitress. "As I recall you were a lager man."

Musgrave drained the last of his beer, then pushed the empty glass across the table. "That's right, Frenchy. I always said you had an exceptional memory."

Time past. The more the conversation wore on, the clearer the balloon incident became in Musgrave's mind. Then as Albert Delahaye rose to leave, it struck. The perfect idea! Musgrave thumped a large bony hand on the table, turned to his companion.

"Say Frenchy, I wonder if you would do an old comrade a favor."

Albert Delahaye nodded. "Why sure Rutherford, if I can. What do you have in mind?"

"My friends and I are having this little get

together this evening. Nothing special you understand, just an informal dinner and some lively conversation. We call it the Wednesday Night Club. I would deem it a personal honor if you would join us as my guest."

Delahaye hesitated. "Oh I don't know, Rutherford," he said shaking his head. "Never was one to intrude."

"Oh, not at all, not at all, old friend." Musgrave groomed his great walrus mustache with the back of his hand. "You see there's this fellow I'd like you to meet. Name's Willaby. He's the editor of the village newspaper. He's always pestering me for accounts of the Great War. Now I'm sure he'll be interested in hearing of our daring adventures."

"Well ... since you put it that way. Now you're sure I'll not be intruding?"

Musgrave leaned back in his chair and smiled. "Not in the slightest, old friend. Not in the slightest."

This was the opportunity Colonel Musgrave had been waiting for. That old doubting Thomas, Willaby, was always quick to disparage his stories of the war years. Now, at last, here was a man, a fellow soldier no less, one who had served with him and could bear witness.

After all, it isn't everyday a soldier disregards his own peril, crawls into no man's land under relentless, hail of enemy fire to lead a mortally wounded comrade to safety.

Albert Delahaye rose to leave.

"Now you won't forget tonight?" cautioned Colonel Musgrave. "Dinner's at six, in the hotel's restaurant."

"Looking forward to it," relied Albert Delahaye over his shoulder as he hobbled off.

With his newfound comrade's departure, Colonel Musgrave returned to his dinner, a smile on his face.

Who knows? There could be a newspaper article in it. Maybe even a photograph of him posing next to the man he saved. He wondered if he could still manage to fit into that old uniform of his. Oh well, he would pay a visit to Miss Molly, the village seamstress, first thing tomorrow morning. Maybe she could let out the seams a tad.

Chapter Seven
Hankin's Dry Goods Emporium

Relay, like other towns along the Patapsco, had its mercantile. In the smaller, mill-owned towns, mercantiles were plain and known simply as the company store. Relay on the other hand was different. Relay had Hankin's Dry Goods Emporium. On this particular afternoon, Mr. Thomas Hankin, proprietor and third generation storekeeper, was busy attending to a customer.

Mr. Hankin moistened the tip of the lead pencil against his tongue. Rice, beans and a slab of fatback bacon, there was little profit to be reaped there. Still, as he watched Brother Nathan peeled several dollars from the thick roll of greenbacks, Mr. Hankin saw an opportunity to increase his profit.

"The rice and beans might prove too cumbersome to tote," he said. "I can have your order waggoned out to the campgrounds first thing tomorrow morning, if that's agreeable? Only cost a solitary dollar more."

"Won't be necessary," Brother Nathan grumbled. "The Prophet has seen fit to provide his faithful with a sound beast and a sturdy wagon to harness it to."

Mr. Hankin's spirits sank, but he tried to maintain a jovial face. "Well, if you're sure."

"I am. Just set the sacks off to the side." Brother Nathan's eyes narrowed. "I don't expect there's a charge for that, is there?"

"No," Mr. Hankin said. The smile dwindled as he watched the roll of bills disappear back into the folds of

Brother Nathan's robe. "No charge for storage."

"So be it. I must return to my flock to prepare for tonight's sermon. I'll send the wagon in the morning to pickup the supplies, if that's agreeable?"

Mr. Hankin nodded.

His business completed, Brother Nathan turned to leave. As he did he collided with Calder who, having entered the store, was approaching the counter. Calder reached out, taking Brother Nathan's arm to steady him.

"Pardon me," said Calder, "my fault I'm sure."

Brother Nathan quickly withdrew his arm. "We are never pardoned in this life, brother," he said in a voice that rang with righteous zeal. "Only on Judgment Day, when we must face the true Prophet shall we find redemption."

Calder smiled, recalling a favorite quotation of his mother. "They that forgive most shall be most forgiven."

"Scripture?" Nathan said, eyeing Calder cautiously. "If so, I don't believe I'm familiar with the verse or passage."

"No. It was the journalist, Bailey."

Nathan's scowl deepened. "Don't have much use for journalists. It's my opinion they're the devil's own scribes. Tell me, Inspector, might I see you at tonight's sermon?"

Calder gave a sad shake of the head. "Sorry," he replied, "I'm entertaining guests this evening."

"A pity," said Brother Nathan. "There's a blue moon tonight ... a Prophet's moon some called it. I tend to give a powerful sermon under a Prophet's moon."

"I'm sure it will be most uplifting."

Brother Nathan nodded. "Perhaps another time then. Well, I must be on my way, Inspector. I'll bid good day to you."

After Brother Nathan's departure, Calder stepped to the counter.

"Good afternoon, Inspector," Mr. Hankin said, looking up from his ledger. "And what can I do for you today?"

Calder laid a handwritten list on the counter. "Mrs. C's weekly order. Could you fill it and send it along, Mr. Hankin?"

"Certainly, Inspector." A quick survey of the items on

the list returned the lost smile to Mr. Hankin's face.

"And Mrs. C fancies lavender soap," Calder added. "I would like to surprise her with a bar or two, something special. I'm not sure of the brand though."

Mr. Hankin gave a knowing nod. "Ah, I know the very one you're referring to, Inspector," he said. He stooped, and reached into the glass display case. His hand started to the right then edged left, to the side containing the more costly toiletries. "I've noticed Mrs. Chaffinch lingering in front of the case on more than one occasion. She's got a good eye, that woman. Here it is." He picked up one of the bars, offered it to Calder for inspection. "Notice the fine scent. Imported direct, all the way from New York City. Now, that was two bars, you say?"

Calder had noted Hankin's deviation to the more expensive items. He was tempted to say, make it a baker's dozen. It would be worth the added expense merely to see Mr. Hankin's reaction, but how would he explain such a large purchase to Mrs. C? True, Mrs. C adored the perfumed aroma of the soap, but she considered it an extravagance and wouldn't accept such a great number. He settled for what he thought was a good compromise. "I believe six cakes should prove adequate, Mr. Hankin."

The lost profit more than adequately restored; Mr. Hankin was transformed into a jovial, talkative mood.

"Glad to see you gave Brother Nathan tit for tat. It's time someone did. I'll say this, he's an odd bird if ever there was one."

"You're not the only one to think that, I gather," said Calder.

Hankin chuckled. "No, not by a long shot." He looked up from his task of wrapping the soap. "He's leased the old carpenter's shop next to the bank, you know."

Calder nodded. "The good sheriff and I met him in the rear of that very same building several days ago. Strange building for a church. I thought he preferred the camp grounds to preach his sermons."

"Oh, It's not a church, Inspector. Brother Nathan uses the shop as some kinda of spiritual headquarters. Sleeps there on occasion, according to Nora Battington." He knelt down, returned the box containing the unsold soap to the display case. "Not that he has it so bad at that camp revival of his," he said as he straighten up. "There I'm told, he has a right proper tent erected on a wooden platform, complete with a freestanding bed. I have it on good authority the bed's encased in the sheerest of mosquito netting."

This Calder found interesting. "Is that a fact? Well, religion has its just rewards."

"For some, perhaps." Mr. Hankin gave a dejected shrug. "But, not so with those misguided followers of his, I fear. They sleep on mats in ragged lean-tos. Trials and tribulations cleanse the soul, according to Brother Nathan." He shook his head. "And the food ... simply horrible. Well, you saw what he ordered, beans, rice and only the scantiest portion of slab bacon. I put it to you, Inspector, how can a body survive on that?"

Chapter Eight
A telegram Arrives
Passenger platform, Relay train station

Inspector Calder,
In urgent need of your assistance. Will arrive on the four-
fifteen from Baltimore, Tuesday next. Mother sends his
regards.
Sincerely,
Priscilla Hopkins

Sheriff Higgins lowered the telegram and looked to his companion.

"So, what do you make of it, Higgins?" Calder inquired.

As usual, when confronted with a problem, Higgins's brow furrowed. "Well, I'm not sure. It's rather cryptic. Obviously the woman is seeking your services, that point is plainly stated. Why, and in what fashion? She doesn't say."

"Go on," urged Calder. "Anything else?"

"Well," Higgins took another look at the telegram. "She does mention your mother."

Calder half-chuckled. "Ah, that she did."

The furrows in Higgins's brow deepened. "But she refers to her as him. That's rather strange, don't you think?"

"Good, good. You noticed that, did you? Excellent!"

"Well, yes. But as I recall, both of your parents

have passed on."

"Indeed. That is true."

Higgins shrugged his shoulders. "Then I can only assume Miss Hopkins's error was due to her highly confused state of mind when she composed the telegram. Still, that doesn't explain how she obtained your name, and why she's traveling all the way from Baltimore to consult with you."

Calder ground his cigarette into the platform's cobbles. "You will soon have all your questions answered." He motioned toward the great stone viaduct. "Here comes the lady's train now."

The locomotive hissed its way across the viaduct and eased to a halt in front of the Village's Victorian station. Calder searched the line of debarking passengers for a glimpse of his mysterious visitor. Through a curtain of steam, a young woman appeared, a handsome young woman in a frock of the lightest summer fabric, topped by a stylish, wide-brimmed hat that sheltered her delicate skin against the harsh August sun.

"Inspector Calder?" she said, holding out her hand.

"At your service, Miss Hopkins," Calder replied, taking her hand and giving a slight bow. "May I introduce my companion, Sheriff Higgins. The sheriff is a trusted friend of mine. You may speak freely in front of him."

"Sheriff," the woman said, displaying a smile that could only be described as bewitching.

Its effect was not wasted on Higgins. Mesmerized by the woman's beauty, Higgins stumbled over his greeting. "I ... that is we, aaaaah..." He paused, cleared his throat. "That is to say the pleasure is all mine, Miss Hopkins," he managed.

Calder came to his rescue. "Your telegram doesn't say what tragedy has befallen you, Miss Hopkins, or how I can best serve you."

"I didn't know how to convey my predicament on

paper, Inspector. It's somewhat awkward, and concerns my brother, Roger. He has ... how shall I put it? He has quite literally disappeared."

Calder sighed, as his head slowly moved from side to side. "Say no more, Miss Hopkins. I'm afraid your journey has been for naught. I sympathize with your problem, but I do not handle missing persons or problems related to the domestic. Those are best left for the police to sort out. Now if you will excuse me." He turned in preparation to leave.

"Oh, but you do not understand, Inspector. This is not a normal disappearance."

"No?" Calder turned back.

"My brother has disappeared, that much is true. Before he did so: he left his employment, giving no notice, withdrew his life savings, and forsaken his betrothed mere weeks before they were to be wed. All without an explanation. Now I ask you, Inspector, is that the mark of a rational person?"

"A rational person? No. Perhaps your brother was having second thoughts about his upcoming marriage, and took the quick, but dishonorable route out."

"I can't believe that, Inspector. Quite the contrary. From all indications, Roger was looking forward with great anticipation to his wedding day. And there is the question of the train he was on, that strikes me as being a bit too opportune."

"Question of the train? Opportune?"

"Oh. Didn't I mention that? It was the same train the Wright brothers were traveling on."

No, she hadn't. The same train as the Wright brothers? Calder pondered the statement. That changed the complexion of things. Could it have been a mere coincidence? No, he quickly dismissed that possibility. He didn't believe in coincidences, not when it came to the theft of the world famous duo's aeroplane. His interest aroused, he studied the young woman.

"You say your brother never arrived in Baltimore?"

he said.

On the verge of tears, she slowly shook her head. "No."

"He has made no attempt to contact you since?"

Again she answered, "No. Not so much as a letter or card."

"Now," said Calder. "Tell me a little about your brother's travel to Baltimore. Are you positive there was no trepidation on his part concerning his upcoming marriage? Perhaps he wanted your council."

"That's possible, of course. Though I have only his roommate's assumption that Baltimore was Roger's intended destination. You see, Baltimore is the family's home and Roger, as was his custom made frequent and often unannounced visits there. The doorbell would ring and there would be Roger. There was no cause to suspect this time was any different."

Calder nodded. "Is there anything else you can tell me? Think. Even the smallest detail may be of importance."

Miss Hopkins fell silent, appearing to ponder Calder's latest question. Finally she spoke, "I don't know if it's of any importance or not, Inspector, but the station master was kind enough to put me in contact with the train conductor, a Mr. Gleason, I believe. It wasn't his regular run, however Mr. Gleason does recall conversing with my brother. With all the ado over the disappearance of the aeroplane, he's not sure at what point Roger left the train."

Calder was puzzled. "How could the conductor be certain it was your brother he had conversation with? From the accounts I've read, there were any number of passengers on the train that day. To recall a chance conversation with your brother seems most improbable. Perhaps Mr. Gleason was mistaken."

Priscilla removed the large floppy hat to reveal a mass of bright copper colored hair. "My brother's hair is several shades brighter than mine, Inspector, though not nearly as long. The conductor was quite positive in his identification." She continued. "When I read in the newspaper the Wrights had retained you to recover their flying machine, I had a brain wave. I thought, might there be a connection between the theft of the aeroplane and Roger's disappearance? Roger may have had the misfortune to chance upon the thieves as they were removing the machine from the flatcar. That is a possibility, isn't it?"

Calder was forced to agree that it was.

"If so, poor Roger could have been kidnapped, or worse. Naturally, I went to the police to voice my suspicions. They were polite, but didn't think very highly of my scenario. Roger is an adult, they said. Without some evidence of a crime taking place they could take no action. An Inspector Eary suggested I contact you."

The tears began to flow quite freely now, compelling Higgins to react. "There, there, Miss," he said, offering his handkerchief. "Don't you fret none. The inspector and I will help you. Won't we, Inspector?"

"Thank you, Sheriff." Miss Hopkins replied, accepting the offer of the handkerchief.

Calder cast a dour look in Higgins's direction. He couldn't in all good conscience condemn his companion's offer of assistance. After all, he had been tempted to proffer the very same offer. Still, he didn't see how he or the sheriff could be of any assistance, and the last thing the poor girl needed was to unduly get her hopes up. But her brother's disappearance did pose some interesting questions.

"Tell me, Miss Hopkins," he said, "you say your brother abruptly left his employment."

Priscilla nodded.

"May I inquire under what circumstances? Do you know if it was an amiable parting?"

Dabbing at the corner of her eye with the handkerchief, Miss Hopkins replied, "I can't say. At least not with any degree of certainty. Roger's a dear, but he's always been a bit of a gypsy, if you know what I mean. Roger has always been a rogue when it came to loyalty to his employers."

"You don't think that is the case here?"

She slowly nodded her head. "No. That is why I sought you out, Inspector. According to his roommate, Roger had devised some grandiose scheme that would land him in the lap of luxury. When pressed on it, Roger grew secretive and refused to speak further on the subject. His roommate thought Roger's sudden departure might have something to do with this scheme. Perhaps Roger was planning to seek a loan from either myself, or our parents."

"Had he done so in the past? ... your brother, borrowing money from you, I mean."

She nodded. "I'm afraid our family has been very tolerant in that regard."

Higgins spotting a redcap excused himself and oversaw the handling of Miss Hopkins's luggage. That task completed, the trio adjourned to the inviting shade of the Viaduct Hotel's veranda, where iced drinks were ordered.

"Perhaps it would help if you would tell me a little more about your brother," Calder said, settling back in his chair as he sampled his drink. "What type of person is he? What were his plans, his ambitions?"

"There's really not much to tell, Inspector. Like most young people, Roger was trying to sort out his place in the world. His latest employment was as a clerk with the telegraph company. As with all the other positions he held, Roger quickly tired of setting at a desk, overseeing dispatches. Too boring ... not venturous enough for him were his words." She stirred her drink and raised it to her lips. "Roger yearned for more."

"So he left his work?"

"Yes." She returned the glass to its ornate doily

coaster. "Roger feels the aeroplane is the wave of the future. In the past he spent a good portion of his wages in attending flyer's school. He wants to be a part of what he calls the brave new world."

Higgins, who had remained mostly silent up to this point spoke, "That's all well and good. But confounded!" he said, pushing his drink aside. "I'm still in a bit of haze."

"Confused?" inquired Calder. "I believe Miss Hopkins has stated her problem quite clearly."

"The problem, yes," Higgins replied. He turned to Miss Hopkins. "But what I am referring to is your telegram. What I would like to know, miss, is why did you refer to the Inspector's mother as he in your telegram? I would have thought even the most unskilled of clerks would have spotted the error and pointed it out. Was it an oversight, and were you acquainted with her?"

"No, I never had the pleasure. Like you, Sheriff, I too am confused on that point."

"Then why-"

Priscilla Hopkins merely shook her head. "I can only tell you the detective I spoke to in Baltimore assured me, that if I included that phrase in my telegram, Inspector Calder would be compelled to receive me."

They both turned to stare at Calder.

Calder set his drink down, smiled. "Perhaps an explanation is in order," he said. "It is a simple matter, really. The inspector Miss Hopkins referred to is in actuality an old colleague of mine, Beecher Eary. Beecher acquired the nickname *"Mother"* as he had a habit of taking fellow coworkers under his wing, much like a mother hen with her brood of chicks. I suspect this is Beecher's quiet way of telling me Miss Hopkins is in dire need of our assistance."

"Oh, I am, Inspector. Truly, I am. Roger has done many foolish things in the past, but I fear this time he may have overstepped himself."

"Let's hope not," Calder said. Seeing the young woman's eyes beginning to well up once more, Calder sought to change the topic. "Have you arranged for accommodations, Miss Hopkins?"

"No." Higgins's handkerchief came once more into play. "I'm afraid in my haste I've overlooked that detail."

"May I recommend the Hotel Viaduct? You'll find the food and service most excellent, and the cooling breeze off the river is quite pleasing in the evening."

"Then you'll help me find my brother?"

Calder looked first to Higgins and then turned his gaze to his newest client. "As the good sheriff has stated, you are not to fret, Miss Hopkins. Rest assured, we shall do everything in our power to find your brother."

The tears were gone, Priscilla Hopkins smiled. "Then I will accede to your recommendation, Inspector. I shall take lodgings here, at the hotel, and I shall remain here for as long as it takes to get to the bottom of my brother's disappearance."

* * *

"A brave woman," said Higgins, later as they made their way back to the jail. "It takes a great deal of courage to face the uncertainty of what has happened to her brother."

Calder smiled. As usual, Higgins's judgment was based more on Priscilla Hopkins's beauty, than her ability to confront the unknown.

Chapter Nine
The Scarlet Lady Pub

Henry Wadsworth Longfellow paused in his task of polishing of the large, beveled edge bar mirror. He stepped back to survey his work.

Calder, who had been sitting at his customary table, the one in the curve of the window embrasure facing High Street, looked up from his meal of eggs, a rasher of bacon and tomatoes wedges.

"What's that, Longfellow?" he said.

Calder had developed the habit of only giving partially attentiveness to Longfellow's endless ramblings. He deemed that a very sane and sensible approach, as Longfellow could drone on, and on, on the most boring of topics. However, Longfellow's mention of the arrival of a government agent had brought Calder out of his reverie.

"I was just saying, Inspector," Longfellow said, over his shoulder as he rubbed, "We have a new member in our mist."

"Who's that, Longfellow?"

Longfellow applied his cloth to the mirror. "Special Agent Lemuel Percival, direct from Washington," came the reply.

"A government agent you say? Here? In Relay?"

"Oh, yes, Inspector. He was here in this very establishment this morning. And a like proper gentleman he was too," Longfellow added. "Got an appreciative eye, I'll say that about him."

"Why is that?"

"Complimented me on my establishment didn't he. He especially liked the ambiance is the way he put it. Said it reminded him of his recent trip to London." Longfellow retrieved the bar towel from his shoulder and wiped at a freshly discovered smear. "Not only that, but he was most receptive to my notion of changing the pub's name to Longfellow's Pen. Most appropriate move, Mr. Longfellow, he said." Longfellow's eye traveled to a pair of locals standing at the end of the bar. He scowled. "Not like some people I could mention."

Calder ignored the remark. Other than participating in an occasional good-natured joshing of Longfellow, he took little interest in the perennial battle raging between the villagers and Longfellow over the pub's name. However, he had to admit he was more than a bit curious over this appearance of a government agent in Relay. This was the second ... no make that the third mention of the agent's existence he had heard this morning. Already he could see sides were forming.

First, the sheriff had ventured out the five miles from the village, interrupting Calder's morning toast, to tell of the agent's arrival. It was obvious from Higgins's remarks that he had no use for the man.

"Came in on the seven-o-eight train," Higgins had huffed, his face beginning to turn a beet-red. "Marched into my office, threw his gold-plated badge on my desk, and demanded to see my case folder on the Wright affair." Here Higgins's expression clouded. "And something he called trace evidence, whatever that is."

Calder chuckled to himself. Demanding wasn't the way to confront Higgins, who could be as stubborn and headstrong as they come. "How did you handle that?"

"I looked him straight in the eye," Higgins growled. "Told him this wasn't Washington and I didn't have to be obliging to the likes of him. Besides, if he had bothered to check his facts he would have known Mister Wright's aeroplane was stolen outside my jurisdiction, and I had no say so in the investigation."

"Have you eaten?"

"No. Been too worked up to eat. Besides I thought you would want to know about this Washington fellow right-away."

Calder reached for the servant pull. "I appreciate your effort, Grandville," he said, motioning for Higgins to a seat, "So, Washington's sent an investigator, have they? Good! I'm sure the Wright brothers will be pleased."

The Wrights may be pleased, but Higgins wasn't. "Confound it, Inspector. I don't need some gilded, Johnny-come-lately telling me how to run my office. I tell you, I see only trouble in him being here."

Then, there was Nora Battington. Nora had stopped Calder on his way to The Scarlet Lady. Damn! That woman could ramble on, he'd grant her that. She had a tongue that ran on well-oiled ball bearings. It would be a simple matter of where to place Nora - she was decidedly in the Percival camp.

Now, here was Longfellow. Seems as if everyone in the village was either singing the praises of, or cursing the presence of Special Agent Percival ... everyone that is except himself. He would reserve judgment until he had met Special Agent Lemuel Percival *"I wonder,"* he mused, *"what side of the tally line I'll fall on?"*

Calder pushed his now empty plate away, reached for his tin of Turk cigarettes. "What type of character is this Agent Percival, Longfellow?"

"Special Agent," Longfellow corrected, applying particular emphasis to the special. "I guess you might say he's been brought up silk-lined. That's plain enough to see. Well-educated he is. Speaks on a variety of subjects and knows his authors. Just the sort of sophisticated patron the village needs." Longfellow glanced up at the wall clock. "You can soon judge for

yourself, Inspector. I've invited him to partake of my ploughman's lunch, and it's nigh on the noon hour."

The ploughman's lunch. Every noonday, Longfellow set out a rather large, silver tray, laden with a selection of mellow and sharp cheddar cheeses, crusty bread rolls and a selection of pickled vegetables. Calder could find little fault there. This delicious combination, accompanied by a foamy pint of Old Stoudt, could be had for the nominal price of two bits. It was little wonder that the ploughman's lunch had quickly gained popularity among *The Lady's* regulars.

Longfellow scowled whenever a patron requested butter, or God forbid, mayonnaise with his meal. "A swath of Gordon's Old English is all that's required," he would reply begrudgingly giving the butter crock a push, sending it down the length of the bar.

Calder exhaled a thin stream of blue/gray smoke into the air. "Coming again, is he? Well, in that case perhaps I should wait and meet this sterling, upstanding fellow for myself." He held up his empty glass. "That being the case, another pint of your lager, Mr. Longfellow, if you please."

Midway through his second pint, Calder's patience was rewarded. From his spot on the fireplace hearthstones, Bounce cracked a sleepy eye. He loosed a low growl. Calder looked up from his copy of *The Sentinel.*

Entering the pub was a man of medium height and slender build. He removed his straw boater's hat to reveal dark hair, plastered down and parted in the middle, with a touch of gray forming at the temples. Despite an August heat that threatened to wilt his heavily waxed mustache, he wore a buttoned up suit and a stiff, cellulose shirt collar. *"A real Dapper Dan,"* thought Calder, *"a dandy or what the English might call a swell."*

The man crossed the floor to the bar, where Longfellow stood wiping the counter with his bar rag.

After engaging in a brief conversation, Longfellow nodded in Calder's direction. Taking his ploughman's lunch and goblet of beer, the man turned and started in Calder's direction.

"Inspector Calder," he said, setting the glass on the table. This was said in the form of a statement, not posed as a question.

Calder nodded. "I am."

"I'm Special Agent Lemuel Percival, of the War Department. May I join you?"

Chapter Ten
An Unlikely Alliance

Special Agent Lemuel Percival toyed with the contents on his plate.

"Not hungry, Mr. Percival?" inquired Calder.

"Agent Percival if you don't mind, Inspector. And no I'm not ... at least not for this ... this." He probed the offering of cheese, boiled eggs and pickled vegetables with his fork. "What is it Longfellow calls this conglomeration? ... A ploughman's lunch?"

Calder nodded. "Longfellow brought the recipe with him from England. The locals have developed quite a liking to it."

Agent Percival's face wrinkled. "Pure garbage," he said pushing his plate away and reaching for the goblet of beer.

"Now that's too bad," Calder replied. "Old Longfellow will be disappointed. He was counting on a ringing endorsement from you to help lure customers away from The Boar's Head Tavern."

Percival inched the plate further away. "Not likely," he grumbled.

"Odd. I was given to understand you had developed quite a liking to it during your recent visit to England."

Percival toyed with his waxed mustache. "I'm disappointed in you, Inspector"

"Oh?"

"You're a bright fellow; didn't you smell a con in the offing?"

Calder arched an eyebrow. "Con?"

"I've never been more than a hundred miles away from the capitol, let alone across the Atlantic. I only led Longfellow to believe that in order to establish a ready source of information."

Calder was quickly developing a dislike for his pompous companion. He shook his head in dismay. "You lied to Longfellow? Why?"

Agent Percival nursed his beer. "I'm fresh to this one-horse village. I needed to develop a reliable source of information." He turned an empty palm. "What better source could an investigator have than the eyes and ears of the local barkeep?" Seeing the displeasure registering on Calder's face, he said, "Oh, come now, Inspector. Surely you employed the very same tactics when you patrolled the wharfs and piers of Baltimore."

Calder ignored the comment. He studied his companion. "For a Washington bureaucrat, you seem well-informed of my past."

Percival merely shrugged. "Nothing personal, Inspector. It's all part of the job. Before I took on this assignment I took the liberty of inquiring into your service record." He removed a paper from an inside jacket pocket, and unfolding it scanned the contents. "Distinguished career, several commendations. Promising future." His head bobbed in approval. "Ah yes, in line for chief Inspector, I see. All in all quite an impressive career, Inspector. Too bad a felon's bullet put an end to it all. Still," he leaned back in his chair, refolded the paper, and stuffed it back into his jacket, "you can't complain. By all standards, you've done all right for yourself. A man of comfortable circumstances, a generous inheritance, fine country house and I'm given to understand a bit of a celebrity status among the locals. What more could one ask?"

"I see the government's done its usual thorough job. Mind telling me why the great interest in my career?"

Percival leaned forward, lowered his voice. "Look, I'll be frank with you, Inspector. You had a good run at things, so far. Even solved a few cases of local significance along the way, I'm told. But this Wright business," he slowly shook his head in dismay, "is way out of your league. Now if you'll heed my advice, you'll take the easy road and leave the more challenging cases to the professionals?"

"Meaning you no doubt."

Percival drained the contents of the goblet. "I'll not deny capers of international consequences are, quite naturally, better suited to a man of my particular talents and skill."

Calder cautiously eyed his companion. "Are you telling me Washington would prefer I didn't inquire into the aeroplane's disappearance?"

"Ah no, no, Inspector. In fact, quite the contrary." Reaching into his jacket pocket, Percival removed a silver cigarette case and opening it offered its contents to Calder.

Calder peered at the row of small, dark-colored cigarettes. "No thank you. I'm afraid Egyptian tobacco is a bit too strong for my liking."

Percival extracted a thin, oval cigarette, and lightly tapped it against the side of the case. "You've gotten a hold of the wrong end of the stick, Inspector. I'm merely suggesting you don't have all the resources or facts at your disposal to make the proper choice. Let me take you into my confidence." Putting a match to the cigarette, he exhaled a stream of strong, aromatic smoke into the air. "Perchance, do you know the aerial distance to Camp Meade?"

"If I had to venture a guess, I'd say twenty miles. Why? Is it important?"

"Is it important? Well you may ask, Inspector. It's exactly twenty-seven and a half miles, as the crow flies. And do you know what is scheduled to take place there shortly?"

"No, but I assume you're about to tell me."

The sarcasm was lost on Percival. "Mind you, it's not for general consumption, but on September the first a high-level conference of ambassadors from several European powers will convene there. Their agenda is to attempt to form the groundwork to resolve the tense situation in Europe."

"And just how does your investigation of the Wright brothers aeroplane figure into this?"

"As I have stated, the distance to Camp Meade is twenty-seven and one half miles." Percival held a finger up, much in the manner of a schoolmaster commanding attention. "More importantly, that translates to a mere twelve minutes flying time for a machine such as the Wright brothers aeroplane. I assume you are aware of the bomb release mechanism the Wrights installed on their machine."

The significance was not lost on Calder. He nodded, indicating he was. "Mr. Wright has advised me of its existence. However, I'm given to understand it's merely in the prototype stage and not very accurate at this time."

Percival's expression grew stern. "Accuracy is not important, Inspector. What is important is that certain foreign interests would like nothing better than to disrupt that conference. If an explosive device dropped by an aeroplane should explode anywhere near the building while the ambassadors are meeting, it would have disastrous repercussions for our government. It's my job to find the aeroplane and see that doesn't happen."

Calder eased back into his chair. Percival was correct, of course. Still, he couldn't resist the temptation to tweak the pompous Percival's nose if only just a little. "Oh," he said. "I wouldn't stray too afar afield, if I were you, Agent Percival."

"Meaning what?"

Calder shrugged. "Only that I'm a very simple man.

74

I tend to believe the simplest, most obvious of explanations is oftentimes the more likely to have occurred."

Percival scoffed. "Surely you're not suggesting common thievery is behind the machine's disappearance?"

Calder withdrew a Turk from its tin. *A common theft? No, it was much more complex than that*, he mused. He struck a match and put it to the Turk. *Damnation!* He now faced the very real possibility that an international ring of thieves were operating near Relay.

Percival wasn't happy. It was obvious he took Calder's silence as a dismissal. He ground his cigarette into the ashtray.

"That's sheer claptrap, Inspector - just plain lunacy; any third rate detective worth his salt can see that. Take my word for it; international forces are at work here. Just look at the thoroughness and efficiency in the way the operation was carried out - a well-oiled deed if ever there was one."

Calder was deliberate in his reply. "Well-oiled, yes. However, you haven't presented any unalterable evidence to indicate international involvement."

"Depend on it, Inspector, there is an aura of international conspiracy attached to this caper." Percival studied Calder's features. "Perhaps you have a better scenario to offer?"

"I dare say I could," replied Calder. "For example, a competing company might hope to wreck the Wright's chances of obtaining a government contract by simply hiding the aeroplane until after the contract is awarded. Two, an enterprising group may have stolen the machine to ransom it to the highest bidder. Or perhaps, an aspiring, but penniless, young aviator may simply wish to possess the very latest model of flying machines. I offer these only at the spur of the moment, if pressed I could put forth several more."

Percival was becoming increasingly irritated. "Do not try my patience, Inspector. I've consented to take you under my wing, keep you abreast with any new developments, *only* at Mr. Wright's insistence. But let me make myself clear, Inspector. This is my case and my case alone. I intend to solve it with or without your assistance." Then after a few moments of silence, he gave a wry smile. "However, to show you that I'm not an unreasonable man, I'll make you a generous proposition. Keep your ears and eyes open, keep me informed of any developments, and when I wind this case up, there will be glory enough for all. I'll see to it that your name is mentioned in the right corridors in Washington." He leaned back, smiled. "Can't be any fairer than that."

Calder was not impressed. "Glory? Having my name bantered about some corridor in Washington holds little enticement," he said. "I'll tell you this, Mr. Percival. I intent to find Mr. Wright's aeroplane simply because that is what I promised him I would do." Calder rose. "Now if you will excuse me."

He rose. As he turned toward the door, the question had been answered. He now knew what side of the ledger he fell on.

Chapter Eleven
The Art of the Deal

Leaving The Scarlet Lady, Calder made his way along High Street in the direction of the village jail, Percival's words ringing in his ears.

Mention my name in the proper halls of Washington, would he? The very audacity of the fellow!

This wasn't Washington. What did he hope to accomplish? Darting here and there about the countryside in those fancy clothes of his wasn't going to produce any tangible results, much less solve a mystery as puzzling as this. Still, despite his massive ego and abrasive manner, Percival was right about one undeniable fact. The theft of the Wright brothers' machine had been carried out with a remarkable high degree of skill and efficiency; trademarks you wouldn't ordinary associate with common thievery.

On the other hand he, himself, had precious little to show for his efforts. A week had come and gone and he was still no closer in locating the famous duo's aeroplane than Percival. Perhaps the good sheriff might be persuaded to accompany him on a little excursion to Grinder's Ridge. He needed to get a close look at the ground surrounding the water tower, maybe speak with the station's aging caretaker. Now that the elderly gentleman had had time to reflect on the incident, he might have recalled something ... an obscure tidbit perhaps, or a forgotten incident, maybe a chance conversation with a stranger inquiring about the train's schedule, anything that would point him in the proper direction.

Down a narrow side lane, his path took him past the green grocer and the massive wooden doors of Parlor's Livery Stable.

"Oh, Inspector."

Calder turned, tipping his hat in greeting as Oney Parlor, proprietor of Parlor's Livery Stable, emerged from the shadows of the building's cavernous interior.

"Got a minute to spare, Inspector?" Oney called.

"What's on your mind, Oney?"

"Got a proposition I think you might be interested in."

Proposition? Calder silently chuckled to himself. This, he knew from past experience usually resulted in, at best an offer of dubious worth. The more likely scenario would be a much-depleted purse.

Despite his better judgment, Calder hesitated. "And exactly what proposition might that be?"

When it came to trading in livestock, Oney Parlor was a force not to be taken lightly. One would be wise to stand guard over his purse strings when dealing with the likes of Oney Parlor. It wasn't that Oney was dishonest exactly, for it could truthfully be said that Oney Parlor was a cut above most purveyors of horseflesh. No, it was his zest for the trading process itself that made Oney Parlor such a formidable opponent. Oney relished in the give and take of negotiating.

Oney paused, peering cautiously about for eavesdroppers. Despite finding none, he lowered his voice to little more than a whisper. "I got some fresh stock in over the weekend."

"Oh, I don't know, Oney. I was on my way to see Higgins. Perhaps another time."

"Won't take but a minute, Inspector." Oney hooked a thumb in the direction of a row of the stables and beckoning Calder to follow. "This one's special, real special," he said over his shoulder as he turned, retreating back into the building's interior. "You'll see."

Calder reluctantly followed the stableman into the barn. Walking to the far end of the stable where the better animals were stabled, Oney continued his spiel. "There this little gelding, you see. Understand, not your run-of-the-mill grade horse. No siree bob," he said, inserting a thumb under the strap of his bib overalls and giving a boastful tug. "A pure Standardbred, that's what this fine beast is. Got all the proper paperwork to prove it." Only when he was sure Calder had had the time to digest such a vital piece of information did Oney continue. He cocked a doleful eye toward Calder, gave a sad smile. "Seeing as how things are a little tight right now, I'd be tempted to let him go for a shameful low price."

So that's it, chuckled Calder, *another one of Oney's offers for a hackneyed horse.* As for the money, if one were to believe Oney things were always in a state of imminent financial collapse. Well versed in Oney's tactics, Calder refused to be drawn in.

"Now, I wouldn't want it said I took advantage of your dire financial situation, Mr. Parlor. However," he conceded, "I am in the market for a proper carriage horse."

Stopping before a stall, where a magnificent black beast stood gazing out, Oney said, "Then look no further, Inspector. You have the perfect animal standing before you." Then, adding the correct amount of regret to his voice, he added, "Although it would break my poor mother's Irish heart, God rest her soul," he said, removing his cap and holding it over his heart. "I'll let him go for a fraction of his true worth." Returning the cap to his head, he added, "Only if it's to a good home, you understand. He deserves better than to spend his days hacking for the miserable likes of me and that's a fact."

Irish mother my foot! thought Calder. Oney was no more Irish than the old mongrel asleep in the stable corner. Still, after taking careful measure of the horse, he was pleased in what he saw.

Oney seeing Calder's apparent pleasure decided to play his trump card. "By the way, Inspector, that housekeeper of yours, Mrs. Chaffinch, would she still be keeping an eye on that poor motherless boy? What's his name? Willie, is it not?"

The reference was to William. Hardly a boy, as the lad was gone fourteen. Still an orphan nevertheless, that much was true. Calder had taken him on as stable lad along with his purchase of Old Dunham House. In itself this might seem a strange act, as there were no horses stabled at Old Dunham House. But, with the constant stream of guests and visitors arriving, some in carriages and others on horseback the task of tending to their care fell to William's capable hands. As for himself Calder made due with the occasional rented mount from Oney.

"It's William, Mr. Parlor, and you're quite right Mrs. Chaffinch has graciously taken the boy under her wing."

Oney's head bobbed in agreement. "Ah yes, that's it, William. Always liked that lad's temperament. The lad has a way with horses, there's no denying it. Some say William has the touch. Yes, sir, he'll see to it that this horse will get the proper care and grooming."

They had entered the stall. The gelding stood quietly, offering no objection as Calder walked about, inspecting as he went. First came the mouth, all was in order. Next he ran a telling hand along the animal's withers and over the hindquarters. Finally, lifting each leg he examined the hooves.

His cursory exam complete, Calder stepped back. "Well, he's not head shy, Mr Parlor, that's a good sign." He nodded. "Quiet. Sound conformation. Good temperament as far as I can tell."

"Oh, he has that, Inspector, never fear. Perfect

road manners and responds well too. You'll see, he'll give you no cause for concern. I'll stake my hard-earned reputation on that."

"Mind telling me how much you paid for him?"

Oney spat a wad of tobacco juice onto the stable's sawdust floor, rubbed his chin. "I'll not lie to you, Inspector. Paid eighty-five, hard-earned government greenbacks for him over at the county auction in Hanover."

Calder, a hand on each side of the halter, continued to study the gelding. *Eighty-five dollars?* thought Calder. *Seems a paupery sum for such a fine animal.* He cast a suspicious eye at the stableman. "Has the vet taken a look at him?"

"He did, and that's a fact. Now I know what you're a-thinking, Inspector, and I can't say as I blame you. But, old Doc gave him a thorough going-over. Gave him a clean bill of health too, got the receipt on my desk to prove it."

Calder knew Doctor Wilson was a righteous man and would not knowingly affix his name to a false document. Still, he was puzzled. This was an exceptionally fine-looking animal. "Then how do you account for such a low price, Mr Parlor?"

Oney merely shrugged, removed his tattered cap and scratched his balding head. "Can't rightly say. Reckon it might have to do with all them noisy automobiles chugging about, cluttering up the roads and belching that infernal oily smoke. Seems people no longer got much use for the horse, even one such as this here one." He sighed. "Might as well face it, Inspector; times, they're a-changing."

This was a calculated play on Oney's part. He knew full well that Calder, despite having lived in the big city, had little use for the automobile.

"Fact is," Oney continued, "I been thinking of getting out of the horse trade myself. Feller past though here a while back, offered to set me up selling Mercer runabouts ... might just take him up on it too. Now, you would be doing me a favor taking this horse off my hands, Inspector. You'll treat this old boy right, I know that. Like I say, he deserves better than end up hacking or pulling a plow."

Calder wasn't convinced. "How much is this act of charity going to cost me?"

"Ah, pay it no-mind, Inspector," Oney said with a dismissive wave of the hand. "A mere pittance for a man of your considerable means."

"How much, Mr. Parlor?"

"Hardly worth squabbling over, Inspector. Now if you'll-"

Calder persisted. "The price, Mr Parlor, if you please."

Seeing that Calder would not be denied, Oney sighed. He reached into his shirt pocket and pulled out a worn, dog-eared notepad along with a stub of a pencil. "Naturally I'll need to recoup my purchase price, plus the usual expenses," he said, wetting the tip of the pencil against his tongue. In a large round hand, he began to jot down a column of indecipherable scrawls. "First, there's fifteen dollars," he peered over his half-glasses. "That'll cover transportation from Hanover to here, bill of sale and the notary public fees. He paused. When Calder offered no objection, he continued. "Now let's see, there's the veterinary bill. That'll come to say, ten dollars. Feed, grooming and oh, don't forget the farrier charges. Had to put on new shoes." He cast a calculating eye - an eye worthy of a Mississippi gambler sizing up his opponent - toward Calder, "Shall we say, twenty dollars?"

To this he received a nod in return.

"And finally, only the barest of profit for my labor." Oney scratched the week's growth of stubble at the tip of his chin. "Tell you what, Inspector," he said, closing the notepad and putting it away not bothering to total the column, "one hundred and seventy-eight dollars.

How's that? Sound about right to you?"

At slightly more than double the purchasing price, the figures were a bit on the excessive side, but well within Calder's ability to pay. Still, ritual demanded that some degree of dickering be conducted before the sale could be properly concluded. It wasn't so much the dollar amount, but the art of dickering that mattered. And as everyone knew, that was the part of the transaction Oney Parlor enjoyed the most.

Calder did not immediately answer. Instead he ran a noncommittal hand along the horse's withers, and gave a series of reassuring pats. "By the way, Mr. Parlor, does the animal have a name?"

Oney merely shrugged. "The auction papers listed him as Marine's Black Sultan, out of Sultan's Surprise and Black Mar-Lou. Seems a right fancy mouthful to saddle such a spirited horse with. Don't see the need. I took to calling him Blackie. He don't mind none and it's easier on me."

"A hundred and fifty, you say?"

"One hundred and seventy-eight, Inspector." Oney corrected, quickly brushing aside Calder's feeble attempt to lower the price. "Tell you what, I'll throw in a complete set of my finest tack and the free afternoon loan of my best surrey. How's that? That way you can take him out for a run before you decide."

Oney spat into his palm, and extended it in the old English custom, asking for a return handshake to formalize the transaction. Calder looked at the spittle-laden hand, then to the timeworn and somewhat dubious condition of the tack dangling from a rusty nail. He withheld his hand.

"How old do you make him out to be?"

Oney wiped his spit-covered palm on his trouser leg. The dickering continued. "Papers don't say. Not long in the tooth I judge. Seven, maybe eight, not much more than that."

"I'll tell you what, Mr. Parlor. Make it one hundred

and seventy, and you deliver him freshly curried and brushed."

"You're killing me, Inspector." Oney turned his empty trouser pockets out, as an open display of his dire financial straits. He cast a rueful glance at Calder. "All I'm trying to do here is make carfare and lunch money. Now you wouldn't deny a feller that opportunity, would you? How's about we split the difference? One hundred seventy-five dollars and fifty cent." He hesitated. "But you'll have to return the tack."

Calder surrendered.

Of course he was going to purchase the horse, but tradition dictated that he couldn't give in so readily. He stepped back, pretending to study the animal. "Mmmmmm, I don't know, Mr. Parlor. I'll have to think it over. Tell you what, you hitch him up to that best surrey of yours, and I'll take you up on your offer of an afternoon ride. If he's as good as you say, I'll pay your full asking price."

Oney beamed with satisfaction. "You won't be sorry, Inspector. No Sir! Old Blackie here is gonna make you a fine carriage horse, you'll see."

Exiting the stable, it didn't take Calder long to alter his original plan. Grinder's Ridge and the proposed station attendant's interview were quickly pushed aside. Now as for Higgins, there was no doubt he would be the better candidate to judge the worth of the horse and to accompany him to Grinder's Ridge. But, matters of the heart easily overshadowed that. What better way to spend a lazy summer afternoon than a pleasant ride along the banks of the Patapsco with a beautiful woman at his side? His course altered, veering from the direction of the sheriff's office toward the village post office, where he found Victoria Byron engaged in conversation with Priscilla Hopkins.

As the conversation concluded, Priscilla turned to leave, slipping an official-looking envelope into her pocketbook as she did.

"Oh, Inspector Calder," she said, startled to find Calder standing to her rear. She quickly recovered adding, "My what a pleasant surprise." She snapped the pocketbook closed. "I was intending to call upon you later this afternoon to inquire about my brother. Tell me, is there any news?"

Calder could only shake his head. "I'm afraid not, Miss Hopkins. Fear not, the sheriff and I are very hopeful something will shortly turn up."

Priscilla Hopkins gave an appreciative nod. "Let us hope that will be the case, Inspector," she said. "Now if you will excuse me, I have a luncheon engagement with that wonderful government agent, Special Agent Percival. I shall be at the hotel later if there are any developments."

Calder watched her depart, and then turned his attention toward the teller's cage where a watchful Victoria sat.

"Good afternoon, Inspector," she said, her violet eyes alight with mischief. "To what do I owe your presence this glorious afternoon - business or pleasure?"

"Perhaps a little of both," Calder replied.

This pleased Victoria for she smiled. "And what pleasure might that be?"

"As you say it is a glorious afternoon, and it's pleasant weather we're having."

Victoria nodded. "Most pleasant."

"So pleasant," said Calder, "that I thought an excursion along the river might be in order." He looked around at the empty post office. "I was hoping you could be persuaded to join me."

Victoria cautiously eyed Calder. "You said both business and pleasure."

"So I did," replied Calder. "I need to pass judgment on a gelding Mr. Parlor has for sale. He's a handsome, upstanding beast, but knowing Oney's zeal for horse-trading, I'm not quite convinced. A second opinion is what's called for. That's where you come in."

"Well...."

"Say yes. We could picnic by the dam."

"You go on, Miss Byron, enjoy yourself," urged Anna, Victoria's assistant clerk. "You've been cooped up too long and can do with a spot of fresh air. Don't worry; I'll manage just fine. Now you run along."

Victoria glanced at the long-case clock. It was well past the lunch hour. Removing her apron-coat and hanging it on a nearby peg, she said, "Just give me a minute to prepare us a proper basket and you can call for me at my door."

Chapter Twelve
The race

Victoria emerged from her cottage door, picnic basket in one hand and her frilliest parasol in the other. Placing the wicker basket in the space behind the buggy's seat, she paused to admire the new horse.

"Oh, you were right," she said, nodding approvingly. "He's magnificent and as coal black as a moonless night. Does he have a name?"

"Marine's Black Sultan, according to the transfer papers. Oney thinks Blackie is a more suitable name."

"And what do you think?"

"Oh, it doesn't matter to me. One name is as good as another."

Victoria gave a violent shake of the head. "No, no. That simply won't do," she said. "Blackie is such a common name, seems every black horse is called Blackie. Besides, Blackie is hardly a suitable name for such a regal animal." Accepting Calder's hand she climbed into the surrey. Settling herself in the seat, she added, "This animal deserves a more befitting name. I'll have to give the matter some thought."

They continued north, along the tree-shaded river road, following the Patapsco as it wound its way towards Bloede Dam. Blackie - true to Oney's prediction - proved to be an exceptional well-behaved animal, exhibiting perfect manners and responding instantly to Calder's slightest command.

All was proceeding smoothly until the fast cadence of hoof strikes could be heard overtaking them.

Instantly Blackie's ears twitched. Like a probing antenna, the right ear swiveled rearward, focusing on the approaching hoof strikes. As the buggies drew alongside, the other driver, a dapper young fellow driving a spirited dapple gray, tipped his hat in greeting. He raised a slender whip, and with a flick of the wrist, dispatched a sharp crack over the gray's head. Immediately the gray complied and slowly began to pull away.

The challenge had been issued and Blackie, despite Calder's efforts to the contrary, responded to the challenge. He didn't break stride. Indeed, to his credit Blackie held it, merely increasing his own cadence to match the other animal. Down the tree-shaded lane the two buggies thundered with Victoria dearly holding on, one hand grasping the edge of the seat and the other her newly purchased bonnet. Blackie not only matched the gray's gait, stride for stride, but effortlessly increased his own high-stepping stride to a point the gray could no longer match and was forced to fall behind. It was only after he had soundly outdistanced the other buggy that Blackie slowed, returning to his normal placid self.

Once more in control, Calder maneuvered to the side of the lane. He dismounted. Victoria quickly followed suit. In the distance, the roar of the Patapsco as it spilled over Bloede Dam could be heard.

Victoria was first to speak. "I can't imagine, what got into him?"

"I can," replied Calder. "It's obvious. Damn horse is an ex-trotter, fresh off the racetrack. No wonder Oney was able to pick him up for a mere pittance. Well," he said, "there's nothing left to do but return him. A pity too, he's a fine horse."

Victoria wouldn't hear of it. Reaching out, she stroked the horse's muzzle, and received an appreciative neigh in return.

"No! You can't," she said. "I like this horse. Poor beast! If what you say is true, he's spent his entire life cooped up in some horribly confined stall, not once able to taste freedom or country air. He deserves better. You just can't take him back, Calder, not now, you simply can't."

"But what am I to do? He's an ex-race horse, for God's sake. You just can't-"

"William," Victoria said with steely determination. "Young William has a way with animals, you said much the same yourself. You can't deny that. Surely he can work his magic on Midnight."

"Midnight? I thought his name was Blackie."

"I think Midnight is a much more suitable name, don't you?" She smiled. Her head tilted slightly, allowing the sun to filter through the thin fabric of the parasol to cast a kaleidoscope of colors onto her delicate skin. "Now isn't there a rule that you can't return a horse once he's been named?"

"Not that I've heard of," Calder replied.

Yes, he knew he was being manipulated, but happily so. Since his arrival in Relay, he had been mesmerized by Victoria's beauty and grace. On more than one occasion she had worked her charms on him. Taking the newly named Midnight's halter, he turned the buggy back toward town. This gave him much needed time to reconsider.

"Perhaps you're right," he said, climbing back into the buggy, and picking up the reins. "I'll have a talk with William when I return. Maybe some arrangement can be worked out."

He held out little hope for this, of course. Racing was a hard trait to counter. Once it seeps into a horse's blood, that's all they seemed to know. Still, like Victoria, he had developed a certain fondness for the animal, and he had no wish to disappoint her. He would try.

Lunch in a shady grove near the dam was

everything he hoped it would be. The food, cold chicken, sliced tomatoes and potato salad was excellent. More than once he found himself stealing a stolen glance at Victoria. As with the first day he saw her, her beauty mesmerized him. It was easy to envision a life that includes Victoria at his side.

Time passed and all to soon it was time to return to the village. Not willing to risk an additional encounter with another would be sulky driver, Calder opted for one of the little used inclines that serpentine their way out of the river valley to the open fields above. From there it would be but a short drive to Relay. Midway up the pathway the roar of the dam's waters began to recede, only to be replaced by the distant roar of a powerful engine as it sputtered then sprang to life.

"Whoa," Calder said, drawing the buggy to a halt.

Now out of the shade of the sycamores lining the river, Victoria was in the process of opening her parasol against the glare of the afternoon sun. She turned. "Why are we stopping?"

Calder held a quieting finger, as he sought to determine the direction and distance the echoing reverberations were emanating from. It was a fruitless act. The narrow confines of the valley acted as a sounding board successfully masking the origin of the sound.

Then, abruptly as it started the roar of the engine ceased. The tranquil sounds of nature returned.

Victoria couldn't see what all the fuss was about. "Oh, it was just a farmer's tractor," she said, dismissing Calder's attention as somewhat extreme. "After all, there are a lot of farms here about, and it is the height of thrashing season."

There was validity in Victoria's assessment. Still Calder wasn't convinced. "No," he said. "That was the roar of a gasoline engine. I'm certain of that. I may be a city boy, but I know farmers use steam engines for their thrashing duties. What we heard was an unthrottled gasoline engine." Extracting a Turk from the cigarette tin, he fumbled for a match. "If I didn't know better, I could almost swear that was an aeroplane engine."

"Aeroplane engine?" Victoria gave a half-smile; it was becoming clear where Calder was heading. "Come now. Surely, you're not suggesting that was the Wright brother's machine, we heard?"

"It's a possibility."

"Not Likely. Whoever stole that aeroplane has certainly transported it miles from here by now."

"Perhaps," agreed Calder, releasing a thin stream of blue/gray smoke into the air. "Perhaps."

For the next several minutes they waited, anticipating a resumption of the roar to guide them to its source. When that failed to occur, Calder glanced down at his watch. "It's grown late," he said, urging Midnight onward. "We better get you back to the post office. Anna will be wondering what happened to you."

The meandering pathway took them past the site of Brother Nathan's tent revival. Attached to a fence post was a crude, hand-lettered sign inviting God fearing and sinners alike to attend the nightly gatherings. In the distant Brother Nathan's thunderous voice reverberated.

"Repent! Repent, I say! Repent sinners, lest ye be doomed to burn for eternity in the fiery bowels of hell."

Shouts of Alleluia and praise the Lord rose from the faithful.

The voice of Brother Nathan responded. "If you feel the spirit moving, Can I have an amen?"

"Amen, brother, amen."

Something didn't set right, not when it came to Brother Nathan. Calder's thoughts went back to the words on the sign, "Welcome to God fearing and sinners alike," it read. He smiled. *Perhaps I might just take Brother Nathan up on his invitation."*

Chapter Thirteen
Old Dunham House

"Then," Calder said, "there's the vexing problem of Miss Hopkins's brother, Roger."

Higgins, relaxing in the leather wingback chair, a tumbler of Dr. O'Keefe's famous sipping whiskey in his hand, seemed only too pleased with himself. "Oh that," he said, puffing out his chest ever so slightly. "I've been working on that, and if I must say so I believe I've come up with a very plausible theory to explain his alleged disappearance."

Calder looked to his guest. "Alleged disappearance? I would be interested in hearing your theory, Grandville."

"Oh, it's quite simple," replied Higgins. "I don't believe Roger Hopkins' disappearance is anything but a well thought out, preplanned act."

"In what manner?"

"I'd say he's run to ground ... most likely to avoid tying the knot."

This wasn't a new assertion, as Calder had suggested the very same possibility at their first meeting with Priscilla Hopkins upon her arrival in Relay. He slowly shook his head.

Higgins, misinterpreting Calder's reaction, said, "I know what you're thinking, Inspector. If Roger Hopkins has staged his own disappearance, then where is he hiding? I put it to you," he said, tapping his forefinger against the side table to emphasize the point, "he's right here. In Relay, under our very noses."

"Here in Relay," mused Calder "That's an unusual theory, Higgins. Mind telling me what you based your conclusions on?"

"Well, you remember that day Clem came busting into the office, scared half way out of his wits and demanding to be locked up?"

Calder chuckled, recalling the incident. "Ah yes. The infamous angels of death were looking to take him across the River Jordan."

"Angels my foot!" thundered Higgins, setting his drink aside. "I'll bet next month's wages that was none other than Brother Nathan and Miss Hopkins' brother, Roger. The way I see it, Roger Hopkins has taken sanctuary in Brother Nathan's group."

Calder was intrigued. In the past, Higgins often came up with far-fetched deductions. How he accomplished this was beyond Calder. However this one had some plausible elements attached to it. "And how did you come to plot this out?"

Sensing Calder was coming around to his way of thinking, Higgins continued. "Well, we know Roger Hopkins was on the Royal Blue the day it arrived in Relay. We have the conductor's testimony on that. It's my belief that in all the confusion, Roger Hopkins slipped off the train, unnoticed. With all the hoopla going on, that wouldn't be a hard feat to accomplish."

Calder nodded. "True. And his connection with Brother Nathan? How did this come about?"

"I haven't quite figured that bit out just yet, but if you recall, Clem described the angels as wearing flowing white robes, with one having a red/gold halo."

"So?"

"Brother Nathan and his followers wear robes, and Miss Hopkins told us her brother's hair was even brighter than her own. It's obvious. In his drunken state, Clem mistook Roger's fiery red hair for a halo."

Calder wasn't so convinced. "That's fairly shaky evidence to base your assumption on."

"Wait," said Higgins, "there's more. There's Roger's interest in aeroplanes to consider, and what was the last position he held?"

"According to Miss Hopkins it was as a telegraph clerk."

"Bingo!" exclaimed Higgins. "As a telegraph clerk, he was in a perfect position to have intercepted the telegram assigning the flatcar to the Royal Blue. Now, the way I see it, Roger Hopkins and this Brother Nathan are somehow mixed up in the theft of the Wright's aeroplane." He leaned back, released a stream of cigarette smoke into the air, smiled. "You've got to admit, it all fits together nicely."

Calder marveled at Higgins's ability to misconstrue. "In what together, and for what purpose?" he asked. "Granted, there is her brother's interest in aeroplanes to consider. But Brother Nathan's religion forbids anything modern, and an aeroplane is definitely modern.

Higgins was no longer so sure of himself. "Well, I-"

"What good would seeing the telegram do Mr. Hopkins? It doesn't direct the Wright brothers' train to stop at Grinder's Ridge. Freight trains regularly stop at Grinder's Ridge as a normal course to replenish their water. Passenger trains, on the other hand, rarely do. It was only by the purest of happenstance the Royal Blue did so on that day."

Higgins's brow wrinkled. "Ah, Yes. Well, I haven't quite figured out all the parts, but they will come to me in due course."

"Your theory does hold one or two points of interest," said Calder, in consolation. "As you have correctly pointed out, Miss Hopkins's brother was employed by the telegraph company, and he did posses an interest in aeroplanes. This, and the fact that he was on the train during the aeroplane's theft, is highly suggestive. Also there is the fact that he could have slipped off the train unnoticed. But, you failed to take into consideration the lack of motive and the statement Miss Hopkins made to us."

"What statement?"

"She told us her brother's destination was Baltimore, not Relay. Further, according to his roommate, Roger had concocted some grandiose scheme that was to be carried out in Baltimore."

"That's right," said Higgins, recalling the conversation. "One that would land him in the lap of luxury."

"If that were the case, why disembark in Relay? As for Brother Nathan involvement, I don't see his camp revival as providing a basis for any grand, financial scheme, do you?"

Higgins seemed rejected. "Well ... perhaps not. But you'll agree my theory is not as far fetched as Agent Percival's."

"You'll get no argument from me there," said Calder.

Higgins shook his head. "Agent Percival's belief in foreign agents involved in stealing the aeroplane is beyond me. Why the closest thing we have to a foreigner is that balloonist friend of Musgrave. Though I don't believe having a French surname qualifies you as a foreigner."

Calder half-chuckled. "Percival is full of himself. There, my friend, we are in complete agreement. Still, his theory of international involvement isn't without some merit."

"Oh come, Inspector, surely you don't believe in that international conspiracy malarkey."

"Conspiracy, no. But consider, other than Delahaye and the Wright brothers, we do not know what others may have been aboard The Royal Blue the day the Wright's machine disappeared." Don't forget, The Royal Blue is a prestigious train carrying passengers from all walks of life. It would be unreasonable to assume there were no foreign nationals aboard that day.

"Then you believe Albert Delahaye is involved."

"No, I have no basis for that. From all indications Mr. Delahaye is what he appears to be, an old warrior trying to relive his youth."

Chapter Fourteen
The Scarlet Lady

Calder sat in the curve of the bay window. Having drained the dregs of his drink, he returned the empty glass to the table just as the first of a series of off-keyed musical notes assaulted his ears.

"Who's making all that infernal racket?" squawked Longfellow, storming to one of the large, leaded pane windows facing High Street.

Unfastening the latch he pushed the window open. Through the opening flowed the piercing renderings of a lone, but horribly off-key, coronet. It was quickly joined by the crash of cymbals, followed by the deep, thud-thud-thud of a bass drum.

Frowning, Calder looked up from his newspaper. "I'll be damned if I know, Longfellow," he said, turning to look over the reverse lettering advertising Old Stoudt lager. "Some type of parade, I imagine."

"What?" retorted Longfellow. "In the middle of a hot August afternoon? Talk about your mad dogs and Englishmen."

Longfellow had a point. His curiosity aroused, Calder laid his copy of *The Sentinel* aside, rose and went to investigate. Outside, he cringed. His ears, no longer protected by thick walls of *The Lady*, rebelled under the blaring strains of what might had been construed as *Onward Christian Soldiers*, although so badly played one couldn't be altogether sure.

Turning the corner and proceeding down the cobbles of High Street came a motley band of musicians, followed by several individuals carrying placards. Their leader, Brother Nathan, strutted in front, armed with a tall walking staff, which he waved about, like a drum major, in an unsuccessful attempt at directing. Bringing up the rear were several shoeless boys with makeshift stick rifles over their shoulders, pretending to be marching soldiers on parade. A like number of mongrel dogs, roused from their noonday slumber, trudged behind.

"I see Brother Nathan's at it again," said Sheriff Higgins as he joined Calder. "Be thankful you live a respectable distance from town, Inspector. Mayor Hightower's not going to take too kindly to this, I can tell you that."

Almost as if on cue, the door of the small, stone building that served as the village's municipal office burst opened. Mayor Hightower stormed out, making his way across High Street to the Scarlet Lady Pub. As Sheriff Higgins had predicted, Mayor Hightower was not in a jovial mood.

"Now see here, Sheriff," thundered Mayor Hightower spying Higgins. "As mayor I demand you to put an end to this unsanctioned brouhaha this very instance."

Higgins took a deep breath, and slowly let it out. "Now, Mayor, we've been through this more than a hundred times. There's no village ordnance prohibiting the playing of musical instruments. He winched as one of the cornet players hit a particular sour note. "No matter how badly it's done." He turned to survey the nearly deserted street. "As long as Brother Nathan doesn't hinder vehicular traffic, frighten horses, ladies or pass the plate on a public street my hands are tied."

Mayor Hightower's face turned barn red. Slamming his clenched fist into an opened palm he glared at Higgins. "You mark my words, Grandville Higgins! At the very next village council meeting that oversight will be duly rectified. You shall have your ordnance, I'll personally see to that." With that, Mayor Hightower turned and stalked off.

The procession halted before the erstwhile carpenter shop that now served as the headquarters for Brother Nathan and his band of followers. Climbing atop a wooden box, dutifully provided by one of the faithful, Brother Nathan held his hand up for silence. Mercifully the clamor ceased.

"Brothers and Sisters," Nathan shouted, his steely eyes taking in the meager group gathered before him. "Hear me. The true path to righteous salvation shall come only when you return to the old ways, the pure ways ... the way of the Prophet."

Murmurs of amen could be heard coming from the ranks of the faithful.

Brother Nathan waved a bony finger in a sweeping arc. "Repent, I say! Return to the fold, else ye shall ever be doomed to burn in the eternal fires of damnation. Who among you will be first to step forward and renounce his evil past?" The boney finger pointed to an unsuspecting individual. "You brother?"

Startled, the townsman looked up. Cowering under Brother Nathan's penetrating stare he would not or could not respond. Dismissing the man, Brother Nathan's finger next singled out a lone woman accompanied by a small child. "You sister? I call upon you to forsake your wicked past. Repent, seek redemption and you shall gain everlasting entry to the Prophet's house."

"Charlatan!" the woman retorted. Taking a firm grip on the child's hand, she turned and stormed off. The meager gathering of onlookers roared with laughter.

Meanwhile, oblivious to the laughter, a robed follower wove his way through the thinly spaced audience. He spoke not a word as he went from individual to individual, pausing in front of each. Words were not necessary; the offering plate in his outstretched hand clearly indicated his intent. It was only after having gained Higgins's scrutiny that he surreptitiously slipped the plate back within the folds of his robe. A packet of cheap paddle fans replaced the plate. He continued on, distributing fans and offering, "Bless you, brother," whenever he received a stray coin in exchange.

Sweltering under the unrelenting rays of the noonday sun, the townspeople quickly tired of Brother Nathan's preaching and began to drift away. No amount of shrillness in Brother Nathan's voice could stem the tide. Eventually, even the mongrel dogs lost interest and sought shelter under a nearby chestnut tree.

Calder and Higgins took advantage of the occasion to approach Brother Nathan. Higgins wasted little time in coming to the point.

"I thought I made it clear there was to be no passing of the plate on the public street."

"Oh, but we're not collecting, Sheriff."

"Don't hand me that, I just saw one of your followers-"

Brother Nathan produced an empty smile. "Oh, you mean Brother Elijah." He turned an empty palm. "Pay him no mind, Sheriff. Brother Elijah was merely spreading the gospel and dispensing fans to the weary, courtesy of Delbert's funeral parlor. Sometimes he goes a bit too far. Of course, at times some giving souls feel the urge to contribute to the feeding my flock, but that is entirely of their own choosing. I trust that is acceptable?"

"Volunteer donations are one thing, outright soliciting is another," warned Higgins. "A fine line, Brother Nathan. Make sure you don't cross it again."

Brother Nathan closed his eyes, his head bobbed in rhythm with Sheriff Higgins' words. "Yes, yes, Sheriff," Nathan said, in a weary voice. "I know, I know. Mayor Hightower has made his feelings well known on that subject several times. I will speak with Brother Elijah." Then, giving a dismissive flick of the hand to indicate the matter was settled, Nathan turned his attention to Calder. "So Inspector," he said, "have you given any more thought to attending one of our nightly services? Your presence among the faithful would be a welcome addition."

"No thank you," Calder chuckled. "I'm afraid camp revivals are a bit too rustic for my taste. I'm more of a traditionalist when it comes to religion. A sturdy oak pew is more to my preference."

"Aaaah, with Miss Byron seated by your side no doubt." Brother Nathan's grin produced a row of well-maintained teeth. "A lovely creature, is she not? Surely one of the Prophet's most beautiful creations. Of course the invitation is extended to her as well."

The expression did not change on Calder's face. Whether it was Brother Nathan's words or the tone, he felt an uneasiness stirring inside. He did not like the look in Brother Nathan's eyes when he spoke Victoria's name. "Perhaps another time," he said.

"You'll change you mind should you chance a visit. I preach a mighty powerful sermon, some say."

"Odd that you should mention that."

"Oh, why is that?"

"Only that Miss Byron and I have the opportunity to drive by your revival grounds recently. She said nearly the very same words. She suggested we stop and pay a courtesy call."

"Do tell!" Brother Nathan seemed genuinely pleased by the latter statement. "When was that?"

"Several days ago," replied Calder, seeing no reason to be more specific. "It was a most pleasant of afternoons. Victoria and I were enjoying a peaceful carriage ride. That is we were enjoying ourselves, until the hellacious roar from some machine spooked our horse. Nearly bolted as a result. Being high strung, he refused to settle back, and we were forced to return to town without stopping."

"A pity," said Brother Nathan giving an understanding nod. "I also have heard the vile contraption you speak of ... spewing out its hellish song, belching oily fumes, polluting the serene air the Prophet has so graciously granted us. Still, what can one do? It's farming country and such abominations are to be expected."

"I'd like to give its owner a piece of my mind," said Calder. "You wouldn't by chance know who owns that machine?" Calder watched to see what type of response the latter statement would elicit.

If the words bore any significance for Brother Nathan, it did not show. He merely shrugged, and gave a sad shake of the head. "Afraid not, Inspector. I have neither the time, nor the desire to seek out the owner or the machine's whereabouts."

"Still," Calder said, "on occasion it must prove disruptive to your services."

"True, but we all have our crosses to bear, Inspector. The Prophet's teachings tell us of man's weakness ... of his willingness to succumb to the lure of the use of the devil's tools." He smiled. "Still, I suspect our church's feelings on that subject are well known to you."

Before Calder could reply, Higgins spoke. "Speaking of that church of yours, maybe you can help me."

Nathan turned back to Higgins. "Certainly, Sheriff. How can I be of service?"

"I've been looking for a missing lad. He was last seen getting off the train several days ago. I was wondering might he had sought shelter within your group."

Brother Nathan turned an empty palm. "A wayward lad, you say? Well, that's possible Sheriff, of course. Many pilgrims come seeking comfort and shelter from the storms of life in the Prophet's house. What does this wayward lad of yours look like?"

"I don't have a photograph of the lad but he shouldn't be hard to recognize; he's blessed with full head of bright red hair." Higgins unconsciously ran a hand through his own thinning hair. "His sister describes him as being young and rather adventurous. Has a particular fondness for aeroplanes. Name's Roger Hopkins. Of course, he is most likely using a alias."

"Hopkins?" Brother Nathan repeated the name. "The name is not familiar to me," he said, "but there are many sheep in the Prophet's flock. I shall make the necessary inquires. Why don't you and the inspector join me later this evening after the service? We could talk further then."

"Perhaps another time," replied Calder, cutting Higgins short. "Mrs. C is preparing one of her special dinners tonight and we dare not disappoint her."

Nathan nodded. "And rightly so, Inspector. One mustn't be tardy when the Prophet's bounty is placed on the table. Now if you will excuse me gentlemen, I must tend to my flock. It's getting late and there's tonight's sermon to prepare."

Higgins's face bore a satisfied expression as he watched Brother Nathan depart. "Well, Inspector," he said, turning to Calder. "What do you think of my little theory now?"

"Your theory?"

"Come now. You got to admit old Brother Nathan was quick to come up with that weak denial of his. Join me later? Bah! That was merely an excuse for him to slip away without committing himself. My money's still on Miss Hopkins's brother being in Nathan's camp."

"Perhaps, Higgins. We shall see."

"Ah, but there's one thing I don't quite understand, Inspector," Higgins said. In reality the expression on Higgins's face was more of disappointment then puzzlement.

"What's that?"

"You didn't say anything to me about a special dinner tonight. You know how I do enjoy Mrs. Chaffinch's cooking. Sure would hate to miss one of her special meals."

"Oh, I apologize Grandville. There's no special dinner tonight."

"No special dinner?" Higgins was taken back. "Then why didn't you take Brother Nathan up on his offer? Seems to me like a perfect opportunity to snoop around that camp of his. How are we going to find out if Roger Hopkins is there or not if we don't go?"

Calder shook his head. "A waste of time and we would achieve little for our efforts. If Miss Hopkins's brother is there, and I don't suspect he is, he doesn't want to be found. Announcing our visit would only serve to forewarn him. Better we should arrive unannounced."

A smile crept unto Higgins's lips. "You're a crafty devil, Calder. I'll give you that." He rubbed his hands together in gleeful anticipation. "So you're going anyway, eh? What's the plan? What time should we meet?"

Calder returned the smile. "I think seven o'clock should prove sufficient, don't you? Now as to Mrs. C. While she isn't preparing one her special meals this evening, I'm quite sure whatever it is; it will meet with your approval. We'll discuss our plans over dinner, and set out for the revival grounds at first dusk."

Chapter Fifteen

Precisely at seven o'clock the dirt lane leading to Old Dunham House erupted in a column of dust. The unmistakable chug-chug of a one cylinder automobile engine and the goose-like honking of a hand-squeezed horn quickly followed this. As the rapidly approaching dust cloud neared, a familiar voice boomed from within.

"Stand clear, Inspector. I haven't quite got the hang of stopping this machine."

Calder retreated, seeking refuge on the manor's steps. After several erratic maneuvers the machine slid to a halt, coming to rest mere inches from Miss Chaffinch's prized bed of perennials.

"Well? What do you think of her?" said a triumphant Higgins, as the dust began to settle. He pushed the steering tiller aside, climbed from the driver's seat and stood back admiring the machine. "A rare beauty is she not?"

Calder shook his head in bewilderment. "Higgins, what in heaven's name are you intending to do with this, this ... this thing?"

"Why I thought it would be plain enough, we'll travel by auto this evening. You got to admit it's much more faster than a horse. As it stands we'll be late enough in returning."

As Relay's lone officer of the law, Higgins had somehow persuaded the town council to grant him authority, should the need arise, to lease an automobile from Oney Parlor. Oney, true to his word to seek another field of employment had taken to exploring the world of automobile leasing. The machine in question, a 1906 curved dash Olds, was Oney's first step in that direction. It was kept in the rear of the livery stable, hidden away under a canvas tarp, for fear it might unduly frighten the horses.

Calder wasn't so convinced. He didn't think much of automobiles and said as much. "You know my feelings on the automobile, Higgins. Your machine may be faster, I grant you that, but I would feel more comfortable with a horse attached to my buggy."

But Higgins wouldn't be dissuaded. "Think of it as a horseless carriage, Inspector," he urged.

This wasn't a hard task to accomplish. Indeed, it seemed by all outward appearances that the blasted contraption was exactly that ... a carriage without the benefit of a horse being attached.

Sensing Calder weakening, Higgins pressed home his argument. "Oney's charged the carbide lamps, and he's polished the reflectors until they were shining like a pair of freshly minted pennies. Even put in new igniters. Why, it will be practically like driving in daylight."

"Well...."

"Come on Inspector, be a sport. What'd you say? It would be a shame to waste the taxpayer's money."

Calder wasn't thrilled at the prospect of yet another automobile ride, especially since Higgins hadn't quite mastered its control. Still, Higgins had a point. Transgressing narrow country lanes at night in a horse and buggy held little appeal, even for a horseman such as himself. In the end he was forced to concede the Olds, with its twin carbide lamps illuminating the way, would prove a much more faster conveyance.

"We shall see," said Calder. "In the meantime stash your driving coat and come inside. Mrs. C's got our dinner waiting."

Over dinner, plans for investigating Nathan's camp

were discussed and debated. Higgins continued to press home his case for usage of the automobile, and promptly at dusk the two set out.

"Mind you," Calder cautioned, easing himself into the machine's passenger seat, "you agreed on ten miles per hour, and not a hair's breath more."

Higgins lowered his driving goggles into place. "You have my solemn promise on it," he said. "Ten miles per hour it shall be and not the barest breath more."

How he was going to accomplish this impossible task, Higgins hadn't the foggiest. The machine wasn't equipped with a speed indicator. Besides, navigating country lanes at night, even with carbide lights, would require his constant attention. There would be precious little time for needless monitoring of some gauge.

As it turned out there was no cause to worry. The darkness kept the machine's speed within an acceptable range and the trek continued without incident. Arriving at the revival grounds Higgins, at Calder's urging, closed the valve extinguishing the lamps and throttled the machine's noisy engine. They coasted silently to a halt in a small pine grove. Alighting from the Old's, Calder surveyed his surroundings. Good! The machine's silhouette blended in quite nicely. It would take an unerring eye to differentiate it from the other carriages and buggies parked near by.

"Now what?" said Higgins, removing the driving goggles.

"We'll leave the machine here. Mingle with the congregation. Try not to attract attention, no sense announcing our presence just yet. If possible, I'd like to take a look around backstage while Brother Nathan is at the pulpit preaching."

Keeping to the rear of the congregation, Calder and Higgins opted for a slight rise of ground that offered an unobstructed view of the service. Under the fiery glow of torchlight, they watched as a robed deacon began the process of working the faithful into a frenzy. Suddenly

Calder stiffened. He stepped back into the shadows drawing Higgins with him.

"What-" said Higgins.

"Shhhhhh." Calder held his finger to his lips, and motioned off to his left. "Look there."

Following Calder's stare, the unmistakable form of Agent Lemuel Percival stood not more than ten feet away.

"What in holy tarnation is he doing here?" hissed Higgins, mindful to keep his voice low. "You think he's out here investigating Miss Hopkins brother's disappearance too?"

"That remains to be seen," replied Calder, as he watched the impeccably dressed Percival, his upheld arms swaying back and forth in time with the mesmerizing chanting of the faithful. This, surmised Calder, was Percival's crude attempt to blend in with the congregation. If it was it failed, for Percival's eyes were not on the stage. Instead, they were systematically combing the sea of faces as if he were searching for someone or something. "Whatever it is," Calder added, "he's not here for spiritual enrichment."

The music reached a fevered pitch as Brother Nathan mounted the steps to the stage. He held his arms up to silence the congregation. The music ceased.

"Brothers and Sisters!" Nathan commanded. "Can you feel it? The spirit of the Prophet, do you feel his presence entering your souls? If you do, can I hear an amen?"

Calls of Amen rose from the body of the faithful.

"Come," said Calder. "It's time."

With attention focused on Brother Nathan, Calder, closely followed by Higgins, made his way to the rear of the stage - to the collection of tents that served as supply, and dining facilities for the Prophet's faithful.

The area appeared deserted. It was not difficult to locate Brother Nathan's tent. It sat off to the side, apart from its neighbors and sheltered by a line of sycamore trees. As described by Mr. Hankin it had been erected on a raised wooden platform and far grander than any of its neighbors.

"I'd give a month's wages to take a gander into that tent of his," said Higgins. "There's got to be a record book. If Miss Hopkins's brother is here, his name's sure to be recorded on some kind of membership roll."

Calder was quick to agree. "Excellent plan," he said, "but far too chancy. Especially for an upstanding officer of the law like yourself."

"What do you mean too chancy?"

Calder ignored the question and patted the still-mending knee. "I, on the other hand, am well-equipped for such an undertaking."

"Your knee?" A frown appeared on Higgins's face. "I don't understand. What's your gimp knee got to do with searching Brother Nathan's tent?"

Calder smiled. "It will serve a plausible reason for my presence, should Nathan return unexpectedly and discover me in his tent. After all," Calder said, "was it not Brother Nathan, himself, that invited me to visit this very afternoon? Now, should he return and find me, I'll feign discomfort. I'll claim the knee had suddenly flared up and became unbearably painful. And while it was rude of me to invade his tent, I couldn't resist the temptation to trespass and seek the comfort of a chair to sit and relieve my suffering. Now, what can he, a man of the cloth, say?"

"But-"

"No buts. Now station yourself nearby and be prepared to intercept anyone approaching. I won't be but a minute."

As he turned, Calder detected a movement off to the side. From out of the shadows, a figure rounded the corner. Spying the two men, the figure jerked to a halt. Instead of challenging their presence, as one might expect, the figure tugged at the edges of the garment's hood drawing the coarse material about his features in an attempt to conceal his identity. Whirling about he quickly retreated.

"Something's not right," said Calder, alerting Higgins. "You take that side and I'll take the left, and we'll see if we can find out what our elusive friend is up to."

"Right," called Higgins, as he sped off in the direction the figure was last seen.

The narrow passageways between tents proved a remarkable maze, and the figure quickly eluded Higgins. Calder's pursuit proved more fruitful. He managed to work himself into a position where he could intercept the figure.

Hearing approaching foot strikes, Calder ducked into the darkened recess between two closely spaced tents. He didn't have long to wait. Within moments the fleeing figure scurried past. Calder reached out, intend on capturing the figure. The figure, in his haste to escape misjudged the guide rope securing the adjoining tent. He stumbled. Thrown forward, he was catapulted headfirst into the communal laundry vat.

"All right my lad," said Calder, reaching into the sudsy water to retrieve the thrashing figure. "Lets have a look at-"

Calder stopped in mid-sentence. The figure's violent thrashing action caused the robe's hood to fall away. Sitting in the sudsy mixture was the unmistakable, but thoroughly drenched, figure of Priscilla Hopkins.

Chapter Sixteen

"You?" they both said in unison.

Calder recovered first. "And what pray tell are you doing here?"

"Me?" Priscilla Hopkins blurted out. "What about you? What are you doing here?"

"I asked first."

"I was looking for my brother."

"Of all the foolhardy deeds!" Calder swore. "Don't you know it's dangerous for you to go prying around in the dark by yourself. Especially in a place like this. God only knows what could happen."

She was a sight. Still, even the bulky, ill-fitting garment did little to conceal Priscilla Hopkins's beauty. She pushed the wet tangles of curls from her face. "I can take care of myself, thank you," she said.

"In that ridiculous costume?" Calder shook his head in mock disapproval. "I dare say Brother Nathan would not look too kindly on you masquerading as one of his flock."

Regaining some of her composure, Priscilla Hopkins became defiant. "What did you expect me to do?" she demanded. "Sit around that stuffy old hotel room all day? I'm certain my brother is here, he may even be held prisoner. I've come to free him." She eyed Calder. "And you? What are you doing here?"

"It's quite simple. The sheriff and myself are here

at Brother Nathan's personal invitation. Like you, I thought your brother might possibly be here. We were planning to do a bit of snooping when we stumbled upon you."

It was at this point that Higgins joined the couple. "Good Lord in the morning," he said, removing his cap and scratching his head. "What's she doing here?"

"I'll explain later," said Calder. "Right now I think we had better get Miss Hopkins out of here before questions are asked."

"Right." Higgins gestured toward the stage. "Sounds like Old fire and brimstone's winding up his sermon. I saw a couple of his followers heading this way." Turning to Priscilla, he said, "Better rid yourself of that robe, Miss Hopkins. It will only slow us down."

Priscilla quickly shed the crudely made robe. Beneath the coarse garment, she wore an expertly tailored, but equally water soaked, blue frock. Undoing a bit of lace from one of the garment's puff sleeves, she secured her red/gold curls. The robe was discarded, draped over the rim of the galvanized washtub, where it was sure to be retrieved. The transformation complete, the three made their way back to the machine.

* * *

"I fear my actions back there must seem a bit childish to you," said Priscilla, once they had reached the automobile and were safely away.

"No, not at all," Calder said. "You acted out of concern for your brother's safety. I dare say neither the sheriff nor myself would had done differently."

Priscilla gave an appreciative nod, turned to Higgins. "Sheriff, would you be so kind as to take me back to the hotel? I-"

"You can't go back to the hotel," Calder interrupted. "At least not in your present condition."

"Why not, I'd like to know?"

Calder chuckled. "It's clear you're not familiar with the wagging tongues of country villagers. Why the Nora

Battington's of the town will have a field day at your expense."

Priscilla Hopkins spun sharply in her seat. "Wagging tongues, indeed, Mr. Calder," she huffed. "This is 1912. Women suffrage will soon be the law of the land. I care little what wagging tongues of some country village have to say."

"Perhaps not. But you're not in a modern, progressive city like Washington or New York. You are in Relay. Things are different here. Better come with us back to Old Dunham House. I'll place you in the capable hands of Mrs. C; she'll soon have you presentable again."

* * *

"You poor, poor child," Mrs. Chaffinch said when informed of the incident. She wrinkled her nose. "My lands," she said, leaning close to Priscilla's still damp clothing and sniffed. "Whatever did they have in that tub ... swamp water and tar soap?"

Priscilla blushed. "It is a bit strong. I'm afraid I must smell frightfully terrible."

"Never you mind," Mrs. Chaffinch said, putting her arm around Priscilla's waist, and leading her out of the room. "You just come with me, child. First, we'll get you out of those wet clothing. Then I'll fix us a nice hot cup of tea. You'll be right as rain in no time."

To Mrs. Chaffinch and her English sensibility, tea was the perfect solution to every predicament, no matter how dire. Everything from a broken arm to a broken heart could be summarily cured by a freshly brewed cup of Twinings.

"You're most kind, Mrs. Chaffinch. Really you are, but I don't want to be a bother. I can-"

"No bother at all," hushed Mrs. Chaffinch waving off further conversation. "Now you just hurry along and freshen up while I see about that dress of yours. I'll lay out some fresh clothing on the bed. Oh, and you'll find a fresh bar of lavender-scented soap next to the wash basin." She cast an appreciative glance in Calder's direction.

* * *

Later, as the three sat discussing the night's events, Mrs. Chaffinch entered the library. "I've laundered your dress, dear, though a devil of a time I had ridding it of that tar soap smell. It's out airing on the garden line. Come tomorrow morning it will be fresh as a daisy."

"That's very kind of you, Mrs. Chaffinch. I don't know how I can ever repay you."

"Never you mind, Dearie. There's little labor on my part."

This was true enough. With Calder's purchase of the great house came a modern scullery, equipped with green tiled walls, two soapstone soaking vats ... and that most modern of inventions, an electric powered Thor washing machine.

"It is getting late," said Calder, looking up at the long case clock. He turned to Priscilla. "Since your dress won't be ready until tomorrow, and you can hardly return to the village dressed in Mrs. C's robe, may I suggest you stay the night as my guest. Mrs. C will see to your room, and I'll drive you to town first thing in the morning."

Priscilla started to protest, then reconsidering the offer, acquiesced. "That will be most kind," she said.

Higgins, setting his empty glass aside, rose from the wingback chair. "Speaking of the hour, it's late. I best be getting back to town. Oney will want to charge the town another dollar rental if I'm tardy."

"I'll see you to the automobile," said Calder rising to see Higgins off. Once they were far enough away from the house that their conversation could not be overheard, he said, "I find Agent Percival's presence at tonight's revival most puzzling. It might prove helpful if we could find out what he was up to."

Higgins nodded. "Any ideas?"

"Check with Longfellow. He's practically made a case study of Percival's movements since his arrival in Relay. If anyone's privy it's him."

"Will do," Higgins responded.

"And Higgins, I needn't add this should be *on the QT*. No need to involve anyone else, especially Longfellow."

"I'll be the model of discretion," Higgins said giving several rapid turns on the Olds' hand-crank. The engine, spurted into life, amid a series of loud, unevenly spaced backfires. Reaching for the spark control, Higgins quickly adjusted its setting and the engine settled happily down into a rhythmic chug-chugging.

Higgins slid behind the tiller, as he did he chuckled. "Let's hope Nora Battington doesn't catch wind of Miss Hopkins stay at your home." Lowering his driving goggles into position, he added, "If she even suspects, neither your or Miss Hopkins's good name will be worth a plugged nickel."

With that he shifted into gear and the machine roared into the night.

Chapter Seventeen
Wednesday Night Club
Conspiracies Abound

As usual, The Viaduct Hotel's dinning room was the setting for The Wednesday Night Club's weekly gathering. Tonight its membership had increased by one.

Professing tiring of the fare at his own establishment, The Scarlet Lady, Longfellow had intruded on the gathering. In due course his true purpose of attending presented itself. It was Victoria's mention of Nora Battington that ignited the brouhaha.

"I had a visit from Nora Battington today," she remarked during a lull in the conversation.

"Ha!" grumbled old Colonel Musgrave. Sitting his drink aside he turned to Victoria. "I knew things were too quiet. What's that old tabby up to now?"

"She's circulating a petition. Wanted me to sign."

"Petition?" said Father Meguiar. "What kind of petition?" With only the hint of foam remaining in his glass of Old Stoudt, and his purse nearly depleted, the old priest turned to probing the depths of his timeworn cassock. As usual the quarry was his ever-elusive packet of cigarettes.

"I'm not quite sure," replied Victoria. "You know how she re-lacquers that straw bonnet of hers every summer?" To this, Victoria received several nods of acknowledgment.

Nora Battington, unlike the younger generation, still clung to the old ways. Instead of purchasing a new bonnet whenever the current color fell into disfavor,

Nora would buy a dime size bottle of hat paint and lacquer last year's hat. Her present bonnet bore three, perhaps four, coats of varying shades of lavender and blues. This year's color was a delicate hue of robin's egg. Only recently applied, the lacquer emitted a strong wave of irritating fumes that enveloped anyone venturing close.

"My poor eyes were tearing something dreadful," continued Victoria. "So nearly overwhelmed by the fumes, I barely managed to get through the first few lines of the petition. Something to do with dog licenses, I believe."

Calder's suspicions were immediately aroused. He paused in the act of sliding his tin of Turks to Father Meguiar. "Dog licenses?" Turning to Longfellow, he said, "By chance, do you have anything to do with this, Longfellow?"

"Me? Me?" chirped Longfellow. "Certainly not!"

Calder's eyes narrowed accusingly. "Are you sure? This has all the marks of an out and out conspiracy between you and Nora."

Longfellow drew himself up to his full height. "Conspiracy? Why it's nothing of the sort. I have, on occasion, provided Mrs. Battington with the fruits of my English grammar school education, and I may have proffered a suggestion or two. But, I can assure you, Inspector, the document was her idea alone."

Calder wasn't satisfied. "Just what was the subject matter of this document you may have proffered a suggestion on?"

Longfellow, his nose tilted slightly upwards, replied, "I dare say a matter dear to hearts of all civic-minded citizens of Relay ... ridding our fair streets of unlicensed and uncontrollable beasts."

"Aaaaah. I see," said Calder. Longfellow's intent suddenly became crystal clear.

"See what?" said Victoria.

"This petition," said Calder. "Its got little, if

anything, to do with licensing of dogs. This is nothing more than an underhanded attempt to get rid of Bounce."

Now, whether Bounce was a stray, as most townsmen would agree, or, whether he had been set upon Longfellow by Marvin, owner of the Boar's Head Tavern, as Longfellow so firmly believed, mattered little. Either way Longfellow had no love for the dog. He saw Nora's petition as a golden opportunity to rid himself of the scruffy little terrier once and for all.

"I just happened to have a copy of the petition," said Longfellow, withdrawing a document from inside his jacket and producing a fountain pen. He looked hopefully around the table. "Now, who would like to be the first to sign?"

"Not I," snorted Willaby.

"Nor me!" declared Sheriff Higgins. "Why, there's not a drop of malice in that dog. Old Bounce merely likes to romp about, same as any dog would."

"Easy enough for you to say, Sheriff, retorted Longfellow. I've been the victim of his vicious assaults on more than one occasion. And I'm not the only one. Why, only several days ago the inspector himself witnessed such an unprovoked attack on one of Relay's citizens."

"Attack?" said Calder. "When?"

"Just last Sunday. At the alley's edge, next to the bank. Surely you haven't forgotten, Inspector. Poor Mrs. Battington nearly suffered a stroke."

"Stroke? My foot!" huffed Calder. "Let me see that paper." Grabbing the document from Longfellow's hand, he began to read. After several minutes he tossed the paper aside, glared at Longfellow. "This is nothing but a bunch of hogwash," he declared. "You'll never get this past the town council."

Longfellow gave a triumphal smile. Producing another petition form, he said, "I wouldn't be so sure, Inspector. As you can see, this one is completely filled.

Already there are more than the prerequisite twenty-five signatures needed, ensuring its presentation before the council. I'm sure being learned men, the council will be compelled to find in our favor."

Calder passed the petition around for all to read. Higgins, next in line, was not at all pleased with the document's wording. As sheriff he would be charged with the ordinance's implementation and enforcement.

"We'll see about this," growled Colonel Musgrave when he had read the petition. He glared at Longfellow. "An old army comrade once told me, 'Be careful what you wish for, it may just come to pass.'"

"It can't come a minute too soon," retorted Longfellow. "Good riddance is what I say! That beastly animal has preyed upon the defenseless citizens of Relay once too often." He turned to Higgins, wagged a finger. "Once this ordinance is enacted, I'll expect you to do your duty, Sheriff."

"It's not passed yet," growled Higgins.

Longfellow rose. He returned the completed document to his jacket pocket, leaving the blank one where it laid on the table. "A mere formality," he said. He gestured to the blank form. "I'll leave that in case any of you come to your senses and wish to reconsider signing."

After Longfellow's departure, the plotting began.

"What are we to do?" said Victoria.

Father Meguiar stubbed his cigarette out. "I don't know, child," he said. "It's all too confusing. When those two get their heads together, it's the devil's workshop at full tilt. Anything is possible."

"Well, we better come up with something fast," declared Higgins. "I don't fancy myself as being the town dog catcher."

"Maybe we could start a petition of our own," suggested Victoria. "I'm sure we can collect enough signatures to challenge the legality of their petition."

"Won't do," replied Higgins. "I've checked their

petition. Everything is in order. The council's compelled to consider all petitions legally presented to it."

Victoria flushed with anger. "This is Nora's doing," she declared. "Longfellow's not that devious. Nora never did like Bounce. It's her way of getting revenge and maybe rubbing salt into the wound. Mark me, Nora's the driving force behind this." She turned to Colonel Musgrave, occupying his usual seat at the head of the table. "Don't you agree Colonel?"

As with everything else in his life, the military figured prominently in Musgrave's response.

"I do Madame," he said. "I do indeed. Now as I see it, what this calls for is a decisive plan, an order of battle if you will. First, we'll need to elect a leader." His chest puffed, ever so slightly, "Preferably someone with military experience to draw upon."

He wiped the ends of his great, walrus mustache positioned beneath the beak-like nose with the back of his hand. There could be little doubt in anyone's mind who Colonel Musgrave thought that person should be.

"Next, we'll probe the enemy's defenses," he said, jabbing the empty air with his fork. "Seek out his weak points. Then we attack! Attack! Attack!"

He thumped a large boney hand on the table to drive home the point. Well-pleased, he pushed back from the table and surveyed his companions. Just what, or how this great plan of his was to be implemented and carried through, he didn't know. He would tend to that minor detail at some later date, after he had assumed command.

Willaby's face suddenly lit up. "I have the perfect solution!" he said, with an air of smugness. "One of us will simply have to adopt Bounce. No longer a stray, the petition wouldn't apply to him. That will resolve the whole problem, wouldn't it?" He crossed his arms, looked about, pleased that he had come up with the solution first. "Now, who will it be? Which one of us will volunteer to adopt Bounce?"

"Not me." It was Sheriff Higgins speaking. "As much as I would like to, Jeremiah and Bounce don't get along."

Jeremiah was the official jailhouse mouser. A female cat of unknown pedigreed, she had been presented to Sheriff Higgins as a kitten by the widow Collins. Although most certainly a female, she bore the most unfeminine of names... Jeremiah. Higgins, hoping to find favor with the young widow, had no wish to inform her of the error. Besides, wasn't one name as good as another? And as far as he could tell, Jeremiah didn't seem to mind.

The question of who would adopt Bounce passed around the table, from one occupant to another - each time receiving a negative response. At last it came to Calder. All eyes turned expectantly to the inspector.

"What about it, Inspector?" Willaby said, encouragingly. "You can't deny that Bounce does seem to favor you over the rest of us."

Calder had said nothing during this exchange. Still, if the gleam in his eye was any indication, his brain had not been idle. He gave a wry smile. "I have a better plan. As law abiding citizens of Relay, I think we should bow to the will of the people."

"What!" exclaimed Willaby. "You know what that will mean. You've read the petition. You know the consequences, without a legal owner Bounce will surely be put down."

A stream of protests followed, with each new member's voice rising above the preceding one.

Taking a piece of silverware, Calder lightly tapped the side of his water glass. The noise subsided, and heads turned to a still smiling Calder. "I'm not suggesting we permit the demise of our good companion, Bounce. To the contrary, what I am suggesting is that we reread the ordinance...only this time with a more critical eye." The smile widened.

Chapter Eighteen
An old adversary returns
High Street - Midday

It was well past the noon hour when Agent Percival, a large twine-bound package under his arm, exited the tobacconist shop. He tipped his hat in greeting.

"Good afternoon, Inspector," he said, effortlessly falling in step with Calder. "Mind if I walk with you a ways?"

"No, not at all," replied Calder.

This was a lie, of course, for it was plain Percival and he hadn't seen eye to eye since their first meeting in Longfellow's. Events had not altered. However, being in particularly amiable spirits this day, Calder added, "I was just on my way over to The Scarlet Lady, if you care to join me."

Percival ran a finger under the rim of his celluloid collar, gave a tug, then peered up into the searing glare of the midday sun. "Don't mind if I do, Inspector," he said. "A cooling draft from one of Longfellow's taps would do wonders for this parched throat of mine."

The two men continued on until they reached Hankin's Dry Goods Emporium. There they paused, relishing in the cooling shade of the mercantile's massive, canvas awning. Before them the cobbled streets of Relay, sweltering under a hot August sun, were all but deserted. Only the melodious clacking of a horse's hooves against the stone cobbles disrupted the afternoon calm.

"I have a confession to make, Inspector," confessed Percival.

Calder turned. "Oh."

"Yes. You see, this wasn't exactly a chance meeting, my bumping into you like this."

A look of feigned confusion showed on Calder's face. "No?"

"No," replied Percival. "I had been waiting inside the tobacco shop. Twenty minutes, if you must know, on the off-chance you might pass by."

This revelation held no great surprise for Calder. Since his arrival in Relay, Percival had proven to be a resourceful and calculating individual."

Traversing High Street Calder paused at the entrance to *The Scarlet Lady*, his hand resting on the pub's louvered half-door. He surveyed his companion. "And why was that?"

Percival hesitated, a sheepish expression spread across his features. "I find myself in a rather awkward situation, Inspector. A bit embarrassing. You see, a pressing matter has presented itself and I feel the need to consult with you."

"I see," said Calder, nodding his head in agreement. He pushed the door open, and then turned back to Percival. "Well, the invitation to join me still stands. I suggest we discuss it inside, away from this heat."

Moments later they were seated in the relative coolness of *The Scarlet Lady's* interior. Only then did Percival permit himself the luxury of removing his boater hat and loosening the stiffly starched collar. He ran a hand along his pomade-scented hair, paying special attention not to disturb the precisely groomed center part.

"So," began Calder, "this pressing matter you mentioned, tell me about it and what is it you wish of me."

Percival raised the heavy gobbet of lager to his lips, draining nearly half of the gobbet's contents before returning it to the table. "I'm afraid it's a bit past the pressing stage, Inspector," he said, wiping the slight foam residue from his thin, heavily waxed mustache with a handkerchief.

Calder said nothing, preferring instead to let Percival proceed at his own pace.

Percival carefully refolded the handkerchief, returned it his jacket pocket before continuing. "You'll recall our earlier conversation? My reason for coming to Relay. The upcoming international conference at Camp Meade and the government's fear the Wright's machine might somehow be used to disrupt it?"

Calder nodded.

"Well, my superiors are becoming somewhat concerned. They're seeking assurances that I've got this missing aeroplane caper under control."

"That's quite understandable. What did you tell them?"

"A response straight out of the Field Investigator's Manual. That progress, while slow, is being made. Further, that we're conducting an intensive, barn by barn search of the surrounding countryside in an effort to locate the Wright's missing machine." Percival paused. "And lastly, that I expect a break in the case shortly."

"And do you?"

Percival sighed in frustration. "No, not really," he said. "I'm afraid I might have overstated my position and therein lies my problem. I'll concede the case is proving more difficult than I originally perceived." He glanced about making sure Longfellow, who was known for his ability to lend an attentive, but uninvited ear toward any unguarded conversation, was not lurking close by. "Mind you, there's nothing I can lay my finger on, but I have a growing suspicion Brother Nathan and that ragtag flock of his may somehow be involved in this caper."

"*So,*" thought Calder. "*Once again, it comes back to Brother Nathan.*" He and the young agent were at odds over the course of the investigation, but on this they were in complete agreement. He struck a match allowing the flame to flare, then die back before putting it to his cigarette. He reached for his drink. "So, that accounts for your presence at the revival campgrounds Sunday. Tell me, what did you hope to accomplish by your appearance there? Take that suit and straw hat of yours for instance. A bit too conspicuous for a fundamentalist gathering don't you think?"

"You saw me then."

Calder nodded. "Lets just say you were a bit out of place."

Percival gave a nervous half-chuckle. "Not one of my better performances, I'm afraid."

"And your purpose of being there? You don't strike me as being a particularly religious man."

Percival smiled. "Oh, I'm not, Inspector. As the reason for my presence, that can be attributed to the receipt of a note."

"A note?" Calder's ears pricked at the words. "What sort of note?"

"A rather strange note," Percival concluded. "Unsigned and covertly slipped under my hotel door sometime during the night hours."

"This note," said Calder. "What did it say?"

"Not much," replied Percival. "It contained just a single line. *If you want to recover the aeroplane, attend tonight's revival meeting.*"

Calder shook his head in dismay. "Along with the lure of the rouge-cheek doxy, one of the oldest ruses in the book. Naturally you saw it for what it was."

Percival was taken aback. "Of course I did," he huffed. "I knew I could be walking into a trap, but I was in a quandary. I wasn't making any headway locating the aeroplane on my own, and it was too good of an opportunity to pass over. I took the proper precautions though." He gave a reassuring pat to his jacket pocket. "Yes sir, had my government-issued revolver with me, just in case."

"And what happened?"

"That's the queer thing, Inspector ... nothing." Percival slumped back into his chair. "Absolutely nothing." He reached for his drink. "Not a solitary soul approached me, no note was pressed into my hand. Nothing."

"I see," said Calder. "Then that leads us to the second part of my question, what is it you wish of me?"

Percival squirmed in his seat. It was evident he wasn't comfortable with what he was about to propose. "I know we didn't get off on the right foot, Inspector. However, I was hoping we might be able to mend our differences, maybe even cooperate." He paused. "Perhaps we might join forces. You know, share information and the like."

"*Not very likely*," thought Calder. Any exchange of information would likely be a one-way transaction, with me receiving the short end of the stick. "That might be a possibility," he replied, careful not to fully commit himself.

From his seat across the table a smile formed on Percival's lips. "Splendid Inspector! To show my good faith," he said, "I'll share an interesting tidbit gained from my little excursion. You see, despite coming up empty-handed on my end of the investigation, my trip wasn't totally for naught."

"Oh?"

From a tin, Percival withdrew one of his trademark, hand-rolled Egyptian cigarettes and began fumbling for a match. After accepting the offer of a light from Calder, he continued, "As I was saying, Inspector, I did stumble upon an interesting tidbit during my little foray."

"What would that be?"

"A glimpse of red hair protruding from the edge of a hood of one of Brother Nathan's followers." Percival paused. "Yes, sir, bright copper/red hair," he added, with a look of satisfaction. He inhaled, taking a deep drag of the foul smelling cigarette as he watched to see what reaction his words would draw. When Calder didn't immediately respond Percival leaned forward, "As you know, Inspector, Miss Hopkins's has reported her brother missing, and I'm told he possesses a particular shade of red hair."

"You think this person you saw may be Miss Hopkins's brother?"

Percival exhaled a stream of stark, blue/grey smoke skyward, sat back, a wry smile clinging to his lips. "Perhaps. I can't say for sure, but there it is. In any case you must admit it's an intriguing possibility."

"*A flash of red hair,*" thought Calder. "*Certainly isn't much to go on.*" Still, after two weeks his own investigation had produced little more.

Percival continued. "While missing persons are normally not the sort of thing the government takes an interest in..." Percival let the thought dangle as his smile slowly deepened.

"Yes, go on."

Percival didn't answer directly. Instead he said, "But then one doesn't often come across a delicate creature such as Miss Hopkins. Like many of the lads in the village, I've developed a certain fondness for that young lady."

Calder's patience was wearing thin. It seemed Percival enjoyed the annoying habit of dispensing information out in bits and drabs. "Well?" he said. "Are you going to tell me, or am I suppose to guess what happened next?"

The smile dwindled. "Here's where I'm afraid we run into a bit of a disappointment."

"What do you mean, disappointment? Was it Miss Hopkins' brother or not?"

"I don't know. You see, upon observing me, this fellow turned and disappeared back behind the stage." Percival turned an empty palm. "As you can well imagine, in my attire it would be an impossible task to shadow him and remain undetected." He shrugged. "There was nothing left for me to do. I was forced to let him go."

It was apparent Percival had no knowledge of Priscilla Hopkins's presence at the revival grounds, or had he considered the possibility of her masquerading as one of Nathan's followers.

"You referred to this robed individual as a he. Are you certain it was a male you observed and not a woman?"

Percival considered. "I suppose," he said. "I mean, I just naturally assumed. One wouldn't expect the gentler sex to go traipsing about in such a costume, would he?"

"No, I guess not," said Calder, deciding not to tell of his encounter with Priscilla Hopkins.

There were now two distinct scenarios before Calder. One, the more likely one, Roger Hopkins was not a member of Nathan's group. Percival had simply stumbled upon Miss Hopkins as she went about in search of her brother and mistook her for Roger Hopkins. In which case he was back to square one. Then there was scenario number two, the one he considered the more perplexing one. In this scenario, Roger Hopkins had indeed ventured to Relay and for some unknown reason, sought and been granted refuge within Brother Nathan's church. If this proved factual, what was Roger's purpose in seeking out Brother Nathan? Surely there was no possibility of him amassing a great fortune with the eccentric preacher. Why was he hiding from his sister? And lastly and the more intriguing part, given Roger Hopkins's interest in flying, was his affiliation with Brother Nathan somehow connected to the theft of the Wright's aeroplane?

The answers to these and other questions were as

elusive as the machine's whereabouts. Calder made a mental note to check with Mother in Baltimore. Maybe he could be of some assistance.

Percival reached for the parcel lying beside him. "Oh, and speaking of my attire, Inspector, I almost forgot." Placing the parcel before him, he untied the string and peeled back the brown paper wrapping. "My best suit jacket," he said, spreading the jacket out upon the table. "Nearly ruined it during my attendance at the revival."

"I inquired of Miss Victoria, seeking a recommendation for a local seamstress to properly mend it. Puzzling thing, despite the damage being relatively minor, she seemed rather beside herself. Said I should show it to you before I have it repaired."

A jacket in need of repair? thought Calder. *Hardly seems the sort of thing Victoria would concern herself over.* Nevertheless he examined the jacket. "I see no damage," he said after a quick examination of the jacket.

"There," said Percival, indicating the most minor of imperfection in the garment's outer fabric, chest level near the outer edge. As Percival had stated the damage was ever so slight, consisting of an inconsequential snag - much like one would receive passing a thorny branch. While the tear may have been inconsequential, the jacket lining was what intrigued Calder. Crafted from the finest silk, it contained an almost imperceptible, but perfectly formed hole directly corresponding with the location of the snag in the jacket's outer fabric — a hole whose diameter was no larger than the diameter of an ice pick's shaft.

An ice pick's shaft.

The words sent a wave of apprehension sweeping over Calder. Without looking up, he said, "Tell me, how did this occur precisely?"

Percival frowned. "Precisely? I don't know. Is that important? It's only a minor snag."

"It's very important. Now think."

I'm not really sure, Inspector. Must have snagged it on a nail or something."

"Do you recall someone bumping against you?"

Percival seemed confused. "You mean intentionally?"

Calder nodded.

Percival thought long and hard. "Hard to say, Inspector" he said finally. "As you can well imagine, a lot of jostling goes on in a crowd like that. When the faithful feel the spirit moving inside arms flail, and bodies start swaying to the ring of tambourines." A surprised look came over Percival's face. "Ah. Now, I know what you're thinking, that there were pickpockets working the crowd. That's the case isn't it? Well, not to worry, Inspector. I'm not some lad fresh from the farm. Before I left the hotel, I took the precaution of placing my wallet in my front trouser pocket where it would be safe from pickpockets."

"Damnation, man. I'm not worried about your wallet's safety. It's your life I'm concerned about."

Percival's brow furrowed. "Me? Why in heaven's name should you have cause to worry over me?"

Calder did not answer. He slumped backward into the chair, his eyes glued to the jacket. One name racing through his mind... *Fernell!* Could it be possible? Had his old nemesis returned?

Percival pressed home his demand. "Inspector, you haven't answered my question. Why should you have cause to worry about me?"

Why indeed? The damage to Percival's jacket wasn't definitive proof of Fernell's presence, and might well have been the result of a common nail snag. However if Fernell were present, Percival's life was in danger. Still the question remains, why Percival? That egocentric idiot presented no threat. Without revealing the possible existence of a master assassin in their midst Calder felt compelled to warn Percival.

"It is mere speculation on my part at this stage," he said. "However, until this case is solved, you would do well to guard yourself. Trust no one and above all avoid crowded situations. They could hold tragic consequences for you."

Thoroughly confused, Percival merely nodded. "I will, Inspector. Now what about our cooperating? My superiors in Washington..." He managed a weak smile. "Can we at least agree to keep each other apprized of new developments?"

This arrangement Calder found agreeable. "Your concern is concentrated solely on preventing any disruption to the Camp Meade conference. My objectives are somewhat different. However both our concerns hinge on the recovery of the Wright brother's flying machine." He lifted his glass. "To that end should I come across any information involving the Camp Meade Conference, I will be sure to contact you."

This seemed to satisfy Percival as he rose and offered his hand. "Thank you, Inspector, thank you very much. And now I must be off; my daily progress report to Washington is due."

After Percival departure Calder had time to reflect. Could Fernell have returned? The Camp Meade Conference, with representatives from a host of nations attending, would present a tempting target for someone of his particular trade. Should this proved true; it was not only Percival that would have to exercise care. He, along with Victoria, would also be in danger.

Chapter Nineteen
Village Post Office
Several days later

Victoria looked up from her work. Across the narrow space that served as the post office lobby, the arthritic form of Albert Delahaye stood gazing at the wall containing a selection of wanted posters.

Relay, unlike larger cities, did not have a great number of wanted posters displayed on its notice board. As the town postmistress, the selection of photographs to be displayed fell to Victoria. Relay was a small village, she reasoned. A tranquil village, the sort of place where everyone knew everyone. A place where there were few strangers and still fewer crimes. Visitors, be they hotel guests or fleeing felons, stood little chance of going unnoticed in Relay.

What was displayed were the obligatory number to satisfy the postal authorities should they chance by, plus the occasional poster that by its very nature piqued Victoria's fancy. The remainder of the space was given over to what was considered more important postings – notices of upcoming community events, the occasional lost property notice, and one mustn't forget the annual adverts for field laborers at harvest time.

Victoria laid her pen down, pushed her work aside. She found herself taking pity on Mr. Delahaye. She watched as the old man inched closer to the board, squinting as he did in order to get a clearer view of a poster. She slowly shook her head. *"Poor old Mr. Delahaye,"* she thought. Since his arrival in Relay, Colonel Musgrave had done everything he could to monopolize the old gentleman's time, traipsing about from one battlefield to another, reliving past skirmishes and recalling fallen comrades. And for what? As far as she could see nothing more that a futile attempt to catch a fleeting glimpse of one's long forgotten youth.

It was half two ... the quiet part of the day, and the post office was nearly devoid of customers. What was needed, she decided, was some genteel conversation and perhaps a generous offering of her famous sweet tea. That should set things to right! There was a pitcher of tea just a few steps away, chilling in the wooden icebox. She rose, prepared to invite Mr. Delahaye to join her, when the bell over the door jingled. It was Priscilla Hopkins. Priscilla, instead of taking her usual path to the counter, made straight for the old man.

"You must be Mr. Delahaye," she said as she approached the aging veteran.

Albert Delahaye turned. He smiled, pleased to find a beautiful young woman standing before him. He nodded, made a feeble attempt at a bow. "That I am, Miss..."

"Hopkins, Priscilla Hopkins." Priscilla returned the smile and extended a slender hand. "Oh, I can't tell you how glad I am to finally get a chance to meet you, Mr. Delahaye."

"I assure you the pleasure is entirely mine, Madame," replied Albert Delahaye in his most courtly manner.

"Colonel Musgrave has told me of his long acquaintance with you." Laying a hand to her cheek, Priscilla said, "And of the daring balloon rescue."

"Aaaaah yes," said Albert Delahaye trying not to laugh, but failing in the effort. "Old Rutherford takes great pleasure in its retelling."

"That he does," agreed Priscilla. "But I can assure you, Mr. Delahaye, I would have been mortally terrified if I had been in your place. Imagine, stranded high above the ground, amid sheets of shredded canvas and shattered bits of wicker. Lines and rope everywhere ... and the bullets! I think you were ever so brave."

Albert Delahaye shook his head to show he was not in agreement. "I was a very young and foolish lad," he confessed. "Nothing more. But, bravery can assume many forms, Miss Hopkins." With the tip of his walking stick, he pointed to one of the posters. "For instance, I see by that notice you have a brother missing. A terrible tragedy for a woman of your delicate nature to endure." He gently patted her hand. "Takes a brave heart to sit and wait, not knowing the fate of a loved one."

Tilting her head to the side, Priscilla studied the old man's features. She was quite taken by his concern. "Why Mr. Delahaye, how perceptive of you. It's almost as if you have experienced a similar plight."

"Indeed I have, miss. Indeed I have. My elder brother, Vincent, fell at Gettysburg. His mortal remains were never recovered. For a long time I sheltered the hope that someday he might return ... but of course, he never did."

"My sincerest condolences, Mr. Delahaye."

"No need, miss," he said. "Time has a way of tempering the pain. Life continues on and so must we."

Laying a reassuring hand on Albert Delahaye's arm, Priscilla said, "You have such a perceptive outlook, Mr. Delahaye. You must have led an extraordinary life. I think it would be fascinating to hear of your exploits. Perhaps you could join me at dinner this evening and we could talk further."

Albert Delahaye nodded in agreement. "I'd hardly call them exploits, Miss Hopkins, but yes, I would like that. Now I must bid a good day to you." He half chuckled, a mischievous gleam in his eye. "Col. Musgrave is taking me on yet another one of his little field excursions. This time we are to visit the bottom lands near Halethorpe, and I see by the clock I'm already tardy."

"Not another battlefield? Surely, not in this heat."

"Oh no, I shall be spared that tribulation. We will be traveling in the cooling shade, near the Patapsco."

Priscilla started to protest, but Albert Delahaye merely shrugged.

"My time in Relay is limited," he explained, "and Musgrave wants to show me the field Hubert Latham used in his nineteen and ten flight over Baltimore before I leave. He thinks I'd be interested, merely because Latham was a fellow Frenchman." He chuckled. "I'm not, of course, but we mustn't tell Musgrave that."

"I shan't betray your confidence," replied Priscilla, laying a finger to her lips. "It will remain our secret."

"I wouldn't want to disappoint him," continued the old man. "He is so pleased with his narrative on local history." With a smile and a tip of his hat, Albert Delahaye turned. "Still," he said over his shoulder as he retreated toward the doorway, "it must have been a grand spectacle to witness, I'll grant him that."

Victoria watched as Albert Delahaye exited through the doorway, and then scurried across High Street in the direction of the hotel. *"Despite his affliction,"* she mused, *"Mr. Delahaye seems to amble about remarkably well."*

Priscilla approached Victoria. Placing her handbag on the counter, she said, "Good afternoon, Miss Byron. A fascinating individual, Mr. Delahaye, don't you think?"

Turning her attention to Priscilla, Victoria smiled. "Indeed I do, Miss Hopkins. Now, how may I help you?"

Withdrawing a five-cent piece from her change purse, Priscilla said, "Five, one penny postage stamps, please. And I wonder, has there been any response to my newspaper insertions?"

Victoria shifted through the stack marked general

delivery, shook her head. "Sorry, nothing so far."

Priscilla sighed. "Oh dear. I was so hoping, if not Roger, then perhaps someone knowing of his whereabouts might heed my appeal and contact me."

"There is still the evening post to sort," consoled Victoria. "Oh!" She reached to a row of pigeonholes, removing a rather cumbersome large envelope with a red wax seal on the rear flap. "I almost forgot. This came for you." She slide the envelope under the screen opening. "It looks important. I was going to send it over with the hotel's mail, but seeing as you're here."

Priscilla took the envelope and looked at the return address. Her face fell. "My solicitor," she said, tucking it unopened into her handbag.

"Not bad news, I trust."

Priscilla, seeing the concern on Victoria's face said, "Oh, it's nothing of consequence, Miss Byron."

"I must apologize," said Victoria, her cheeks turning an embarrassing pink. "I didn't mean to intrude. Official letters tend to disturb me, particularly ones from a solicitor's office. They're oftentimes harbingers of unpleasant news."

"Not in this case. The firm of Baumgartner and Owens has been my family's advisors for ages. I've arranged for them to transfer sufficient funds to cover my financial needs during my stay in Relay." She snapped the clasp on the handbag closed. "I dare say this contains nothing more than some forms to sign."

"Oh," said a visibly relieved Victoria. "I see. Any thought on how long that might be? Your stay, that is."

"No. I really can't say. Until the fate of my brother is revealed, I suppose. Well, I must be on my way, Miss Byron. By the way, have you seen Inspector Calder?"

Victoria shook her head. "If he's in town, he's most likely with the sheriff. Sometimes those two are as thick as thieves. Have you tried *The Scarlet Lady*?"

Gathering up her stamps and handbag, Priscilla said, "No. Is that the type of establishment a lady dare venture into?"

"Have no fear, Miss Hopkins. Longfellow maintains a respectful establishment. I can assure you no woman's reputation has ever been soiled there."

"Then that's where I shall look for him. Good day, Miss Byron."

After Priscilla departure, Victoria found it difficult to concentrate on her work. Something was troubling her. Had it been Priscilla's letter, something Priscilla said or was there something else? Perhaps it was merely guilt. Official letters had never upset her. As postmistress, she had seen her share of bureaucratic mail. She had only used that ploy in an attempt to ascertain why Priscilla had been receiving like letters on an almost daily basis. But Priscilla had offered a reasonable explanation, hadn't she? Still....

After a few minutes she again laid the pen down. Perhaps it was a touch of stiffness settling in and a little movement was all that was needed. Stifling a yawn, she exited the teller's cage, and crossed the flooring leading to the display of wanted posters. She busied herself removing several outdated notices and rearranged those remaining. She then turned her attention to the posters, reinserting a dropped thumbtack. As she had done a thousand times before she reviewed the crimes, taking note of the dozen or so stiffly posed for photographs. Suddenly her eyes widened in disbelief.

Chapter Twenty
Old Dunham House
The Farewell Dinner

It was late afternoon when Victoria turned her bicycle onto the dirt lane leading to Old Dunham House. Mrs. Chaffinch answered the doorbell.

"Good afternoon, Mrs. Chaffinch. Is the Inspector about?"

Mrs. Chaffinch liked Victoria. A fine young woman was Miss Victoria. Of all the eligible women – not that there were that many in Relay – for the Inspector to choose from, she liked Victoria the best. She secretly hoped the inspector would soon ask Victoria for her hand in marriage. Wouldn't it be grand to hear a women's laughter about the place?

Mrs. Chaffinch nodded. "He'll be out in the stable with William. He's overseeing the training of Midnight. I'll just go and fetch him for you, miss."

Victoria's eyes danced with mischievous delight. "No, no. Not just yet, Mrs. Chaffinch. It's really you I came to see."

"Me, Miss?"

"Yes, Mrs. Chaffinch. Do you think you could recognize Mr. Gregson if he should return?"

Mrs. Chaffinch puzzled, nodded.

"Even if he wore a disguise?"

"The eyes aren't what they used to be, but yes dear, I think I would."

"Good. I have a little plan and it will require your help. Might we have a private, girl to girl talk before you announce my presence to the inspector?"

Mrs. Chaffinch was both puzzled and flattered. "Plan? Certainly, Miss. I'll just get us some fresh lemonade and we can talk undisturbed in the library."

* * *

The library doors swung open and Calder, buttoning the shirtsleeve, entered. "Victoria, what a pleasant surprise. It's always a pleasure to see you. Tell me, what brings you out here?"

"Oh, nothing special. It was such a pleasant day and I was tired of being cooped up in that stuffy old post office. I thought I might do with a bit of exercise and bicycled out."

"But you must be thirsty after your trip. I believe Mrs. C has some fresh lemonade in the ice box, I have her bring us a glass."

Calder turned to reach for the servant pull.

"Perhaps later," Victoria replied, carefully sliding her now empty lemonade glass behind the globed table lamp. "To be quite frank there's more to my visit than a need for exercise."

Calder eased himself into the wingback and lit up a Turk. "I thought so." He smiled. "Go on, what can I do for you?"

"It's about that nice old gentleman, Mr. Delahaye."

"The Colonel's friend?"

"Yes. I happened to overhear him mentioning to Miss Hopkins that his time in Relay is drawing to a close."

Calder chuckled. "The colonel and he do seem to get along well. Like peas in a pod, one might say. Still, I know it will sadden old Musgrave to see his friend go."

"My thoughts exactly. I was thinking, won't it be grand if Mr. Delahaye were to be given a proper send off. Sort of a pleasant remembrance of his stay in Relay. After all Colonel Musgrave did save his life."

Calder nodded in agreement. "That would be a fitting gesture. What do you have in mind?"

"A farewell dinner. I thought we might hold a dinner in his honor. Would you attend?"

. "Most certainly. When is such an event scheduled?"

"I was thinking this Friday, at the hotel."

At the mention of the hotel Calder frowned. "Oh, I don't know. This Friday? That would be nice, but the hotel's dinning room is rather crowded, especially on a Friday evening. Couldn't you possibly choose another date?"

Victoria's lower lip turned down ever so slightly. She sighed. "I'm afraid that's the problem. According to the Colonel, Mr. Delahaye will be leaving this weekend."

"That does present a problem." Calder pondered the problem. "I have the solution," he said after several minutes of reflection. "We'll hold it here, at Old Dunham House."

"Oh!" said a surprised Victoria. "On such short notice? Do you really think that's possible?"

"Well," said Calder. "We'll have to check with Mrs. C first. As you say it is short notice and a majority of the work and planning will fall upon her."

Calder reached out and pulled the servant's cord.

Mrs. Chaffinch appeared almost instantly bearing a tray with two glasses of sweet tea on it. Setting one before Victoria, and producing a roguish wink, she said, "I know you'll be thirsty, Miss Victoria after all your bicycling."

Taking his drink, Calder outlined his plan. "So, what do you think, Mrs. C? Could we manage it?"

"Oh, it'll be no burden at all. How many guests will you be having?"

"I really don't know. We haven't gotten that far along with the plan." He turned to Victoria.

Victoria began to count. "Naturally there would be Mr. Delahaye. The colonel, of course. You and me. Then

I think Higgins and that nice young widow he has his eye on. That's six. Let's see, your table has place settings for eight. We really should have another couple to complete the seating arrangement." She looked to Calder. "How about Priscilla Hopkins and Agent Percival?"

"Percival? Why in heaven's name would you want to invite that fellow? He's full of himself. Enough to drive one insane with that ego of his."

Victoria smiled. "Especially Agent Percival. He'll add a dash of intrigue to the evening.

"Eight people? I don't know. I was thinking of a smaller, more informal affair. What say you, Mrs. C?" He turned seeking corroboration from his housekeeper. "Wouldn't a party of eight be too large on such short notice?"

"Oh, no sir," Mrs. Chaffinch beamed. "Plenty of time. Hardly any problem at all. It'll be good, preparing a formal dinner again."

Calder wasn't convinced. "But eight people," he said. "You'll need assistance in the kitchen, I'm sure." He held up a hand silencing Mrs. Chaffinch's planned protest. "No, I insist Mrs. C, Victoria can procure temporary help in the village."

Only after she saw that Calder would not retreat did Mrs. Chaffinch reluctantly agreed. "Only for the serving and vegetable preparation," she warned. "The kitchen is still my domain. I'll not be having any strangers fooling with my spices and stirring my pots. I'll just go tell William. He'll need to be make extra provisions for the horses."

"Then it's all set. I'll leave it to you and Victoria.

With Mrs. Chaffinch's departure, Calder proceeded to the library's desk where he set about preparing a draft to cover the cost of the dinner and the hiring of additional staff.

Absently accepting the draft Victoria's thoughts appeared to be in a distant place.

Calder, in the process of returning the ledger to the desk drawer, paused. "Is something wrong? The draft, if the amount isn't sufficient enough I could increase-"

Startled from her thoughts, Victoria looked up. "No, no," she said, forcing a quick smile. "I'm sure it's quite adequate," she added without checking the amount.

"Then what?"

Victoria blushed. "You may think me foolish, but I couldn't help thinking about that horrible fiend, Fernell."

"Fernell?" Calder cast a suspicious eye at Victoria. "What made you think of that villain after all this time?"

"Oh, I don't know. Maybe it's just being in this house. After all it was his home for some time, and as I recall the library was his favorite room." She gave an involuntary shutter. "I can almost sense his presence here."

Calder looked around at the walls lined with books. "Perhaps. I never thought of it in that vein. I suppose the room could conger up past feelings for some."

Victoria sipped her tea. "Does Mrs. Chaffinch ever speak of him?"

"No."

"To think our Mrs. Chaffinch was here, under the very same roof with that monster. I shutter to think what could have happened to her."

Calder quickly pooh-poohed the idea. "Oh, I can't imagine Mrs. C was ever in any real danger. The last thing Fernell would do is harm Mrs. C, It would point the finger directly at him."

"Do you think she would recognize him?"

"Recognize him?"

Victoria looked up. "I mean if she should chance upon him again."

"Oh, I don't know. Hardly any chance of that ever happening."

"I'm sure you're right." Victoria rose. "Well, I must

be on my way, there are a thousand things to tend to before Friday evening. Lest of which is employing kitchen and domestic help for Mrs. Chaffinch."

"Naturally," smiled Calder.

After Victoria had left, Calder sat for some time reflecting on her visit. Of course it was all planned out before hand, between Victoria and Mrs. C ... that whole dinner party business including the guest list. He had quite easily seen through that charade. Exactly what Victoria was planning, or the reasoning behind it, he didn't know. And what was behind her bringing up the subject of Fernell?

"*I wonder what she is up to now,*" he thought.

Chapter Twenty-one
Along the Patapsco

Their tour of the lowland bordering the river complete, Colonel Musgrave eased the buggy into the shade of one of the numerous weeping willows that clung to the river's bank. Alighting from the vehicle, he said, "Won't be but a minute, Frenchy. Just going to dip my handkerchief into the water. I feel the need to cool my fevered brow before we begin our journey back."

Albert Delahaye, his shirt sleeves rolled up and his jacket relegated to the corner of the buggy's seat, puffed contentedly on his cigar. He nodded, gesturing with his free hand. "Take your time, Rutherford. If it's all the same to you, I think I'll just sit here and enjoy the breeze."

Musgrave shrugged. "Suit yourself," he said, as he made his way down the narrow path leading to the river edge.

The willow's branches, like the listless tails of a dozen kites on a summer's afternoon, bent to sweep the water's edge. Under the canopy formed by its boughs, Colonel Musgrave paused to allow his eyes to adjust to the dimness. Kneeling at the river's edge, he dipped his handkerchief into the swirling current. Moments later, he let out a startled scream and scampered back up the bank.

"What in tarnation!" exclaimed Delahaye from his seat up in the buggy. He searched his companion's

147

ashen face. "What's gotten into you, Rutherford? You look like Lucifer himself has reached out and taken a hold of you."

Musgrave pointed a shaky finger back toward the river. "Worse than that, Frenchy. Oh Lord, much worse. I bent down to splash some water on my face and there … in the water."

"Yes, yes. For God Sake man go on. Out with it, what happened?"

Musgrave grasped Albert Delahaye's arm, his fingers digging into the flesh. "In the water, entangled in a mess of tree roots, I swear Frenchy, there was a face."

"What?"

"Yes, yes. A face I tell you. A horrible, death mask of a face staring squarely back into my eyes. Oh it was horrible!"

"Oh, Rutherford." Delahaye laughed, pulling his arm away. "You old fool, the heat's finally done you in. You've merely seen your own reflection in the water, nothing more." He looked at his companion, wild-eyed, hair disheveled and face dripping river water. "Though I can't say as I blame you, you look a poor sight."

Despite the accuracy of Delahaye's statement, Colonel Musgrave became indignant. He drew himself up to his full height. "Not unless I've lost a good fifty years and grew a full head of copper-red hair."

The laughter drained from Albert Delahaye's voice. "What?" He eased himself down from the carriage. "Maybe you better show me."

Moments later Delahaye rose, looked around. "Doesn't look good, Rutherford. A terrible tragedy. Looks like the poor chap's must have fallen in and drowned himself." He turned and started back up the incline.

"But, what about the body? We just can't leave him like that. We'll have to tell someone."

"Leave him. He's caught fast. But, he's a strapping lad and it'll take someone stronger than we two to free him from those roots. There's nothing we can do for him."

"But-"

"The authorities will have to be notified, of course. We'll notify Sheriff Higgins the moment we get back to town."

"No," replied Musgrave, who by this time had regained some of his composure. "I've got a better idea. The inspector's house is just down the road apiece. He's on the telephone circuit. It will be faster if we go there."

* * *

A short time later found Colonel Musgrave and Albert Delahaye in the library of Old Dunham house, sipping on iced-laden drinks heavily fortified with brandy. Calder was on the telephone.

"Higgins, Calder here. I've got Colonel Musgrave and Mr. Delahaye with me. They say they discovered a body in the river, at the foot of Halethorpe Farm Road. Would you be so good as to put a call to the county sheriff and then perhaps you'd better arrange to meet us at the scene."

"Halethorpe Farm, you say?" Higgins transferred the earpiece to the other ear where his hearing was better. "That's a good ways out of my jurisdiction. Why not notify the country sheriff direct? I take it something's amiss?"

"You could say that." Calder paused. "Musgrave says the corpse is that of a young lad with bright copper-colored hair."

The line went silent.

After a few moments, Calder said, "And Higgins."

"Yes?"

"Mum's the word. Don't say anything to anybody, especially Miss Hopkins. I don't want to involve her ... at least not at this point. This may, or may not, be her brother. No sense alarming her until we can check for identification."

"Right. Did Musgrave say what the cause of death was?"

"No, only that he's not been in the water long."

"I see. Doctor O'Keefe's with me. We were going over to Longfellow's for a bit of lunch, I'll bring him along."

"Good. Might speed things along."

Chapter Twenty-two
At the scene

Kneeling over the body, Dr. O'Keefe worked the corpse's lower jaw, and then slowly moved the head side to side. Both moved freely. "Musgrave's right," he said. "He's not been in the water long. No signs of rigor having set in."

"How long, Doc," asked Higgins, taking up a position close to the body.

"Hard to tell. Not long. Probably not more than a couple hours, would be my guess."

"Accident?"

Snapping the clasp on his medical case closed, Dr. O'Keefe rose, brushed the bits of vegetation from his trouser leg. "You taking a personal interest in this, Grandville?" he said, addressing Higgins by his Christian name, as oftentimes was his habit. "A bit out of your jurisdiction isn't it?" This was said not with any animosity, but merely out of curiosity on the doctor's part.

"I've got no official standing, that's true," Higgins replied, his eyes drawn to the country lane and the approach of a lone horseman. "Still, somebody's got to inform Miss Hopkins if it turns out to be her brother. Best she hears it from me than some stranger."

The doctor nodded in agreement. "Suppose so," he said. "Well," turning his attention back to the body, he added, "for the present I'll spare you all the medical

terminology. In layman's terms, it could go either way."
He motioned toward the ugly gash to the rear of the
corpse's head. "Suffice to say, that appears to be the
primary cause of death. It may or may not been
delivered prior to his entering the water, difficult to tell
at this point."

Turning his attention from the rider, Higgins said,
"You mean someone could have smashed him with let's
say a cudgel of some sort, then threw his body in the
river?"

O'Keefe shrugged. "It's conceivable. A cursory
examination of the body shows no outward signs of a
struggle. On the other hand, and the more likely
scenario in my opinion, it was sustained when his body
tossed about by the river's current stuck against a rock.
An autopsy might clear that point up."

"No puncture wounds to the chest area?"

Dr. O'Keefe stiffened. He spun to face Calder.

"Puncture wounds! What in God's name-" Realizing
his voice was fast reaching a crescendo, the doctor
stopped, cast a leery eye in the direction of Colonel
Musgrave and Delahaye. To his relief they were at the
river edge, and safely out of earshot. Regaining control,
he hissed, "Mind telling me what's going on, Inspector?
The only puncture wounds I've encountered involved
that fiend, Fernell. Don't tell me you think he's
somehow involved in this?"

Calder shrugged. "Let's just say I want to keep an
open mind. Now, what about those wounds?"

Doctor O'Keefe wasn't satisfied with the
explanation, nevertheless he complied. "Naturally, I
checked for the obvious signs of foul play ... a gun shot
or knife wound. Not something as minute as an ice pick
thrust to the rib cage. That sort of thing will require a
more thorough examination, more than I'm prepared to
perform out here. I'll have a more complete answer for
you after we get back to town."

"You Higgins?" the booming voice said.

Higgins, who had been listening attentively to the exchange, had failed to note the arrival of the rider. He turned at the sound of the voice to find himself staring up into a rubicund face. The five-pointed star, pinned to the figure's lapel, glistened in the bright sunlight.

"That's right," Higgins said, shielding his eyes against the August sun. "You're Jones, I take it."

"Leander Jones, County Sheriff," the rider acknowledged. "I was over Lansdowne way, serving a writ when your telephone message reached me." Dismounting, he walked to where the body lay on the riverbank. Reaching down to examine the coarse linen robe, he said, "Well, well. What do we have here, some kind of religious monk?"

Calder spoke. "By his dress I'd say he's probably part of that camp revival meeting upriver. He's a stranger to us, but the members all wear generally the same type of clothing as their leader, Brother Nathan."

Jones rose, removed his hat and wiped his brow with the back of his sleeve. "Ah yes. Brother Nathan," he said. "Been getting reports on him ... nothing good so far. Fundamentalist preacher with a fiery tongue, they tell me." He looked to Calder. "And you sir are?"

"Donahue. Calder Donahue. My home, Old Dunham House, is near by."

"Ah, yes. I've also heard of you. From Baltimore, a retired police inspector they say."

Calder nodded. "And those two gentleman," he motioned toward Musgrave and Delahaye, who having taken note of the sheriff's arrival, were making their way up the riverbank, "are Colonel Musgrave and his friend, a Mr. Albert Delahaye. Musgrave's the one with the walrus mustache. They discovered the body and used my telephone to notify Sheriff Higgins." He turned to Doctor O'Keefe, "And this is our mutual colleague, Dr. O'Keefe."

Said Higgins, "I took the liberty of bringing the good doctor along. He's given the body a cursory examination. Hope you don't mind."

"No, not at all." Removing a note pad from his shirt pocket, the Sheriff Jones turned to Dr. O'Keefe. "And what's your verdict, doctor? Accident drowning, I suppose."

With a sideway glance in Calder's direction, Dr. O'Keefe replied, "I found nothing so far to contradict that finding. Of course, a full postmortem will be necessary to-"

Jones snapped the notebook closed. "Let's not be too hasty in that respect, doctor. Not on a simple drowning case. The county doesn't like spending good, hard-earned taxpayer money on needless autopsies. I think I'll stop and see what this Brother Nathan has to say first, then I'll make a decision on the autopsy. In the meantime, I'm hard pressed for time. Due back for afternoon court. I'd be appreciative if you could arrange transportation of the deceased back to Relay."

Dr. O'Keefe surveyed the empty space in the rear of his buggy. "He'll be at Delbert's Funeral Parlor."

"Much obliged," Jones said. He motioned toward the corpse. "Don't suppose that outfit of his has any pockets in it?"

Higgins nodded. "A single side pocket. I took the liberty of checking it for identification." He shook his head. "Didn't find much though ... several coins, a few soggy scraps of paper and a worn, but serviceable, jackknife. Nothing to tell us of who he might be. I'll keep everything in a bag for you, it'll be at my office."

Remounting, Sheriff Jones said, "I'll stop by on my return from court. Much obliged for the assistance, gentlemen." With a tip of the hat he urged his horse on.

After the sheriff's departure, Higgins turned to Calder. Barely able to contain himself, he wasted no time in speaking his mind. "Now what's this about Fernell? You never mentioned anything about his presence before this."

"Something Victoria said the other day when she

stopped by. It seemed absurd at the time. Then, this body turns up."

"Victoria? What-"

Calder related the details of their conversation in the library. "The woman won't come out and say it, but I'm sure she's convinced Fernell's back."

"And you're of a mind she's wrong?"

"No dammit! That's what so puzzling. Victoria comes off with these far-fetched, scatterbrained ideas of hers, with nothing of fact to base them on. Trouble is, she's nearly always right." He paused, offering an open tin of cigarettes to his companions before continuing. "As for me? I'm not convinced of anything. But if she's right, she's in grave danger. Fernell can't be too happy about that dragon claw of hers being plunged into his shoulder. He'll want to exact his pound of flesh."

Calder's reference was to an incident that occurred in the cave near Old Dunham House. Having being stalked by Fernell, Victoria lashed out, injuring the villain with her gardening tool. The tool, a wicked implement of Victoria's own design, had been constructed to break up the heavy garden clay surrounding her cottage. Its sharply honed talons had proven a valuable weapon in the dark confines of the cave. Fernell escaped, but vowed to return.

"Suppose she's right." It was Dr. O'Keefe speaking. "Did she say who she suspects of being Fernell?"

"No. Knowing her wild imagination it could be anybody."

"What I want to know," said Higgins, his brow pinched tightly together, "if Fernell's back, what's his purpose in Relay? Surely he hasn't returned merely to seek revenge on Victoria."

"Let's hope not," replied Calder. For the first time a worried frown appeared on his face. "Fernell's a cold and calculating killer. His services belong to the person or government willing to meet his fee."

Doctor O'Keefe gave a determined shake of his

head. "But there's no one of stature great enough to warrant an international assassin's presence in Relay."

Calder agreed. "You're right, Doctor. But murder isn't his only trade. Remember his last appearance? His sole purpose then was to recover the plans to *The Winan Steam Gun*."

Doctor O'Keefe shuddered. "Aye, I've not forgotten. Nor have I forgotten Herr Schmidt. His body was recovered from this very same river with an ice pick puncture over the heart."

Calder tapped his cigarette against the side of the tin before putting a match to it. "All the more reason to perform a thorough examination once we get the body back to town. For now the only plausible attraction I could come up with is the Wright brother's aeroplane. Their bomb release mechanism could fetch a considerable amount on the open market, and the embarrassment to our government could go a long way in restoring Fernell's damaged reputation in his failure to recover the Winan's drawings."

* * *

The next few minutes were spent loading the body into Dr. O'Keefe's buggy.

Covering the corpse with a canvas tarp, Calder said, "After Doctor O'Keefe completes his examination we'll need Miss Hopkins to identify the body. I'll leave that to you, Higgins."

Higgins was a bit upset at the prospect. "Normally I would agree with you, Inspector, you know that. But in this case, don't you believe that's being a little too harsh. Miss Priscilla's a delicate creature. It won't be easy for her to view the remains."

"It's an unpleasant task to be sure, but I don't see another way around it. After all it's her brother. She is the only one who can identify him. As difficult as it may be, there's no other way."

The look on Higgins's face indicated he had resigned himself to the inevitable.

"Oh, don't look so gloomy, Higgins," said Calder. "Women are made out of stronger stock than you might suppose."

"Might well be," replied Higgins, "but that doesn't make the task any more easier."

Chapter Twenty-three
Brother Thaddeus and the scrapes of paper

It was late afternoon before they arrived back in Relay.

"Damnation!" Calder swore, as the buggy rounded the corner onto High Street.

Midway down the street, a small group of villagers had assembled in front Murphy's Hardware. Heads turned, alerted by the metallic strikes of horseshoe against the cobblestone. At the center of the group a dainty parasol could be seen protruding above a flowing patch of red/gold hair... Priscilla Hopkins.

Their destination, Dr. O'Keefe's office, lay midway down the alley above the hardware. An encounter seemed unavoidable. This was not the proper time or place, not with the lifeless form her brother laying inches away beneath the canvas in the back of the buggy.

Calder could but only grumble at the insanity. Still, It had been his own doing. In his haste to notify Higgins, he had violated a cardinal rule of village life. While he had rightly cautioned his friend not to speak of the body's discovery he, himself, had failed to take into consideration the perils of the telephone party line. There was no doubt in his mind. Before their conversation ended, every villager within reach of a telephone knew a body had been discovered in the river. The news spread outward from there, and the mention of red hair was sure not to be overlooked.

Seeing the gathering, Dr. O'Keefe simply veered course turning the buggy down Welcome Alley. As a lifelong resident of the village, he took such things in stride. "No sense going on to my office," he said, in his easy, matter-of-fact manner of speaking. "Not with that crowd loitering about. I can finish my examination just as well over at Delbert's Funeral Parlor." The buggy slowed to permit Higgins to dismount. "Give Delbert a few minutes to make the body presentable, before you escort Miss Hopkins over for the identification."

Higgins nodded, and started for the group.

A short time later found an apprehensive Priscilla Hopkins, with Higgins by her side, positioned alongside the examination table. Nervously clutching her purse, she gave a slight nod of the head to indicate she was ready. Dr. O'Keefe pulled back the top portion of the sheet reveling the pale, ashen face. Delbert had toiled feverishly. Under Doctor O'Keefe's guidance, the corpse's facial features were carefully cleaned, the soiled robe removed, and the gash skillfully hidden beneath neatly combed hair. Still his efforts failed to dampen the effect.

Priscilla Hopkins, an audible gasp escaping over her lips, recoiled in horror. "No," she whispered, shaking her head and turning to look away. "It's not Roger."

Calder, who had been sitting at the undertaker's desk examining the scraps of paper taken from the corpse's pocket, looked up. "Not Roger? You're sure? The red hair-"

"Yes. Quite sure, Inspector. There is some resemblance, of course. The hair for example, but Roger was of much slighter build. And the face..." She shuttered. "No, I'm quite positive."

"Easy," said Higgins, laying a gentle hand on her shoulder. "Sorry to put you through this, Miss Hopkins. If there had been another way."

Priscilla turned. "I quite understand, Sheriff. You're very kind. Thank you for your concern. Now, if you'll excuse me gentlemen, I would like to return to my hotel."

"I'll see you home," said Higgins.

"That won't be necessary." She gave a nervous smile. "I'm perfectly fine."

"You're sure?"

"Quite. It was just the possibility it could have been Roger, and the shock of seeing that poor man. I'm quite all right now, really I am."

Higgins walked Priscilla Hopkins to the door and standing by the doorway, watched her safely across the street. "A fine upstanding woman, Miss Hopkins. She certainly put on a brave face."

As usual when it came to women, Higgins was guided more by his heart than his head. It was obvious he was smitten by Priscilla Hopkins' beauty.

"You think so?" mused Calder.

"Certainly," said Higgins. The look of admiration quickly turned to a scowl. Turning back to Calder, he said, "And if ever a brave face is needed, it is now. Yonder comes Brother Nathan."

Calder rose from the desk. Taking a copy of the Sentinel, he placed it over the pocket's contents. "Quickly, doctor," he said. "Your examination, did it reveal any sign of a puncture wound?"

"No. For the present, it appears just as Sheriff Jones says, a simple case of accidental drowning." He stared at Calder. "Are you still harboring thoughts Fernell is somehow involved in this?"

Before Calder could answer, the gaunt frame of Brother Nathan entered the doorway.

"I understand you have recovered an unidentified body."

"That's right," said Higgins. "What is your interest in it?"

"A member of my flock has strayed. If I may be permitted to view the body."

"This way," replied Dr. O'Keefe. He proceeded to

the examination table and drew back the top portion of the sheet.

Brother Nathan nodded, showing little emotion. "It's as I feared. It's Brother Thaddeus. He went missing right after breakfast this morning."

"We found him in the river, about a mile downriver from your camp," said Higgins. "Fortunately his body got tangled up in some tree roots, or he might have been carried all the way to Baltimore."

"In the river, you say? That's odd. As you can see he's was a strapping lad, and a good swimmer. I don't understand how he could have drowned. Musta been a accident." Nathan nodded his head. "That's surely what happened. Most likely he slipped and fell into the river."

"Perhaps," replied Higgins. "It's only of the purest of chance he was found at all. Why didn't you report this sooner?"

"I thought he had gone to the meadows. He's often done that, seeking solitude and a quiet place to meditate before the workday begins. I had no reason to suspect other."

"Next of kin?"

Brother Nathan thought for a moment. "No, no one close. There is a distant aunt I believe, somewhere in Ohio."

"And his remains?"

Naturally the congregation will want to pay their respects. I have my wagon. If I may, I'd like to take his body back with me."

Dr. O'Keefe spoke. "I'm afraid that won't be possible, not at this point. I haven't completed my examination."

"Perhaps this evening then?"

"It's not for me to say. The county sheriff is charged with making that determination. He's due in later today if you would like to stop back."

"I see, doctor. Well, I suppose the laws of man must be satisfied. By the way, Sheriff, I couldn't help noticing Miss Hopkins leaving as I crossed the street. She processes an interest in Brother Thaddeus's death?"

"Thankfully no." Higgins's eyes burned with irritation. "And that's another thing. Why didn't you tell us a member of your church closely matched her brother's description?"

"You mean the red hair?

"Damn right!" His finger wagged in an accusatory fashion "You were aware of her brother's disappearance. You could have spared her the ordeal of having to view the body.

"Ah yes, I see your point. Perhaps in hindsight I should have, but it never occurred to me it would result in something like this." If there was any compassion in Brother Nathan, it did not show in his voice or his gestures. "As for my reasoning for not notifying you, there never was any question Brother Thaddeus was Miss Hopkins's brother. He has been a member of my flock from the beginning, joined our crusade out in Ohio." He looked down at the lifeless body. "Pity," he said. "He was a resourceful lad. Kept the wagons and all things mechanical in a good state of repair. I don't know how we're going to replace him. Tell me doctor, did he suffer greatly in the end?"

Dr. O'Keefe pulled the sheet back over the body. "It doesn't appear so. You may have noticed he sustained a nasty gash in the back of the head. Probably from striking a rock in the river. Death would have been swift."

Brother Nathan closed his eyes, his head bobbed in acceptance. "We must take solace the Prophet has seen fit to be merciful to Brother Thaddeus in his hour of need."

Merciful? Thought Calder. *"The man's dead for God sake. Struck down in his prime. I rather think if Brother Thaddeus could speak, he would have a different view on the matter.*

From his shirt pocket, Higgins removed a notepad

and the stub of a pencil. "About the funeral, Brother Nathan. I assume your church will attend to the cost of laying your fallen brother to rest."

Nathan turned an empty palm. "We'll provide the spiritual service, of course. But, we are pilgrims of simple means. We hold no title for an earthly plot to lay our fallen brother to rest, or a proper stone to mark his passing." He smiled, a smile laced with greed and avarice. "Perhaps, with your kind permission, I might prevail upon the good citizens of Relay to help us in our time of need. A collection, perhaps?"

Calder's thoughts went back to their meeting in Mr. Hankin's store and the huge wad of bills Brother Nathan had produced.

Higgins was equally unimpressed. "Now, about the interment itself."

"There is a Potters field, is there not?"

* * *

After Nathan's departure Calder returned to the undertaker's desk. Using a pair of tweezers obtained from desk drawer, he set about the process of attempting to reassemble the bits of still damp paper. His progress was slow, hampered by paper's fragile condition and its tendency to stick to itself.

From his position next to the body, Dr. O'Keefe said, "I suppose it would be too fortuitous for it to be an envelope bearing his name or address?"

Calder, engrossed in placing the last piece in its proper spot, replied, "No, doctor. Not an envelope." He turned his head this way and then that, attempting to make sense of the jumble mass of squiggled lines before him. "It appears to be some type of mechanical drawing."

"Let me have a gander at it." Higgins moved to join Calder at the desk. After a few moments, he gave up. "Beats me," he said. "Appears to be someone's random doodling. Doubtful it's of any consequence."

Calder wasn't so sure; he refused to surrender.

"You may be right," he said, idly drumming his fingers on the desk. "What bothers me is it seems to have a definite sense of order about it."

"Order?" said, Dr. O'Keefe, looking up from his note pad where he had been recording his findings. "If that's the case, let a scientific mind have a go at it." Removing a pair of rimless spectacles from a leather case, Dr. O'Keefe wrapped the wire ends around his ears. Like Calder and Higgins before him, he studied the tangled mass of pencil lines. "It reminds me of a crude diagram of the human circulatory system, much like a first year medical student would render," he said after some deliberation. He pointed to one of the darker lines. "Take this line for example, see how it returns to a central point, like a vein returning to the heart muscle."

"Not likely our corpse was a medical student," scoffed Calder, dismissing the idea. "You noticed the hands? By their looks, he was never near a medical textbook. What did Brother Nathan say he job was?"

"Something to do with wagons, I believe" replied Higgins. "A wheelwright perhaps."

Wheelwright? Thought Calder. *Yes. That would account for the callous, scarred hands ... but there was something more. What were Brother Nathan's words? 'He kept the wagons and all things mechanical in a good state of repair.'*

Rising quickly from the desk, he rushed to the opened doorway.

"You there, boy," he called to a lad playing nearby. "You know Oney Parlor?"

The boy looked up from his game of marbles. "Mr. Parlor? Over at the livery stable?"

"That's him," Calder said, flipping a coin to the boy. Here's a nickel, and there'll be another waiting when you get back. You tell Mr. Parlor he's to come right away. Right away, boy, you understand!"

"Yes, sir."

Chapter Twenty-four

It was only a few moments later that a confused Oney Parlor stood before Calder. He looked first to the mortuary table containing the sheet-covered body, and then to Calder. Oney scratched his head in puzzlement. "You wanted me, Inspector?"

Calder indicated the reassembled bits of paper before him. "Yes Oney. Take a look at this drawing and tell me what does this remind you of."

Oney glanced at the paper, shrugged his shoulders. "Nothing. Just a bunch of squiggled lines on a scrape of paper."

"Look harder."

"Harder?"

"Yes. Use your imagination. What does it remind you of?"

Oney studied the paper in earnest. "Wellll," he said, scratching the three-day growth at the tip of his chin. "If I had to venture a guess, I'd say it looks kind of like a wiring diagram for some kind of a gasoline engine."

"Excellent! Exclaimed Calder. "Go on."

Bolstered by Calder's encouragement, Oney quickly warmed to the subject. "See here." Oney's finger moved across the paper, pausing on a box-shaped symbol. "This could represent the magneto. And here, these are the wires running to each of the cylinders."

"And here?" said Calder, pointing to a line of

numbers.

"The firing order."

"And this?"

"That upside down triangle is ground. And this symbol represents the ignition kill switch." Oney tilted his head to the side. "But I've got to tell you, Inspector, it doesn't look like any engine I've ever worked on before. Everything is doubled ... every wire, ground, spark plug. Every switch or connection. Everything."

"It's not important, Oney," said Calder. "It's just a doodle and I was merely curious. Thanks for your help."

After Oney's departure, Calder settled back in his chair and looked to his two companions. He smiled. "Well, gentlemen, that certainly cast a different light on our friend's drowning, don't you think?"

Both men stared at Calder. "How so? It's merely someone's aimless doodling. You said as much yourself. I don't see how it has anything to do with the drowning." It was Higgins speaking, but from the bemused look on Dr. O'Keefe's face it was clear he was in complete agreement with the sheriff.

"Ah," replied Calder, "but a special kind of doodling."

"The duplication?" ventured Dr. O'Keefe.

"Exactly," said Calder. Tapping a fresh cigarette against the side of the tin, he said, "And that's because it's a wiring diagram for a very special application."

"A aeroplane engine," blurted out Higgins. "That's it, isn't it?"

Calder carefully collected the assembled bits of paper, placing them into an envelope. "Stands to reason. Whomever took the Wright's aeroplane wouldn't want to risk an engine failure at five hundred feet."

Chapter Twenty-five
Dinner at Old Dunham House
Friday evening

Dust was just beginning to fall as Priscilla Hopkins, accompanied by Albert Delahaye stepped from the carriage in front of Old Dunham House. Calder, with Victoria in her role as hostess, greeted the couple at the manor's entrance.

"Good evening, Miss Hopkins, Mr. Delahaye," Victoria said, welcoming the newly arrived guests. "So nice of you to come."

"Why my dear lady," Albert Delahaye said, taking Victoria's hand, "I wouldn't miss tonight's gala for the world."

"Nor would I," added Priscilla. "Mr. Delahaye gallantly offered to share his carriage with me."

"My pleasure," replied Albert Delahaye performing a slight bow. Turning to Calder, he said, "And to you, sir, my deep felt appreciation for the opportunity to again visit your magnificent home. Thankfully this time it is under more pleasant circumstances."

The latter remark was in reference to Colonel Musgrave and Delahaye previous visit, in which they reported their discovery of the red haired body in the river.

"Not at all, Mr. Delahaye," replied Calder. "Victoria and Mrs. C have planned a very special evening in honor of your visit. Let me add however that while taking no active part, I wholeheartedly concur with their agenda."

Albert Delahaye's brow wrinkled slightly. "Madame C?"

At this point Victoria interceded. "Pay the inspector no mind, Mr. Delahaye. Mrs. C is the inspector's diminutive name for Mrs. Chaffinch, the guiding force behind the smooth functioning of Old Dunham House."

"And I might add the most fabulous of cooks," said Calder. "I'll introduce you later. It would be a shame if your stay in Relay drew to a close without partaking in one of her culinary creations. Speaking of your departure, I understand the time is upon us?"

Albert Delahaye nodded. "Sadly yes. My train departs in the morning."

"So soon?" lamented Victoria. "Surely another day or two won't matter. Why-"

Delahaye held a hand up, gave a gentle shake of the head effectively halting Victoria in mid-sentence. "No, no dear woman," he said. "My task here is finished and I've lingered longer than I should. Perhaps I'll return another time, but for now duty calls and I must answer."

Victoria acquiesced. "Then I trust you enjoyed your brief stay with us, Mr. Delahaye."

"I did, I most certainly did. My old heart felt rejuvenated walking the paths of my youth." He smiled. "And not to forget, there was my reunion with my old comrade, Rutherford. It was the most joyous of occasions to see him once again."

Victoria chuckled softly. "It's strange hearing the colonel referred to as Rutherford. He is somewhere about," she said, turning to glance over her shoulder. "I suspect he's cornered Agent Percival and relentlessly bending his ear. Probably instructing him on the proper methods of conducting an investigation."

The elderly veteran joined in with the laughter. "Somethings never change. Rutherford could always talk a blue streak even as a young recruit."

"I've taken the liberty of seating the colonel to your left tonight. I thought you two might want to continue your military reminiscing over dinner."

Albert Delahaye was quick to reply. "No, no, dear lady. Not on a momentous occasion such as tonight. Very gracious of you, but, given such genteel company the retelling of old battlefield sagas really should be dispensed with, don't you agree?"

"As you wish, Mr. Delahaye," Victoria said with a smile.

Turning, the old soldier took in his surroundings. His eyes swept over the foyer's parquet flooring, then onto the finely crafted furniture and oils of pastoral farm scenes that graced its walls. His head bobbed in approval. "If I may be permitted, Inspector, allow me to compliment you on your excellent taste." Moving to a magnificently carved sideboard, he paused to admire its beauty. "I was once steward of a fine piece of furniture, very similar to this one." He ran an appreciative hand along the sideboard's edge. "It's obvious you spent years acquiring such treasures."

"It is a beautiful piece," agreed Calder. "Regretfully I can take no credit for any of the manor's acquisition." Noting Delahaye's puzzled expression, he said, "I'm a relative newcomer to Relay, Mr. Delahaye. My original home was in Baltimore. With no immediate family and a demanding career, a sparsely furnished set of rooms fulfilled my simple needs."

Delahaye paused to reassess his surroundings. He shook his head in dismay. "But how can this be? Everything appears so established, so well ordered. The furnishings, the carpets and the paintings all seemed to exhibit a certain permanence about them, as if they had been carefully garnered over a lifetime."

"Undoubtedly that was the case," Calder said. "However all the home's furnishings were acquired by the previous owners. They were conveyed with my purchase of the property."

"Nevertheless," Albert Delahaye pronounced, "it is an undeniable fact, this is a very beautiful home. It reminds me of my boyhood home in France. If I may be so bold would a short tour be possible?"

"Certainly." Calder turned to Victoria and Priscilla. "Perhaps the ladies would care to join us?"

Victoria shook her head. Looking to Priscilla for conformation, she said, "I'm sure Miss Hopkins will want to freshen up before dinner. You two run along. We'll join you later in the library."

* * *

As the two men meandered through the manor's first floor rooms, Calder told of the history of Old Dunham House ... and of its former owners Joshua Burrows and his two sons Cain and Abel.

He summed up by saying, "A very learned trio, the Burrows, but I'm told a more vile family one would be hard pressed to find. Their deaths were a cause for celebration among the villagers. After their passing the house lapsed into receivership, during which a Mr. Gregson held a short-term lease on the property. Some of the minor pieces you see are his, this painting for example." They had paused and were standing before of a miniature English landscape.

"A Milair, if I'm not mistaken," said Albert Delahaye, moving closer to examine the painting.

"You have a good eye," replied Calder. "An excellent example of one of his earlier works, I'm told. It, along with several other paintings, were left when Mr. Gregson was suddenly called away."

Turning his attention from the painting, Delahaye said, "That's odd. Here we have a man who obviously enjoys fine art and I assume is aware of its worth, yet he simply abandons it." He shook his head. "Very strange indeed. Still, there must be some explanation."

Pausing to straighten the miniature's frame, Calder said, I'm not in position to speak to Mr. Gregson's reasoning. Nevertheless you're correct in your assessment, Mr. Gregson was known to be a bit of an eccentric."

Albert Delahaye seemed to take an interest in this statement. "Eccentric, how so?"

"He kept mostly to himself," Calder said. "Rarely ventured into town. Then, on his last day in Relay, he hosted a lavish dinner party. Invited an imposing list of guests, even provided a trio of musicians to accompany the dinner. When the dinner gong sounded and the guests were seated, Gregson's seat remained empty."

"You're saying he failed to attend his own dinner party?"

Calder nodded in the affirmative.

Albert Delahaye seemed befuddled by this. "But that's absurd. Surely there must be a reasonable explanation for his absence. Could he have suffered an accident or perhaps there was an untimely incident that prevented him from appearing?"

"*Hardly an accident,*" Calder thought, "*but an incident, yes.*" His thoughts meandered back to the past and the master criminal's prior connection to Relay. Fernell had made two separate appearances in the tranquil village, both in the case of Winan's steam gun. Once in Victoria's cottage and later in the blackness of a hillside cave. On each occasion Victoria came within a hair's breath of falling prey to Fernell's viciousness.

Calder looked to the questioning gaze of his guest. There was no need to apprise Delahaye of the Fernell's past appearances. Few knew of the master assassin's existence, even less of his brief stay in Relay or of his masquerade as Gregson.

"Not likely," Calder mused. "While Mr. Gregson's departure might be impromptu, it was well thought out. He took the time to insure the staff was properly compensated. Left instructions for his guest's entertainment and then packed a small valise and vanished before the first guest's arrival. Most prefer to view it as another example of Gregson's eccentricities.

"He just vanished?" Albert Delahaye rubbed his chin, his eyes narrowed. "Fascinating! No explanation, not even a note?"

"None."

"Where?"

"You mean where did he go?"

The old man nodded. "You're a detective. Surely your training must give you some idea to his strange behavior or his destination."

Calder shrugged. "That remains a mystery. Perhaps the answer lays in his profession. I'm told it involves travel to the far reaches. Something to do with finalizing international contracts for the heads of European states."

"International contracts?" Albert Delahaye scowled; his wrinkled his nose in displeasure. "Sounds a bit too highbrow, if you ask me. Never was one to go for all that legal terminology. A man ought to say what he means straight out, and in plain terms. But traveling ... now that's more to my liking."

"Then you travel a lot, Mr. Delahaye?"

The old veteran shook his head. "Sadly, no. At least, not as much as I would like to."

It was at that moment the dinner gong sounded, preventing further conversation and the two men proceeded to the dinning room.

Chapter Twenty-six
Old Dunham House

Dinner was proceeding flawlessly; conversation was both lively and engaging. Calder was forced to admit, Victoria's suggestion to invite Agent Percival had been a near stroke of genius. The dapper young agent held court, entertaining the women and holding them spellbound with his tales of Washington society and fashion.

"What about next season's dress length?" inquired Miss Hopkins.

Agent Percival smiled. "While a man in my position isn't normally privy to such sensitive information, I did manage to obtain some minor tidbits. It's been reported...." Percival's voice faded. "No," he said, after some reflection, "I really shouldn't. After all, I've been sworn to secrecy."

"Ooooh," sighed the widow Collins. A look of disappointment showed on her face. "And I was so hoping..."

Percival sipped his wine. His eyes danced with devilment. "Then, you shall not be disappointed, dear lady." He leaned forward, wagged a finger in warning. "Promise not to reveal your source?" To this he received eager nods of anticipation. "Well," he said, "Its been reliably reported that hemlines will reach mid-calf this season."

"Oh, do tell!" gasped the widow Collins.

Albert Delahaye had little use for such frivolity. He concerned himself purely with the menu, anticipating the arrival of each new course with great delight. Finally, after a second helping of beef Wellington he crossed his fork and knife on the emptied plate, signaling the ever-hovering server that he had reached his limit, and slumped backward in the chair. A smile of utter contentment etched on his face.

"Ah, delicieux." He said, bringing his thumb and two fingers to his lips in a culinary salute. "My compliments to you, Madame Chaffinch. I can't remember when I've tasted such wondrous creations."

A chorus of here, here, echoed from the other guests.

From across the table, where she was overseeing the serving girl in the replenishing of the stray empty wine glass, Mrs. Chaffinch's cheeks glowed pink. "Thank you kindly, sir."

Laying aside his napkin, Albert Delahaye said, "Tell me dear lady, by chance your marvelous skills, they are restricted only to the English fare?"

"Oh, no sir. I can turn out a respectful German dish, if required."

"Sauerbraten?" queried Albert Delahaye hopefully. "Although French, my tiny village was situated quite close to the German border. It was there that I've developed a taste for such a dish."

Mrs. Chaffinch beamed. "My specialty."

"Tell me. Your cut of beef, do you soak it for the requisite three days in the marinade?"

Mrs. Chaffinch stared at the elderly dinner guest in mock disbelief. "Most certainly, sir. Could it be prepared any other way?"

Albert Delahaye sat back and clapped his hands in glee. "Marvelous, dear lady, marvelous!" he said. "With potato dumplings and sweet and sour red cabbage?"

"Don't forget the ginger snap gravy," Mrs. Chaffinch lectured. "Can't be considered a proper sour beef without ginger snap gravy."

"No!" squealed Delahaye with delight. "One mustn't forget the ginger snap gravy. But I must alter my schedule at once. Tell me, Madame Chaffinch, when is such a feast to occur?"

Mrs. Chaffinch merely smiled. "Not for a while. It's too hot in the summer for such dishes, even if I were to use the summer kitchen. You must come visit us again, Mr. Delahaye, but do so in the fall or perhaps the wintertime."

"Oh dear lady that I shall, you can be sure of that." Then suddenly realizing the boldness of his statement, Albert Delahaye gave an apologetic glance in Calder's direction. "That is if I wouldn't be intruding on my host's hospitality."

Calder, watching the delight the topic had caused the old veteran, said, "Certainly not, Mr. Delahaye. Rest assured, you'll always be a welcomed guest at Old Dunham House."

Albert Delahaye raised his glass in salute. "You're too kind, Inspector."

After dinner the guests retired to the library, where over drinks the conversation naturally turned to the search for the missing aeroplane.

Albert Delahaye, from his position between Calder and Percival, said, "Tell me, gentlemen, what progress have you made? Surely, with two skilled professionals such as yourselves on the case, a solution can't be far off."

Percival swirled the contents of his wine glass. "It is a challenging case. Unfortunately, the Inspector and I view the machine's disappearance from two different perspectives. The Inspector is concerned merely with the locating the craft, and returning it to its owner. I, on the other hand, am forced to place our government's vital interest first."

The mild rancor contained in Percival's response, caused Delahaye to arch an eyebrow. "But surely the government's interest, and the inspector's desire to return the aeroplane, are not in conflict. They are one and the same, are they not?"

Percival did not answer. Looking up he noted Victoria's entrance into the room. "If you will excuse me, gentlemen," he said. "It's been a long day and I must thank our hostess before leaving."

"Odd fellow" observed Delahaye, watching Percival make his way across the room. "I take it there hasn't been much progress made, Inspector."

Calder shook his head. "The problem is," he said, holding a match to Albert Delahaye's cigar, "the countryside around Relay is pockmarked with numerous grazing meadows and abandoned barns, each capable of secreting an aeroplane. It will take weeks to properly investigate each one, and time is a commodity that is in short supply. The thieves will surely have completed their reassembly and absconded with the machine before I've completed my search."

Albert Delahaye released a stream of cigar smoke skyward. "I can appreciate your predicament, Inspector. I take it you're of a mind that whoever stole the Wright's machine intends to fly it out of the valley?"

"Without a doubt. In that one regard Agent Percival and I are in complete accord. Besides, the roads are being too closely watched to chance moving it overland. Then there are the reports to consider."

"Reports?"

"From outlaying farms, of a thunderous engine roaring into life in the countryside. By most accounts, usually in the evening hours. I, myself, heard it on one occasion. Unfortunately, it was of short duration and I was unable to track it to its source."

"An aeroplane engine!" Albert Delahaye declared, unable to contain his excitement. He waved an arm in a sweeping motion, causing cigar ash to cascade down his front. He brushed at his waistcoat while he continued to speak. "That fits in with your thinking they're reassembling the machine. It's only natural the scoundrels would want to test the engine before chancing flight."

Calder nodded. "I'm sure it's the Wright brothers machine I heard. Naturally, Higgins and I have made several excursions to seek it out, but so far we've come up empty-handed."

"Old Rutherford and I have traipsed all over the countryside revisiting old battlegrounds. Can't say as we ever heard anything that sounded like a aeroplane engine. Any guess where the sound was coming from?"

Higgins, along with Priscilla Hopkins, had joined the two men.

"We've narrowed it down to an area just south of where Brother Nathan's got his tent revival set up," Higgins said. "There's a stretch where the Patapsco overflows its banks each spring, leaving a flat treeless meadow. A bit rough to be sure, but suitable enough for an aeroplane's use."

For the next few moments Delahaye paced about the room as he continued to puff on his cigar. Leaning against the fireplace mantle, he flicked the ash into the cold hearth. "What's needed here," he said, "is some good, old textbook spying, you know like we did during the war. Now, if I could only step back in time, and there happened to be one of Professor Lowe's aerial balloons handy ... why I'd show you a trick or two about spying." He moved to a position alongside Colonel Musgrave's chair, "We'd take to the sky, wouldn't we, Rutherford? Scour the countryside for miles around, we would." He smacked his fist against an opened palm. "By God, if the Wright's machine is about we'd soon ferret its position out."

"Speak for yourself, Frenchy," Musgrave grumbled, stubbing his spent cigarette out in a nearby ashtray. His glass empty, he rose, headed for the wine cart. "I have no desire to go aloft in one of those infernal flying contraptions of yours. Flies in the face of God, if you ask me. I plan to keep these old legs firmly planted on good old terra firma."

Ignoring Musgrave's remarks, Albert Delahaye turned to Calder. "This Brother Nathan you speak of, what's he like?"

Calder gave brief, concise description of Nathan. "A fundamentalist preacher. Stern. Favors a return to what he calls the old ways. Has a knack of luring hapless, misguided individuals to join his flock with promises of eternal salvation."

Delahaye studied Calder's face. "But I can tell you sense there is more." His eyes narrowed. "Something more sinister I'll wager."

Calder turned an empty palm. "Nothing I can prove for the present. It is said he coerces his followers to pledge all of their earthly goods to his church ... a sign of their commitment to the faith, he claims."

"He'll deny it, of course," Priscilla said entering the conversation. "But I fear my brother has also fallen under his spell and has become one of his converts."

Disposing of his cigar, Delahaye said, "Alas, my dear child, if only there were time enough."

Priscilla, in the act of lifting her glass, paused. "Time, Mr. Delahaye?"

"My leaving in the morning." Delahaye's face took on a rueful expression. "Surely you haven't forgotten."

"No. But I fail to see-"

"Time is a fleeting commodity, is it not? Musgrave and I are to place flowers at the grave of some of the fallen lads in the morning. My train departs shortly thereafter. If this were not so, I would have savored the chance to venture out to the camp of this Brother Nathan and have a look see." He tapped an all-knowing finger to the side of his head. "You see, no one ever suspects an old man like me of being anything but an old man. If your brother is there, I would seek him out and convince him of the folly of his ways. I would return him to the bosom of his family, to you Miss Hopkins."

"That's very kind, Mr. Delahaye."

Draining the last of his drink, Albert Delahaye, with the aid of his cane, eased himself down into a chair. "Not at all, dear lady," he smiled, "not at all."

Chapter Twenty-seven
Saturday Afternoon

It was the afternoon following the dinner party. Calder, having procured a still-damp copy of *The Sentinel* from the tobacconist's counter, set out in search of Higgins. He was proceeding along High Street when he chanced upon Victoria Byron emerging from the town millinery. It was Victoria, struggling under the weight of an armful of parcels that appealed to Calder's sense of chivalry.

"What have we here?" he said, relieving her of a goodly portion of her burden. He shifted his newly acquired load to a more manageable position. "Looks like you just procured Mr. Sanders's complete inventory of yard goods."

Having become accustomed to Calder's wry humor, Victoria merely smiled. "Hardly," she said. "In fact, it's barely enough material to complete my fall wardrobe. There's not a yard to spare."

Insisting that he accompany her to her doorstep, they continued along, chatting about this and that as they went. It was not until they neared the village square that Victoria managed to introduce the name Fernell into the conversation.

"Fernell?" Calder said. His face clouded with puzzlement. This was the second occasion Victoria had unexpectedly introduce Fernell's name into a conversation. The first being in the library at Old

Dunham House. He studied his companion's face. "Fernell?" he repeated. "What made you think of him?"

"Oh, nothing. I was just thinking. Tell me, hypothetically speaking of course, now that we've have grounds to suspect Fernell had returned, who do you think he would masquerade as?"

"Hypothetically? I don't believe for a moment you are speaking hypothetically, not when it comes to the name of the man who came within a breath of killing you, not once but twice. Now, what are you really thinking?"

Victoria smiled. "Humor me, just for the moment. I'll explain later."

Calder cautiously eyed his companion. "I'm really not one to speculate," he said. "Since we're speaking hypothetically, I would say one name does present itself above all the rest."

"Go on," Victoria said, as she transferred another package to Calder's already overloaded arms.

"Well," he said, "if I have to venture a guess I'd say the logical choice would be Brother Nathan."

"Poppycock! That zealot. What makes you think he could possibly be Fernell?"

"Oh, I'm not saying he is, mind you, but there is ample grounds for one to form that assessment." Calder set about relating the incident in Hankin's Emporium. "We collided as he was turning to leave. I reached out instinctively, as a precautionary gesture and took hold of his arm. In doing so my hand brushed against something solid under the sleeve of his robe."

The latter drew Victoria's interest. "Exactly what kind of object," she said.

"Well, I'm not quite sure. It was just the merest of touches, and Brother Nathan quickly drew his arm away."

Victoria stopped. "That's it? That's all you have to base your claim on?"

"No. Beside those long, baggy sleeves, well suited

to conceal an ice pick, there's the timing of his appearance in Relay, mere days before the arrival of the Wright brothers. One mustn't overlook that."

Handing Calder another package, Victoria scoffed. "Ha! That's where you're wrong."

"Oh? And I suppose you know who it would be."

Victoria, a smug look on her face and her nose tilted ever so slightly, said, "Indeed I do. I know for a fact it could be none other than our own Agent Percival."

"Fact? What fact?"

"The look in his eye. You may change your overall appearance by the addition of a pair of spectacles, maybe add a wrinkle or two with the proper make-up, and I'm told it's possible to even change the eye's color ... but you can't change the intensity, and in Agent Percival I see that same intensity as Fernell."

Calder's eyes rolled heavenward. "That's not fact. That's intuition, and female intuition at that. Besides, Percival looks nothing like Fernell. For one thing he's shorter than Fernell."

Victoria merely shook her head. "It is a well known fact women are much better suited at observation than men," she said. "Besides, you don't know what Fernell looks like, *not really*. We've only saw him when he was disguised as Gregson. But if you insist on evidentiary facts, need I remind you Fernell's a genius in the application of theater makeup. So much so that he has been known to have successfully masqueraded as a woman. Now, as for the shortness, it's merely a matter of selecting the right clothing and walk. It's an old theatrical trick, I seen it a hundred times. If he ever stood straight he would be as tall as Gregson."

She had him there. Fernell had successfully posed as an old woman selling flowers outside of Camden Station in the case of Winan's steam gun. He had not told Victoria of this and did not intent to reveal it now. "Masquerade," he scoffed. As a woman! What woman? The only recently arrived female in the village is Miss

Hopkins. Surely you're not going to suggest-"

"Don't be foolish. I only meant he could pass as a woman, not that he is posing as one now. Certainly not someone as young and vibrant as Miss Hopkins. The cleavage is real. I don't think even Fernell could manage to pull that one off."

Calder shook his head in disbelief. "To use your logic, Mrs. C is a woman. If anyone should have recognized Fernell, she should have, remember she was his housekeeper when he posed as Gregson. With her attentiveness to the dinner guests last night, she would have easily spotted him."

The validity of Calder's assessment had struck a nerve and Victoria's face registered her frustration. "You're right about Mrs. Chaffinch. I must admit I was more than a little disappointed in her not being able to recognize him."

Calder spun about. "Aha! I knew it! So that was the reason behind the dinner and your insistence on inviting Agent Percival."

Victoria made no effort to deny the accusation. "Naturally."

"You admit it then. You set the whole thing up simply as an opportunity for Mrs. C to observe Agent Percival at close hand, in the hope she would identify him as Fernell?"

"Can you think of a better test? Besides, you would have done the same thing, you're only upset I beat you to it."

"Horsefeathers! Next, you'll be telling me it's old Delahaye, you suspect."

"Mr. Delahaye," Victoria laughed, pooh-poohing the thought. "The colonel's known him since Civil War times. He's seventy if he's a day. No, you can dismiss Albert Delahaye."

"Dismiss him? I've never considered him."

"Perhaps I may have been mistaken about Percival," Victoria confessed.

Pausing in the shade of the bank's canvas awning, Calder again shifted the unyielding load of packages.

"Why women are so infatuated with constantly altering their wardrobe is beyond me," he said, retrieving a fallen package from the sidewalk. "Are you in competition with Miss Hopkins? You've got enough material here to construct a half dozen new frocks, maybe more."

This was said jokingly, of course. In reality he found Victoria, despite her habit of interfering in his investigations, as every bit as appealing as Priscilla Hopkins ... perhaps more so when Victoria donned a frilly dress and parasol.

Victoria brushed aside the comment. Well, perhaps not completely so, for she smiled. "Now, Mr. Calder, a woman's wardrobe must stay current. Agent Percival has it on good authority that this fall's fashions are certain to contain an abundance of ruffles. Besides," she said, helping him to rearrange the packages, and in the process relieving him of one or two of the lighter ones, "a good portion of your load has nothing to do with fashion. The larger packages contain material for curtains in the front parlor. How, hold still while I-"

Victoria's voice faded from Calder's ears. The sight of Bounce, in the dirt alleyway bordering the bank, captured his attention. As usual, the little terrier was involved in one of his favorite antics, digging at the rim of a mud puddle. Not wishing to risk a repeat of the Nora Battington incident, Calder decided they should continue on as quickly as possible. As he turned, his gaze fell upon the bank's large plate glass window, and inside, to the image of banker Foxworth securing the vault's heavy, metal door.

Time froze.

"Calder!" Victoria said, snapping him out of his trancelike state. "I declare, you've not heard a word I've said, have you? What's wrong with you?"

"Uh? Oh, sorry," he said, turning back to Victoria.

"Nothing. Everything is fine. It just that I've been so unbelievably dense. It's been staring me in the face all of the time, and I been too blind to see it."

"See what?"

"There's no time to explain. If you will pardon me, Victoria, there's something I must tend to. You can manage the rest of the way, can't you?"

Not waiting for an answer, Calder deposited the armload of packages on the nearby bench, and scampered off across High Street, leaving a befuddled Victoria Byron.

Chapter Twenty-eight
Several hours later
The Farmers and Mechanics Bank

Inside the cramped confines of the vault the three occupants spoke in hushed tones. Despite the closeness, Calder had insisted on the vault's massive iron door remaining closed, and the lone oil lamp's wick be kept at its lowest setting. Banker Foxworth, his brow covered in thin rivulets of sweat, was having second thoughts.

"I'll confess, Inspector," he said, rising from his chair, "when you approached me with the idea that the vault was going to be burgled, I was skeptical. Even now, I'm not sure this is the proper way to handle the situation. What would the depositors, not to mention the bank examiners, say if you should be proven correct, but allowed things to go awry." He looked from Higgins to Calder. "You're positive you and the sheriff can manage the situation?"

Calder, who had been lying prone on the vault's stone flooring, an ear pressed against one of the massive three by three foot paving stones, nodded. "Not to worry," he said rising up and joining his companions. "I can assure you, Foxworth, things are well in hand. Grandville and I can handle this end, and in the off chance things should go wrong, Higgins has taken the precaution of stationing several good men at likely escape points."

189

This did little to satisfy the banker. "I know, Inspector, but perhaps we should have notified the railroad authorities." He gave an impatient tap of his cane against the stone floor. "After all it is their payroll that is at risk."

Calder rose. The slightest trace of irritation had begun to creep into his voice. "I must caution you to keep your voice low, Foxworth, and put away that damn cane. No sense telegraphing our presence."

Foxworth wasn't quite finished. "If not the railroad, what about Agent Percival? I see no harm in taking him into your confidence. He could have brought the weight of the government to bear."

"What?" exclaimed Higgins, barely able to contain himself, "and have the village crawling with a dozen new faces. They would stand out like a sore thumb and the burglars would certainly smell a trap. Besides, Percival's more interested in proving his international conspiracy than foiling a bank robbery."

Said Calder, "Relax, Mr. Foxworth. The railroad's payroll is in no danger. And if my hunch proves correct, by this time tomorrow, we will have not only prevented a bank robbery, but recovered Mr. Wright's aeroplane as well."

Unconvinced, the banker removed a large white handkerchief from his pocket and mopped his brow. "That's all fine and dandy, Inspector," he said, "but how can you be so positive someone intends to rob the bank today? After all, all you have is the antics of that fool dog to base your assumption on."

Calder reached over, gave the little dog a pat. "Don't discount old Bounce. His digging in the alleyway indicates our quarry is very close to reaching their goal. Now, if my calculations are correct, they should make their move this afternoon."

"I hope you are right, Inspector." Foxworth turned, his eyes fell on Higgins. "If things go awry, not only my job will be hanging in the balance."

Higgins merely shrugged in return.

Calder withdrew his watch, held its dial close to the lamp's light. Three O'clock. They had been in the vault only one hour and already things were starting to become unraveled. He had to placate the skittish banker's fears somehow.

"Look at it logically, Foxworth," he said. "Saturday afternoon is the most opportune time. The theft won't be discovered until Monday morning when the bank reopens. That gives our man the remainder of today, and all day Sunday to make good his escape. Come Monday morning, he'll be several states away."

"That's another point, Inspector. You never were quite clear on who he is."

That act had been a conscious omission on Calder's part. Was his quarry an ordinary thief … he thought not, or was it as he feared the return of the arch-criminal and assassin, Fernell? In soliciting the banker's participation, he had chosen not to speak of Fernell. Few in the outside world knew of his existence. With the exception of himself, Dr. O'Keefe, Higgins and Victoria, no one in Relay had ever heard his name spoken.

He had handed Fernell his only defeat – the case of the missing steam gun – a feat Fernell would not have taken lightly. Had Fernell returned to extract his revenge? That was a distinct possibility. The man he now waited for, possessed many of the same qualities as Fernell. Indeed, it could be Fernell himself. To counter this Higgins had taken the precaution of arming himself with a revolver.

"Well, Inspector."

Calder chose to continue the deception. "He? Possibly the most cunning type of adversary. A criminal who capitalizes on the goodness of other people, then perverts it to his own advantage. Brother Nathan."

"Nathan?" Foxworth seemed genuinely taken aback. "Surely there must be some mistake. Brother

Nathan is one of our most influential depositors, a man of the cloth. Why, he's even stores his church's records in our safety deposit boxes."

Calder chuckled. "I couldn't think of a better ruse to ascertain the layout of the bank's vault. I'd venture to say when you inspect those ledgers; you would find the pages blank. No doubt Brother Nathan has made frequent trips to his deposit box as of late, has he not?

"Welllll, yes," Foxworth conceded. "Yes he has. Several times this past week in fact."

"Did he by chance have that heavy walking staff of his with him?"

Foxworth seemed to be warming to the thought. "Now that you mention it yes, yes he did. I remember remarking what a resounding thud it made as it struck the floor."

Calder nodded in agreement. "No doubt that was used to give his digging companions a sounding beacon, guiding them to the bank's vault. Or, perhaps it might have been to alert them of your presence in the vault. In which case they would cease their digging activity. You-"

Calder's response was cut short by Bounce. The little terrier had leaped from Calder's side and moved to the center of the floor. With head tilted, ears erect, he stared down at the center paving stone.

"What's he doing now?" said Foxworth.

Calder held his finger to his lips, turned the lamp's wick extinguishing the flame. The vault lapsed into darkness. He handed the lamp to Foxworth and whispered, "Go stand by the doorway. When I give the word, turn the light switch. But not a moment before," he cautioned. "We don't want to alert our guest to our presence until they are out of the tunnel."

From beneath the flooring came the light, almost imperceptible sound of digging. Gradually the sound grew in intensity. Bounce gave a low growl. Calder retrieved the dog, tucking him under his arm. "Easy lad," he whispered, stroking the little dog's head. "We don't want to give ourselves away just yet."

The sound of digging ceased. Moments later it was replaced by a scraping of stone against stone, as one of the floor's large paving blocks, shifted, levitated from its setting, and was pushed aside. A dim shaft of light, created by the stone's removal, filtered up through the floor opening. Calder stepped behind a pillar and motioned Higgins and Foxworth to do the same.

From the void came movement. A head was the first to appear, followed by a hand holding a miner's lamp.

"We're in," a low voice said, as the lamp's beam surveyed the room in a slow sweeping arc. "It's a bit awkward going. Better give me a boost up."

As he climbed from the hole, the figure was immediately set upon by Higgins, clamping a hand over the intruder's mouth as he did so. Foxworth, bursting with anticipation, reached for the light switch. "*No*," Calder mouthed, giving a vigorous shake of the head. "*Not yet.*" Reluctantly, Foxworth's hand fell away.

Moments later a second hand emerged out of the floor opening. "Give me a hand up," a voice echoed from below. Silently taking the place of the first burglar, Calder reached down, grasped the offered hand and pulled.

"Now Foxworth, the lights!"

Instantly the vault's interior was bathed in a stark light. Before Calder stood a surprised and somewhat bewildered Brother Nathan. Foxworth, in his excitement to witness the capture, rushed forward. Brother Nathan quickly recovered. He reached out, seizing Foxworth and shoved him into Calder's path, causing both men to tumble to the floor. Taking advantage of the ensuing confusion, Nathan leaped back into the tunnel.

Extracting himself from beneath the floundering form of the banker, Calder reached for the hole. Too late, Brother Nathan had made good his escape.

"Sorry, Inspector," said a very embarrassed

Foxworth picking himself up from the floor. "That was very foolish on my part. I don't know what came over me. I only wanted to see what was happening."

It was senseless to become all fumed over Foxworth's misactions. It was clear they were accidental. Besides, now that it was confirmed Brother Nathan was the mastermind behind the burglary, the mission before him was clear. Brother Nathan had made good his escape, but that was only a temporary setback. Unless he had missed his guess, he knew exactly where he could be found.

"Don't fret yourself too much, Foxworth. It could happen to anyone."

"But... but what about Brother Nathan? He's gotten away."

Calder gave a gentle shake of the head. "Perhaps not. There is only one place he can flee to."

"You mean back to his camp?"

"No. If my suspicions prove correct that will be the last place he would flee to." He called to Higgins. "You okay over there, Higgins?"

"Right as rain." Removing the gag from the first burglar's mouth and snapping the handcuffs closed, he said, "This one isn't going nowhere."

"Good. After you finish up, you might want to accompany me when I go after Brother Nathan."

"You bet I will! The devil, himself, couldn't stop me."

"Good. We'll have to hurry though, there's not much time. Meet me over at Oney Parlor's as soon as you can."

"Won't be but a tick. All right, my lad," said Higgins, giving his prisoner a nudge toward the vault's doorway, "You heard the man. Let's go. There's a comfortable cell waiting for you."

Chapter Twenty-nine
Oney Parlor's Stables

Leaving Higgins to tend to his prisoner, Calder made his way to Oney Parlor's where Midnight was temporarily stabled. He kept to the alleyways. The last thing he needed was to run into one of the Nora Battington's of the village. His good fortune held. Either the fumes from her hat, or, more likely the August heat had swept the streets free of villagers. In either case, he encountered neither man nor beast en route and in short order arrived at his destination.

His arrival was acknowledged by Midnight's soft neighing, coming from the shade of the structure's overhang. Oney, under Calder's direction, had taken the precaution of ensuring the horse was not only shielded from the heat of the midday sun, but that he was remained hitched and ready to go at a moment's notice. There was cool water available and Midnight's harness, although still attached, had been sufficiently slackened as to cause no discomfort.

Calder set about the task of readjusting Midnight's tack in preparation for travel. Midnight, normally only too eager to be on his way, took the uncharacteristic stance of shying from Calder's touch.

"Easy fella," Calder said in a soothing tone. Reaching out he took Midnight's bridle and ran a comforting hand along the beast's shoulder. "What is it, boy?" he said, giving a series of reassuring pats. "Now what's got you so riled up?"

Midnight snorted. With a nervous flick of his head, he stamped at the dry earth and turned toward the stable's shadows.

"Aha! I thought something was afoot."

Calder spun to face the all too familiar voice. In an open sided lean-to, Oney kept a ready supply of straw for use as bedding material. On a bale, stacked deep within the recess, sat Victoria. Sliding off the bale, she brushed the stray bits of straw from her dress and approached.

"Afoot?" Calder said, quickly recovering. "Nothing of the sort. And what are you doing here? I'd thought you would be at home, sewing a new frock."

Drawn by the sound of their voices, Oney Parlor emerged from the stable, pitchfork in hand. "Sorry, Inspector," he said, in his most apologetic voice. "I told her nothing was astir. But she's strong willed, got a mind of her own. Insisted she was going to wait you out." He shrugged. "Short of running her off with this here pitchfork wasn't much else I could do."

"That's quite all right, Oney. It's not your fault." Despite his predicament and the need to apprehend Brother Nathan, Calder was forced to laugh. "That pitchfork wouldn't have helped in any case. Victoria has the uncanny knack for turning up where she shouldn't."

Victoria balled her hands into tight little fists, and jamming them against her hips glared up into Calder's face. "So you admit it, do you? I suspected as much the minute you went scurrying across High Street, leaving me with all those packages."

"Now Victoria, that's not exactly the case. I-"

If Victoria heard, she gave no indication. "Then, when I checked the jail, the hotel and *The Scarlet Lady*, and you and Higgins were nowhere to be found, I knew you two were up to your old habits."

Calder was pressed for time. Every second spent arguing with Victoria, allowed Brother Nathan that much more time to make good his escape. He had to find a way to rid himself of Victoria's presence before Higgins arrived on the scene. Placing his hand about her shoulder, he gently turned her about and attempted to escort her away.

"Habits?" he said, urging her along. "Why Victoria, whatever do you mean? Now, be a good girl and run along. I'll see you later this evening."

Victoria threw his hand off. "Not so fast." Her head swiveled about. "Where's Higgins?" she said. "What shenanigans is he up to, I'd like to know?" Not giving Calder a chance to reply, she said, "No use denying it, Calder Donahue. Its got something to do with that missing aeroplane, doesn't it?"

At that moment Higgins appeared around the stable's corner. "Well, I'm all set to-" Spying Victoria he immediately drew up short. "What in tarnation is she doing here?"

"Nothing. In fact, Miss Byron is on her way home. We were just saying good-by."

Victoria would not be dismissed so easily. "Oh no you don't, Calder Donahue," she said. "You're not getting rid of me that easily. I demand to know what's going on."

Time was of the essence. Deciding to lay some, but certainly not all, of his cards on the table, Calder replied, "I'm not so sure myself, and that's the truth. If what I suspect is true, it will be far too perilous a trip for a woman," he said. "I'll tell you what I know, only if you will promise you'll go with no further questions."

Victoria eyed the two men. After a few moments she relented. She had no illusions. She would not be getting a full accounting of their devilment, but she had nothing to bargain with and it was obvious she wasn't going to be allowed to tag along. "Very well," she said, "but I want to hear all the details, and no holding back or the deal's off."

"Agreed," said Calder. He gave a brief summation

of the attempted bank robbery and the escape of Brother Nathan. He said nothing of his fear Fernell might be the mastermind behind the theft of the Wright's machine, or of the growing suspicion he might use the machine to disrupt the Camp Meade Conference. He finished by saying, "And so you see, it's imperative that Higgins and I get out to Brother Nathan's camp as quickly as possible. Now there's sure to be danger once we arrive there, and I'd prefer you not to be present."

"But I-"

"Now, no more buts." He reached down, and lifting her chin stared into her violet-blue eyes. "You've promised. Besides there's only room enough for two in the buggy and I need you here."

"Here? What for?" If this another of your tricks I'll-"

"No tricks," said Calder. "Someone is going to have to prevent Foxworth from blabbering everything he knows to Agent Percival. That glory hound will gather up a few of his men and come charging in like the U.S. Calvary. That will only serve to destroy my chances of catching Brother Nathan unawares."

"*Damn!*" she cursed, as she watched the buggy carrying Calder and Higgins disappear around the corner. She had surrendered much too soon. There was more, that she was sure of. Next time she wouldn't be so quick to agree to Calder's smooth talking. Still, she had to admit there was truth in his logic.

She had given her word. She smiled. Well ... not exactly her word. She had merely agreed to ask no more questions, and she hadn't. She was positive Calder hadn't told her everything, and her promise hinged on that very condition. "*I'll not be ignored so easily,*" she thought. She looked down at her costume. "*Still, I'd only be a hindrance in this frilly frock.*" No matter. A quick change into something more appropriate, then she would seek out banker Foxworth. She smiled. "*I'll worm the rest of the story from him.*"

Chapter Thirty
A strip of land bordering the Patapsco

With the buggy safely hidden out of sight, Calder, closely followed by Higgins, made his way through the pinery. Several minutes later the two stood at the edge of a grassy meadow. A short distance away, nestled in a grove of thickly boughed pines, sat a disused hay barn. Vine covered, and constructed of weathered board and batten, the old barn blended flawlessly with its surroundings, escaping all but the closest of scrutiny.

Calder crept to the edge of the building. Cautiously rising up, in the dirt-encrusted window. *"Damnation!"* There was no sign of Brother Nathan, or the missing aero machine.

Still, the barn wasn't completely abandoned.

In a far corner, at a makeshift desk, sat a robed figure hastily stuffing papers into a leather traveling case. *"Another member of Nathan's followers,"* judged Calder.

"We're too late," hissed Higgins, joining Calder at the window edge. "Damn barn's empty. Looks like Nathan's already made good his escape in the machine." His eyes traveled to the desk in the corner. "Maybe we can squeeze some information out of that fellow."

"Not likely," said the familiar voice.

Spinning about they found themselves staring at the hooded, but unmistakable gaunt silhouette of Brother Nathan, a large caliber revolver in his hand. "I thought you two might come nosing about," he sneered with great satisfaction. "So I took the precaution of preparing a little reception in your honor. Now, since you're so eager to see what's inside the barn..." The wave of the revolver's barrel completed the sentence.

As Calder and Higgins were herded through the barn's doorway, the figure at the desk looked up. "What the-" he swore, springing from his seat and reaching for the revolver lying close by.

"No need for the gun," said Nathan, stepping in view from behind Calder. "Just a couple of uninvited guests. Nothing I can't handle." He motioned Calder and Higgins into a corner.

The figure at the desk cast a nervous glance from Calder to Higgins, and then back to Brother Nathan. It was clear their sudden appearance was unnerving. "I-I don't know, Nathan," he said. "This ain't good. Our orders were to-"

"I said I can handle it!" growled Nathan, cutting his companion off in mid-sentence. "Now hurry up and take that case out to the aeroplane. I'll be along as soon as I finish up here." Turning back to Calder, he said, "But first, Inspector, perhaps you'll tell me how you manage to find our little hideaway?"

The willingness of Brother Nathan to engage in conversation could only work to Calder's advantage. He shrugged. "It was simple enough. Reports from travelers of the engine noise narrowed it down. Then Willaby, over at *The Sentinel*, happened to recall this meadow had on occasion been used as a landing field. It was simply a case of putting the two together."

"I see," said Nathan, nodding his head in agreement. "Granted, running the engine was a risky venture. But necessary you'll agree to ensure it would perform correctly once in the air." His finger tightened on the trigger. "No matter, I'll correct the consequence of my misactions. Now turn and face the wall."

Higgins, not wishing to turn and face the prospect

of a certain death, was quick to interject. "Since the Inspector answered your question, perhaps you might satisfy my curiosity?"

Nathan hesitated. He mulled over the "Fair enough," he said. "What is it?"

"Aaaah," said Higgins stumbling over his words. He hadn't expected Nathan to agree so readily, and he struggled to come up with a suitable subject. "Er. That is... Well, I, I've often wondered, Fernell," he said, finally settling on a subject. "That's an odd sort of name. Is that your real name? Or is it, as I suspect, simply a code your clients use?"

"My real name?" Nathan gave a hardy laugh. "I'm flattered you think so highly of me, Sheriff." He shook his head. "No, I'm not Fernell. I am merely one of his faithful lieutenants. As to your question, *The Master* is known by many names. In Berlin he's called *Der Adler* or *Der Meister*. In London, most call him *The Master* or simply *Death*."

"But the bank? You were-"

"Oh, that." Nathan shook his head. "I'm afraid you've got a hold of the wrong end of the stick, Sheriff. The contents of the vault held little attraction for *The Master*. In fact, he had generously decided the spoils were to be divided up among the faithful." He looked to Calder. "By the way, Inspector, they won't be too pleased to learn your interference has deprived them of their just reward."

In answer Calder merely smiled. "Please extend my heartfelt apologies," he said. Calder could not let the conversation end there. As long as Nathan was willing to talk, there was a chance of figuring a way out of their predicament. All he had to do was to keep him talking. "I assume the primary reasoning for the machine's theft was to obtain the bomb release mechanism."

Nathan nodded. "Once its accuracy is demonstrated, its sale will bring a tidy sum on the open market."

"And what better audience to demonstrate the device to than the representatives of the world governments gathering at Camp Meade?"

"And the aeroplane?" said Higgins.

"Merely a means to demonstrate the device. Once the device has proven its worth, it will be removed from the aeroplane and the machine abandoned."

"I see," acknowledged Calder. "But indulge me, the bank. You went to a lot of effort merely to gain entrance."

Nathan shrugged. "Perhaps. I'll admit the tunneling did display a touch of theatrics. But I assure you the method of the robbery was intentional, it did have a role to play."

"And that would be?"

Keeping the revolver firmly trained on Higgins, Nathan smiled. "At this point I see little harm in telling you, Inspector." The smile deepened. "Especially since the theft of the machine and the robbery were conceived with you in mind."

Calder said nothing, but merely nodded in acknowledgment.

Nathan continued. "Both the theft and the robbery were intended to be The Master's personal requital ... revenge, if you prefer that term." Seeing the confused look on Higgins's face, he said, "Come now, Sheriff. Surely, you must realize The Master's never quite gotten over the Inspector's meddlesome interference in the steam gun case."

"I thought as much," said Calder. "Fernell didn't seem the type that would go quietly into the night."

Nathan nodded. "After the bank was relieved of the payroll, I was instructed to leave a small memento. Something appropriate. Something you would recognize as coming only from The Master. By the way, how was it you came to be waiting for me in the vault?"

"The dog. He heard the tunneling."

Nathan gave an all-knowing nod. "Ah yes, that

pesky Jack Russell terrier. It should have occurred to me, I noticed him digging in the alley several times."

Higgins's confusion only grew. "But, if you're not Fernell, then who-"

In the background the roar of an aeroplane engine sputtering to life filled the barn's interior, and prevented further conversation. Nathan paused, allowing the roar to settle back to a rough, throaty idle before he again spoke. "Who?" Nathan merely shook his head. "The Master is like a chameleon, Sheriff, capable of assuming any number of identities. Not even I am permitted to know which one is the real Fernell." The revolver swung from Higgins to Calder. "And now, Inspector, it's time."

Over Nathan's shoulder Calder caught a sudden flash of movement. He blinked, barely able to believe his eyes. At the very same window, where only moments ago he had stood, a mass of curly hair, followed by a set of incredibly violet/blue eyes appeared over the edge of the windowsill.

Victoria!

Holding a cautioning finger to her lips, Victoria motioned towards the barn's massive doorway. Before he could protest she slipped from view

What's she up to? He wondered. His question was soon answered when moments later the curls reappeared at the edge of the doorway.

"*Fool woman!*" he silently cursed, watching her clumsy attempt to peer around the edge of the doorframe. "*If Nathan spots her, he won't hesitate to use that gun.*" He forced his attention back to Nathan.

"One last question," he said, stalling for time. "Surely you can grant a condemned man that consideration."

It was clear the roar of the machine's engine had signaled an end to Nathan's willingness to talk. "Be quick about it," he snapped. Then, perhaps sensing the anxiousness in Calder's tone, half-turned to glance at the opened doorway.

Victoria, her approach masked by rumblings of the aeroplane's engine, had entered the barn. Seeing Nathan beginning to turn, she ducked behind a packing crate.

Calder's mind was now running at a feverish pace. He had to do something and fast. "Camp Meade," he blurted out in desperation.

Startled, Nathan turned, his attention focused on Calder. "Camp Meade? What about it?"

With Nathan's attention diverted from the doorway, Calder permitted himself the luxury of a cigarette, while he figured his next move. Under the watchful eye of Nathan, he carefully removed the cigarette tin from his pocket and extracted a Turk.

Nathan was becoming unsettled. "Never acquired the habit," he snapped, when Calder extended the tin in offering. "Now what's this about Camp Meade?"

Extinguishing the match, Calder released a thin stream of pale blue smoke, watching it waft upward into the still air before he again spoke. He was in no hurry. "This absurd plan of yours," he said finally. "It will never work, you know."

"No?"

Calder shook his head. "I think not. You see, the Army's been alerted. You don't think I'd be fool enough to come out here without first dispatching a telegram, do you? You'll not get within a mile of the conference before a cadre of sharpshooters open fire."

This was a lie, of course. A calculated gamble on Calder's behalf, but it had paid off handsomely. He now had Nathan's undivided attention.

"You're bluffing!" scowled Nathan.

Even with the rumbling of the aeroplane's engine in the background, the distinct, metallic click of the revolver's hammer being cocked was plainly audible.

"Am I? Perhaps. Pull that trigger and you will never know. But, on the other hand, if I'm not bluffing you'll be sending your master into a certain trap. If he survives, which I seriously doubt, he'll not forget who was responsible."

The last was not lost on Nathan. "I could make your own death exceeding slow, Inspector," he said. "I suggest you tell me exactly what you know about Camp Meade."

"Practically everything, I should say," Calder replied, taking a deep drag on his cigarette. "The government's scramble to perfect the bomb release mechanism, before international law prohibits its production, for instance. Of course, Fernell's intent was to use it and the aeroplane to disrupt the conference. Percival's presence confirms that." He paused. "There is one minor facet that puzzles me, however."

"What's that?"

"Fernell's goal. Is it to kill all the participants attending the conference, or, does he intend merely to demonstrate the proficiency of the bomb release mechanism before prospective bidders and drive up the price?"

Nathan did not respond. Indeed there wasn't time. With his attention again centered on Calder, Victoria had crept from her position behind the crate. She silently crossed the gap. With a leap worthy of a circus athlete, she pounced onto Nathan's back, driving him forward and pulling the baggy hood down over his face in the process. The gun discharged harmlessly as it sailed free, and was quickly retrieved by Higgins. Blinded, and taken by surprise, Nathan was powerless to rid himself of his attacker. Around and around they spun ... like two drunken sailors engaged in a tavern brawl, until at last, Calder stepped forward and with one well-aimed blow ended the melee.

Assisting Victoria to her feet, Calder took her in his arms. "You reckless little fool." He grinned. "If I wasn't so happy to see you I'd-"

Victoria, slightly out of breath and hair disheveled, lifted her violet/blue eyes to his. "You would what?" she cooed.

"I'd-"

"Sorry, Inspector." It was the familiar voice of Oney Parlor that broke the spell.

Calder turned to find a panting Oney had entered the barn. For the second time within the hour, the hapless stableman found himself in the awkward position of apologizing for the presence of Victoria.

"I tried, Inspector, I really did," Oney said, managing to regain his breath. "Miss Victoria's the spunkiest female I ever had the misfortune of running into. Barely had time to shut the automobile off, before she lit out into the woods in search of you. It was everything I could do to keep-" He paused long enough to look down at the unconscious form of Brother Nathan. "Well, well," he said. "What'd we got here?"

"I'll explain later," said Calder. "Here, give me a hand."

Together the two men dragged the unconscious form of Brother Nathan back into an out of the way corner. Propping him up against a post, they bound him with a length of rope taken from a nearby bench, but not before he had been stripped down to his union suit.

Oney's nose wrinkled in disgust. "What are you fixing to do with that filthy old rag?" he said, referring to Nathan's robe that Calder was in the process of pulling over his head.

"With any luck, this will be my ticket to capturing Fer-" Calder halted in mid-sentence. Oney knew nothing of the existence of Fernell, and Calder quickly corrected himself. "That is to say whoever is piloting Mr. Wright's aeroplane."

Oney appeared not to have noticed the blunder, and Calder sought out Higgins. Higgins, having taken possession of Brother Nathan's revolver, had stationed himself in the shadow of the barn's entrance. After noting his companion's new wardrobe, he jerked a thumb towards the opened doorway. "The machine's down at the end of the field."

"How many men?"

"Just Fernell and the one with the traveling case, as far as I can tell. If Nathan doesn't show up soon, they're going to get suspicious. What's the plan?"

"It's a bit unorthodox," admitted Calder, "but at this point, I'm afraid we're out of options."

"Unorthodox be dammed! We both can't just waltz down there, not out in the open." Higgins cast a suspicious eye at his companion. "And no matter what you say, I'm not leaving you to your own devices."

Calder pulled the hood up concealing his features. "Not to worry. They're expecting to see Brother Nathan coming from the barn, not me. I'll be all right until I reach the machine."

Higgins's eyes narrowed. He would not be left behind. "And what am I to do?"

Calder looked to his companion. "By now that other one has told Fernell of our capture. No doubt they've heard the gun go off, but it was only one shot. They'll be expecting a second one. Better fire another round."

Higgins quickly complied, discharging the gun through the open doorway.

"Now what?" he said, offering the gun to Calder.

Calder shook his head. "Leave the gun with Oney. Take the back exit. Stick to the tree line and keep out of sight. Work your way around to the rear of the machine. I'll get as close as I can wearing the robe. Once I'm close enough, you take the one with the case. I'll deal with Fernell."

"You're right," said Higgins. "It's not only unorthodox, it's downright foolhardy."

Nevertheless, he moved to the rear of the building, and opening a side door cautiously peered out. Seconds later he slipped through the opening and disappeared into the dense undergrowth.

With Higgins's departure Calder turned to Oney

and Victoria. "You two keep a sharp eye on Nathan," he said. "Should any of his confederates turn up," he gestured to the gun in Oney's hand, "that will serve you well. Use it." For Oney, there was one additional instruction. "There's an extra length of stout rope lying on the bench," said Calder. "Use it if she tries to follow me."

Chapter Thirty-one
An unexpected meeting

Calder exited the barn. The aeroplane, its engine belching black exhaust sat a short distance away. Lacking Nathan's beard, and not possessing the preacher's ungainly posture, Calder kept his head tilted earthward with the sides of the robe's hood gathered 'round. It was chancy. Approaching with the hood up would certainly appear odd, especially in this heat. His only hope was that it would stay his identity until the last possible moment. Then, if all went according to plan, it would be too late for Fernell to react. There would be no escape. *He would have him!*

All proceeded smoothly. As he neared the machine, Calder momentarily lifted his eyes, permitting himself the briefest of glances. As brief as the glance had been, it had been enough. As expected, there were just the two individuals. He recognized the one, the robed individual from the barn. He was standing alongside the machine, engaged in an animated conversation with the machine's pilot. As for the fiend, Fernell, well that was another matter. His true identity remained hidden under the leather-flying cap. With its elongated flaps tied at the chin, and goggles down over the eyes, the cap succeeded in obscuring all but a minor portion of the master assassin's features.

Fernell looked up. Mistaking Calder's approach for that of Brother Nathan, he waved a beckoning arm. "Ah, there you are, Nathan," he shouted over the roar of the engine exhaust. "Better get a move on, there isn't much time left."

Calder's brow furrowed.

That voice. It sounded strangely familiar. Could it be Gregson? After all, hadn't Fernell masqueraded as Gregson during his previous stay in Relay? Perhaps another look might decide the issue. "No," Calder decided, quickly dismissing the thought. He may not be close enough to identify Fernell, but Fernell would surely recognize him. He dare not risk discovery, not until he had narrowed the gap. He waved, acknowledging the call and increased his pace.

Now, mere feet from the machine, he could smell the engine's oily exhaust, and feel the backwash created by the machine's massive propellers swirling and tugging at the tattered edges of his robe. Despite the risk of discovery, he was forced to venture another stolen glance. He lifted his head ever so slightly – not much, just enough to avoid the propeller's lethal arc.

What greeted Calder's eyes was unbelievable. He stumbled, nearly losing his balance, then stood frozen in stark disbelief. On the portion of the wing that contained the pilot's seat sat... *Albert Delahaye.*

"Well? Hurry up, Nathan," Fernell commanded turning to make last minute adjustments on the air/fuel mixture control. "We don't have all day to dilly-dally. Climb aboard."

With Fernell's attention temporarily diverted by the uncooperative engine, Calder maneuvered his way past the sweep of the propeller to the edge of the wing. From the corner of his eye he saw Higgins emerge from the woods. Higgins, his steps masked by the engine's rumblings, was able to approach the robed individual undetected.

"*Good man*" Calder thought, as he watched Higgins drag the limp, unconscious form back into the underbrush. He turned, his attention again fixated on

Fernell. Now, nothing stood between him and putting an end to the master assassin and his evil scheme. Grabbing a strut he hoisted himself onto the wing's surface.

Perhaps sensing the danger, Fernell looked up. "*You!*" he shouted in disbelief. If there was any indecisiveness on Fernell's behalf, it lasted only a moment. He lunged for the cane. This action brought his torso in contact with the throttle, releasing it and shoving it forward. The machine gave a violent lurch, and lumbered forward. Calder was thrown backward, entangling himself in the maze of wire cables securing the wing struts.

Starting its taxiing roll, the machine began to pick up momentum, its wheels seemingly seeking out each and every depression in the meadow's uneven turf. With the control stick unattended the machine swerved, first to one side of the field then to the other, as it slowly worked its way down the grassy field. Despite this, Calder managed to regain his balance. Grabbing another strut, he began inching his way across the wing surface. His progress was agonizingly slow. More than once, he was thrown backward into the cables when one of the machine's wheels slammed into yet another depression.

As erratic as the machine's wanderings were, they were the least of Calder's problems. There was Fernell. Having succeeded in retrieving the cane, Fernell whirled, unleashing his pent-up fury on Calder. In the tight confines of the wing, the cane proved a formidable weapon. Repeatedly it found its mark, striking him across his upheld forearms.

Still, Calder refused to yield his grip. In reality, there was little choice for him but to endure the pain. To do other would cause him to be drawn into the arc of the propeller and certain death

Somewhere in the midst of this onslaught, one of Fernell's blows went astray. The sharpened tip of the cane nicked the fuel line resulting in a minor puncture. Immediately the air filled with a fine spray of gasoline. Occupying the pilot's seat forward of the spewing fuel line, Fernell was spared the consequences. Calder was not so fortunate. Caught between Fernell and the propeller, he was quickly enveloped by the acrid mist. His mouth filled with bitter tang of raw petroleum and his eyes burned with searing pain. Blinded, and no longer able to ward off the blows, Calder released his grip. He slid backward across the wing surface, then plunged downward. Somehow, he miraculously survived, avoiding the propeller's lethal path on his way to a safe, albeit abrupt landing on the meadow's grass. Groggily he sat up, lifted his head. The last he saw was a blurry image of the machine as it lifted skyward cleared a line of trees and disappeared into the afternoon sky. Soon, even the drone of its engine faded.

He uttered a silent curse. Fernell had managed to escape his grasp once more.

Chapter Thirty-two
The Reveal
Library – Old Dunham House

The occasion was Saturday brunch. At the completion of the meal, Calder and his guests retired to the relative coolness of the library where Mrs. C had an ample supply of her delicious sweet tea waiting.

Doctor O'Keefe, spying the latest edition of *The Sentinel* on the sideboard, was first to speak. "I'd say old Willaby really outdid himself this time," he said, gesturing to the bold headline — Respected clergyman arrested in the ill-fated bank burglary. Receiving no immediate response, he turned to his companions. "What's your thoughts on it Victoria?"

Victoria, in the process of selecting the smallest bonbon from the silver serving tray, looked up. "Me? Oh, I don't know. John does tend to sensationalize at times I suppose. Just be thankful there's no mention of brother Nathan's involvement with the machine's theft in any of the narratives. Or," she said, popping a dainty piece of chocolate into her mouth, "that scoundrel Fernell."

Dr. O'Keefe had moved to the teacart. At the mention of Fernell's name he paused, the heavy, crystal tea pitcher tilted precariously midway in the pour. "Let's pray it remains so," he said. "If Willaby had accidentally stumbled upon Fernell's existence, or if there had been even the slightest hint that Delahaye wasn't who he claimed to be, well..." His voice drifted off as he contemplated the insufferable consequents of such an event.

"It would be disastrous," said Victoria, completing the good doctor's thoughts. "Now we must act to ensure he never does."

Dr. O'Keefe, shaken from his reverie, frowned. "Just how do you propose we accomplish that?"

Victoria hesitated. Although normally quite willing to venture an opinion on any given topic, she wasn't prepared to voice her thoughts on this particular problem. This was due primarily to her not having – at least up until this point – considered the possibility.

"I'm really not quite sure," she said, cautiously. Then moving to more familiar grounds, she quickly added, "But I'll tell you this, John Willaby is not your average pressman. If that newspaperman's nose of his senses something's amiss, he'll not be put off or denied. Indeed, I fear he'll not be satisfied until he's ferreted out every last sordid detail."

"Well, yes," concluded Dr. O'Keefe, quick to appreciate the danger, "naturally we'll have to tread lightly there." He eased the pitcher down as he carefully weighed the consequences. "But more to the point," he added, "if Willaby should manage to uncover something our placid village life would be in for a drastic alteration." He shook his head in dismay. "Every blasted reporter from New York to St Louis would descend upon Relay like a biblical plague of locust."

From the opposite side of the room came the familiar voice of Sheriff Higgins. "Grant you, so far providence has seen fit to smile upon us in that regard. But Willaby's discovery of Delahaye's true identity will create another minor, but hellish problem — what to do about the colonel."

Victoria turned to Higgins. "The colonel?" She frowned. "I don't see what's the colonel's got to do with any of this. I thought we were discussing Willaby."

Higgins merely shrugged in response. "We are. "I'm just saying old Musgrave's not going to take too kindly to the situation, should Willaby find out."

His glass filled and the pitcher safely returned to the cart, Dr. O'Keefe retreated to his favorite chair by the fireplace. "Kindly to what, Grandville?" he groaned, easing himself down into the comforting depths of the armchair.

"Welllll..." Higgins smiled. A generous smile, one that graced his broad face from side to side. It was obvious he was taking a great deal of enjoyment in what he was about to reveal.

"Well what?" Dr. O'Keefe insisted. "Come now. Out with it man, stop meandering around the mulberry bush."

Seemingly in no hurry, Higgins stubbed out his cigarette, leaning back exhaled a thin stream of blue/grey smoke. He watched the haze as it carved a lazy path skyward. Finally, leaning forward he said, "I'm just saying it's going to kill the old codger when he finds out that he's been duped, that's all."

"Aaaaaaah." Now it was Dr. O'Keefe's turn to smile. "Now it's becoming clear," he said. "You're referring no doubt the alleged balloon incident and Musgrave role in saving Delahaye's life."

"Precisely, Doc," Higgins beamed. "Precisely."

Dr. O'Keefe frowned. "Let me see if I've got this right, Grandville. No Delahaye," he ticked off one finger, "therefore no battlefield heroics." A second finger appeared. "No battlefield heroics, no fabricated tale for old Musgrave to beleaguer us to death with." The frown transformed, warming into a smile. "I fail to find any misfortune in that," he said.

Higgins nodded but groaned. "As delightful as that prospect may appear, Doc, there's a fly in the ointment. Publicly exposing his battlefield heroics as made up will just about kill the old colonel."

While everyone suspected Col. Musgrave's tales

were, at best, somewhat embellished, the occupants of
Relay were a tolerant lot. Musgrave's unauthorized
assumption of the rank of Colonel was but one example
of the villagers' forbearances.

Reluctantly, Dr. O'Keefe was forced to concede.
"Yes, yes," he said, his head bobbing slowly in
agreement. "An unfortunate consequence of living in a
small village, where one's transgressions are an open
page." The old doctor's face suddenly brightened. He
chuckled softly. "But let's look on the bright side,
Grandville. The fact remains that it's one less
fabrication we'll be forced to suffer."

Higgins warmed to the prospect. "That would be
nice," he said. "Say Doc, you remember the time he
claimed he dined with Abe Lincoln up Gettysburg way?"
He slapped his knee in gleeful delight. "Dang! That was
one whopper of a tale if ever there was one. The old devil
nearly snookered us on that one."

"Do I!" chuckled the doctor in response. "How the
man manages to concoct such out and out fantasies, I'll
never know."

"Shame on the two of you," scolded Victoria.

Her effort to admonish her companions was
tempered by the fact that she also had been forced to
endure untold retellings of the colonel's alleged wartime
exploits. Like Higgins and Dr. O'Keefe, she did not look
forward to additional tales.

"The colonel's stories may be self-glorifying in the
extreme," she said. "That's true enough. But," she cast
an accusatory eye in Higgins's direction, "they're
essentially harmless embellishments of his past and no
more scattier than some I heard you spin Grandville
Higgins. I for one have no wish to see the colonel bear
the consequences of having his past revealed."

"Neither do we, Miss Victoria, said Higgins. "We
were just joshing."

Victoria, her brow knitted into a series of tight little
furrows, said, "Still the dilemma of John Willaby

discovering the truth is a real possibility, and one that we must prepare ourselves for."

"Don't fret yourself none, Miss Victoria," said Higgins reassuringly. "It's nothing that can't be resolved." To prove his point he set about conjuring up a workable solution. "Now, let's see," he said, his chin coming to rest between thumb and forefinger. "Perhaps we could... No, no, that will never do, John will never fall for that." He grumbled. Shaking his head, he slumped back into the depths of the chair only moments later to again spring to life. "Ah! I have it now," he said. "We'll, we'll..." Once more he lapsed into silence. In the end he was forced to concede there was little he could offer in the way of an alternative.

Calder had been content to sit quietly in the background, a silent observer to his guest's discussion. It fell upon him to come up with a workable solution. His plan was a simple one. "I suggest we let matters lay as they are," he said.

The astonished group turned to their host. "What?" they said in unison.

Calder moved to calm his companions. "If we are careful, watch our words, there is no reason Willaby or the colonel need ever to learn of Delahaye's deception."

Higgins spoke up. "Do nothing? Then you're willing to assure us Willaby will never find out."

Calder wasn't quite ready to go that far. He shook his head. "No, but it's not likely, is it? Look at the situation logically. There are several points to consider. One – There's nothing to overtly suggest Delahaye's connection to the machine's disappearance. Two – Delahaye's departure was not an unscheduled event. In fact, it had been previously announced. We had a farewell dinner right here in Old Dunham House with Willaby, himself, in attendance. More importantly, Delahaye's departure occurred days before the bank robbery and Nathan's arrest. Therefore it's not likely to draw Willaby's scrutiny."

"On the other hand, should we now choose to expose Delahaye, it would quite naturally lead to questions of his true identity."

"Or his purpose in coming to Relay and befriending Musgrave," said Victoria, quickly grasping Calder's reasoning.

Calder nodded. "From there, Fernell's existence and his involvement is a mere step away." He hoisted his glass as if to propose a toast. "Until such time Fernell is securely behind bars, I propose we let the colonel continued in bask unabatedly in his self-imposed glory."

"But another round of Musgrave's battlefield tales," moaned Higgins. "Have you no mercy, Inspector?"

Calder smiled. "Come now, Grandville. Surely your silence is a small pittance to pay for the continuance of the village's tranquil existence."

Higgins started to protest. "I hardly consider one of Musgrave's whoppers a pittance."

Calder shook his head, effectively ending further discussion. "Now Higgins, surely we agree the village's interest would best be served if Fernell's existence were kept safely tucked away." His gaze went to each of his companions. "I submit this is not the time to falter. Agreed?"

Reluctantly, one by one, each hoisted his glass in silent accord.

The glasses settled to the table, all except Calder's, his remained aloft. He turned to Victoria. "While on the subject of proposals, I would like to propose a somewhat belated toast to the heroine of the aerodrome incident."

Calls of "Hear, here," echoed in the room as the group turned to Victoria, their glasses raised.

"To Victoria," said Calder.

Caught unaware, but nevertheless pleased by the impromptu announcement, Victoria beamed in joyful anticipation.

"To Victoria," Calder repeated. "Without who's

valiant, though somewhat *scatty deductions,* we might not have-"

Too late! He had not meant to say it. *Shouldn't have said that,* he thought. *An accident, it had sort of spilled out over the tongue and there was no way to retrieve it. But blast-it-all! It was true. Despite serendipitously meandering down perilous paths, without plan or forethought, and with only the most ill conceived assumptions as her guide, Victoria had nevertheless managed to arrive at the correct conclusion, and much to his relief, emerged unscathed.*

The smile faded. Victoria, the blood rushing to her cheeks, whirled to face Calder. Her eyes blazed. "Scatty deductions indeed!" she huffed. "You are no doubt referring to my brilliant deductions on Fernell's presence in Relay?" Not bothering to wait for a response, she continued, "I'll have you know Mr. Donahue, that I had sufficient and good, well-founded suspicions of Delahaye and Fernell being one and the same from the very onset."

"What!" Calder thundered, spilling cigarette ash down the front of his shirt. "Hogwash! Come now, Victoria." He dabbed at his shirt front with his hand. "I'll admit I might have been just a tad overzealous in my assessment, and I appreciate your abilities as well as the next man, but you don't expect us to believe you were early on privy to Fernell's presence, do you?"

Victoria, her nose slightly a tilt, and with a smile on her lips that could only be described as bordering on devilish impertinence, nodded affirmatively. "I do."

"And yet," Calder huffed, "despite the inherent danger, you chose to say nothing to either the sheriff or myself of this miraculous revelation of yours?"

Again Victoria nodded. "Certainly."

"How in God's name did you manage to arrive at such an all-knowing position?"

"Women's intuition," Victoria replied, in a voice that left little doubt as to her conviction. "Now I wouldn't expect a mere man to understand such logic. I realize such comprehensions are well beyond the male of the species. But, if it's proof you require, proof you shall have."

The room fell silent. Only the tinkling of the ice being swirled in Higgins' glass broke the hush.

"Well?" Calder demanded after several anxious moments. "We're waiting."

"It was the eyes."

"Eyes?" stammered Higgins. "What in tarnation does someone's eyes have to do with it?"

"Why everything, of course. I for one took mindful note of Mr. Delahaye's eyes on the occasion of our first meeting."

"Yes, yes," urged Higgins. "Go on. What about his eyes?"

"Well. If you gentlemen will recall there is an artist rendering of Milford Gregson prominently displayed on the post office's board."

"Eyes? Artist rendering?" Higgins threw his hands up. "What the-"

Victoria sighed. "Must I remind you, Grandville? Fernell posed as Milford Gregson during his last visit to Relay."

"Yes, yes," Higgins grumbled, still not fully comprehending. "Your point being?"

Much in the manner of a schoolmaster lecturing a misbehaving class, Victoria balled her small hand into a fist, leaving only the forefinger erect. This she held like a fencer's épée. "If you had taken the time to compare the two," she said, "you would have found the two strikingly similar."

Calder was having none of this. "Poppycock! Pure unadulterated poppycock!"

"Oh," Victoria said, waving a dismissive hand. "Granted our Mr. Fernell is a master of disguise. And at times a dab of theatrical makeup, a false beard, or a pair of eyeglasses can misdirect one's focus. But, to conceal the intensity of one's eyes ... really, gentlemen." Shaking her head, she relaxed into the cooling recesses of the chair's leather and picked up her drink. "I do believe that would prove impossible, even for the celebrated talent of Fernell."

"Ah ha!" exclaimed Calder. "I have you there. As I recall you made the very same, and I might point out unsubstantiated, accusation against Agent Percival, not more than a week ago. Don't deny it now."

"Oh that," Victoria scoffed, quickly pooh-poohing the idea. "I might have mentioned the hypothetical possibility purely in passing. But unlike some people I could mention, I never honestly considered Percival among my list of viable suspects."

"That's all fine and dandy," interjected Higgins. "But as sheriff, my interest lies not in who successfully masqueraded as who, but rather with the more tangible aspects. That body we pulled from the river, for example. Tell me, was Brother Nathan responsible for that black deed or not?"

"Ah yes, the unfortunate demise of Brother Thaddeus," said Calder; relieved to see the conversation's focus had comfortably shifted away from him. "Had the misfortune of falling." Here Calder gave a slight pause. "Or could it be as I suspect, struck from behind and his body then thrown into the river?" He shrugged. "Alas, we may never know, but one should not rule out the possibility of Brother Nathan's involvement."

"And that brings up another question." The confusion on Higgins's face deepened. "I'd thought Fernell's objective was simply to burgle the bank and make off with the aeroplane. Brother Thaddeus's murder, if it was murder, unduly complicates matters. What's the motive, and how does it figure into all of this?"

"Purely a case of greed," explained Calder. "Thaddeus task was to reassemble the Wright machine after it had been removed from the flatcar and stored in the barn. Once that was completed, Nathan had no further need of his services. His demise left one less portion of the robbery spoils to split up. Also, it eliminated the worrisome problem of what Brother Thaddeus might reveal should he fall prey to the authorities. Remember the Wright aeroplane was equipped to carry only two occupants. Brother Thaddeus would quite naturally be left to his own devices once Fernell and Nathan had absconded with the machine."

"Murder? Greed?" mused Higgins. "Yes, yes I can see that connection, especially for someone as villainous as Nathan. However to dispose of the body in such an overt manner," Higgins shook his head, "and so close to the revival's grounds. Rather a foolhardy act I should think, even for the brazen likes of Brother Nathan."

"Not really," cautioned Calder. "As a member of Nathan's church, Thaddeus would have worked and resided at the revival grounds. It would appear suspicious *if* his body was discovered elsewhere. People would quite naturally question his presence away from the camp. Remember, it was only the purest of circumstances that his body became entangled in the roots of the willows lining the Patapsco. Had it not, it would have floated all the way to Baltimore, and eventually out into the bay without the benefit of discovery."

Dr. O'Keefe crushed out his cigarette. "Speaking of Brother Nathan and his role in this, he certainly went to a lot of effort to burgle a small town bank. Why not a daytime holdup like your common criminal would attempt? Much simpler and straight forward, wouldn't you say?"

"Ah!" exclaimed Calder. "Now you are beginning to see the workings of an evil mind. As you might well suspect this was to be more than a simple bank robbery. First dismiss your thoughts of this being a small town bank robbery. According to Banker Foxworth, the railroad's payroll being stored in the bank's vault was sizable, and would yield a substantial bounty to any would be robber. But mere money alone, substantial as it might have been, wouldn't be enough to entice Fernell to return to Relay. No, it was to be the theft and subsequent sale of the bomb release that would serve as his main enticement." He wigwagged a finger. "But there is one more element we must take into consideration, the element of revenge. Extracting revenge against Victoria would be most satisfying for Fernell, and certainly near the top of his agenda."

"Revenge? Victoria?" Doctor O'Keefe said. "Surely you're not suggesting the fiend harbors ill-feelings against her?" When he received an affirmative reply, he said, "But why in God's name? What does Victoria have to do with any of this?"

"Come, doctor. Have you forgotten that little incident in the cave? Rest assured Fernell has not."

"Ah yes," said Dr. O'Keefe, putting a match against a fresh cigarette. "The infamous dragon's claw episode. I confess I had momentarily forgotten about that. Judging from the amount of blood left at the scene, I'll wager its tines inflicted a rather nasty gash on its prey."

The dragon's claw was Dr. O'Keefe's colorful description of Victoria's handheld garden cultivator. A menacing looking weapon, it had been forged to her precise specifications by the local blacksmith out of hardened steel. Its four talon-shaped tines-honed to razor-like sharpness- and mounted on an eighteen inch hickory shaft was used to routinely dispatch the cement-like clumps of clay found in Relay's rocky soil. It was while fending off Fernell in the dark confines of a cave that Victoria had blindly lashed out with the tool. One of her blows found its mark, burying three of its tines into the fleshy portion of Fernell's shoulder.

"And one he'll not likely forget," swore Victoria, her anger, no longer directed towards Calder, had been firmly transferred to Fernell.

Calder continued. "The robbery of the bank would serve as Fernell's revenge. And in case we weren't clever enough and failed to recognize his participation, Nathan was instructed to leave a calling card."

"That's right!" said Higgins. "Nathan said as much when we nabbed him in the bank."

"To bad Nathan decided to stop talking at that point," said Calder. "One can't help but wonder what sort of calling card Fernell had in mind for us."

"Don't fret," said Higgins. "I'll wager a few weeks spent in the county jail with only beans and bread will loosen that pious tongue of his. Running a thumb under a suspender strap, he gave a boastful tug. "Then we'll see just how far Nathan's loyalty stretches. Not very far would be my guess. He'll be more than willing to swap information on that and more of our questions for a more comforting berth. I wouldn't be surprised if he decides to turn nose on Fernell's whereabouts."

"Not very likely," mused Calder. "One must not confuse loyalty with fear. As it stands Nathan has only a finite amount of time to serve. Remember, attempted burglary is looked upon as a minor felony; it doesn't carry a particularly harsh sentence. Eventually Nathan will have to be set free. On the other hand, if he chooses to break his silence and cooperate with the authorities, there will be a much harsher penalty levied on him."

Higgins slumped back. "By that you mean Fernell. It always comes down to Fernell, doesn't it?"

Calder nodded. "His tentacles stretch far and wide. Prison walls would pose no obstacle for a man of his talents. The warden would do well to keep a sharp eye on Brother Nathan. Unless I miss my guess when the time comes, Fernell will come up with a proper scheme to free him."

There was a brief period of silence before Calder again spoke. "There is one more person we have yet to discus."

"Oh, who's that?"

"Priscilla Hopkins."

"Priscilla? You're right," said Higgins. "In all the commotion I've forgotten about her and her predicament. I'll check on her the minute I get back to town."

"I don't think that will be necessary."

Setting aside his drink, Higgins said, "Why not?"

"Unless I miss my guess, I think you'll find Miss Hopkins is no longer a guest of the Viaduct Hotel." Checking the clock on the fireplace mantle, Calder added, "In fact, she's probably at some Washington garden fête, enjoying the lawn tennis and sipping afternoon cocktails."

"Washington? But what about her brother?" said a confused Higgins. "Surely she wouldn't just up and leave without finding him."

"Ah! But you see there never was a brother."

"What? You mean it was all a sham?"

Calder nodded. "I'm afraid so."

"But why?"

"For that we must return to Miss Hopkins's first appearance. My suspicions were aroused when she appeared on the scene so soon after the machine's disappearance. Too quickly to be a mere coincidence. I am not a believer in coincidences, not when it comes to crime. So when we failed to find any evidence to document her brother's disappearance, I had Mother check." Moving to the desk, he removed a telegram from the center drawer. "This arrived this morning.

'*Investigation reveals no record of Priscilla Hopkins or a brother at addresses supplied. Re. Law firm Baumgartner and Owens, not known this city Address is vacant office. Most likely scenario a mail drop. Regards Mother.*'"

Dr. O'Keefe fumbled for his cigarette case. "A pity," he said, shaking his head. "And she was such a handsome girl too. I guess it goes to show you can never tell. Odd though, she didn't strike me as being the type to become entangled with the likes of Fernell."

Calder shook his head. "You've got it all wrong, doctor."

"Then-"

"Miss Hopkins is certainly not a criminal. Quite the contrary just the opposite. Miss Hopkins, although that most certainly isn't her correct name, is in all likelihood a government agent, a confederate of Agent Percival. As I see it she needed a plausible reason for her presence in Relay, something that wouldn't draw attention or arouse suspicion. Posing as the grieving sister of the fictitious Roger Hopkins did that quite well, don't you think? From her position she could report any new developments directly to Percival. All in all a very satisfactory arrangement."

"And what of all those official-looking letters she received?" said Victoria.

"I'm guessing here," replied Calder, "but we can safely assume they were communiqués from Washington. Percival couldn't very well make use of the telephone or telegraph as a means of direct communications with his superiors for fear of becoming compromised. If the letters were addressed directly to him, they ran the risk of being read or intercepted by Fernell's men. However, no one would suspect a poor, grieving young woman of being involved in something as grandiose as the theft of an aeroplane."

"No one but you," said Higgins. "But, what I can't figure out is how Fernell was so dang sure the train would stop at Grinder's Ridge. Passenger trains rarely stop there to take on water."

"Good point, Higgins. I'll attempt to answer that, although certain portions are mere assumptions on my part. To start we know Fernell, posing as Delahaye, was a passenger on The Royal Blue. Orville Wright, himself, confirmed this by his conversation with Delahaye in the dining car, while the engine refilled its water tank at

Grinder's Ridge."

"Ah! No doubt to distract the brothers while his gang of thieves uncoupled the flatcar," observed Dr. O'Keefe.

"Very observant of you, Doctor."

"Delahaye, or Fernell if you prefer, observing the addition of the flatcar at the Point of Rocks station, and the engineer's failure to take on water, made a very shrewd decision. He alerted his gang by telegraph of the train's possible stop at Grinder's Ridge."

There was a light tapping at the door and the diminutive form of Mrs. Chaffinch appeared. "Beg pardon, Inspector," she said. "The afternoon post's arrived. There's a package from a Sheriff Jones."

Calder unwrapped the thin, cylindrical package. "Well, well." He looked to his companions. "It seems at least one of our questions has been answered."

"Oh? Which one?"

"Fernell's calling card." Removing a gentleman's walking stick from the wrappings, he said, "Albert Delahaye's cane."

"Is there's a note?"

"Two, in fact," said Calder. "The first is from Sheriff Jones and tells of the Wright's machine recovery."

"That's good news," said Higgins. "Does he say where?"

Consulting the note, Calder replied, "In a pasture a short distance west of Ollea. It seems the ruptured fuel line caused the machine to prematurely run out of gasoline. Fernell was forced to land and abandon the machine."

"Quite naturally there wasn't a trace of the scoundrel to be found."

"You're right there, Higgins. Fernell managed to make good his escape before the aeroplane was discovered. Upon the sheriff's arrival there was just the machine and the cane. It was left on the seat along with instructions requesting that it be forward to me.

"And the bomb sight?"

"It's safe. Fortunately its size and bulk prevented its removal." Calder looked to Dr. O'Keefe. "There's a post script. Sheriff Jones says to thank Dr. O'Keefe for his valuable assistance in the drowning case."

Dr. O'Keefe gave a gentlemanly nod. "A most knowledgeable fellow that Sheriff Jones." He looked to Higgins, smiled. "If I must say so, Grandville, one who appreciates good sound medical advice when he hears it."

"Spare me," groaned Higgins. Turning to Calder, he said, "You said there was two notes, Inspector. I take it the second is more of a personal nature."

"Yes." For the first time concern registered on Calder's features. Handing the folded slip of paper to Victoria, he said, "It's addressed to Victoria."

"Me?" Surprised, Victoria took the paper unfolded it and began to read. Moments later, visibly shaken she sat back, her hands trembling.

"What is it, my dear?" said a concerned Dr. O'Keefe raising from his seat and rushing to her side.

"I'm, I'm not sure. It's as if someone had just walked over my grave." She passed the paper to Higgins.

Higgins taking the paper began to read out loud. "My wound has healed. However, it will remain a constant reminder of our last encounter. I look forward to our next meeting."

"The unremitting gall of the man," huffed Dr. O'Keefe.

Calder swore. "Then it's as I feared," he said. "We haven't seen the last of the scoundrel."

EPILOGUE
Bounce's Day In Court

The village town council met on the first Monday of the month. Normally the hearings were a sparsely attended affair, predictably dull and devoid of any meaningful controversy. However with Longfellow's thinly disguised petition to do away with Bounce scheduled for review, September's meeting quickly captured the village interest. To accommodate the anticipated large turnout the village schoolhouse was pressed into service. Windows were flung open. Overhead a lone paddle fan droned, swirling the already stale, lifeless air.

With the exception of the presence of Clem Simpson, the proceedings had taken on an almost courtroom-like atmosphere. Clem, oblivious to his surroundings, sat quietly dosing in the far corner of the room. Whether it was from sheer boredom, lack of sleep or too much cheap wine, one couldn't really be quite sure.

Calder, acting as the petition's chief opponent, sat at the opposition's table. Victoria sat to his left. Bounce, freshly brushed and on his best behavior, occupied the chair between. Leaning moral support was The Wednesday Night Club. They occupied the front row and consisted of Higgins, Colonel Musgrave, Father Meguiar, followed by Dr. O'Keefe and John Willaby, editor of the village newspaper.

Longfellow, with Nora Battington at the ready, were the sole occupants of the petitioner's table.

The proceedings had been going on for the better part of an hour. Calder, contrary to everyone's expectations, had not put forth a single challenge to any of Longfellow's numerous and somewhat questionable assertions. Instead, he was content to while away his time drawing mindless doodles on a notepad.

Despite Nora's overbearing presence, and her constant interruptions to correct even the most minor inconsistency, Longfellow had succeeded in establishing a very convincing case. Faced with no opposition, it appeared only a matter of time before the town council would be compelled to approve their petition.

To say Victoria was becoming concerned would be an understatement. Calder had repeatedly assured her he had a plan that would save Bounce. What this plan was, or how it was to unfold, he hadn't said. So far she could see little, if anything, he had done in that vein. True, he had spoken out, but that had been only once and it was not to challenge Longfellow, but merely to inquire if Longfellow was in fact the sole proprietor of The Scarlet Lady Pub. Receiving an affirmative reply, he returned to his doodling.

Even the three town commissioners seemed perplexed by Calder's lack of participation. "Inspector," the senior member on the panel inquired, when Longfellow had raised a particularly dubious point. "Would you care to challenge Mr. Longfellow on *any* portion of his last statement?"

To this, as he had done with prior queries, Calder merely shook his head. "If it pleases the council, not at this time."

"Calderrrrr!" Victoria hissed, jabbing a stiff elbow into her companion's ribs. "For heaven's sake don't just sit there doodling. *Do something!*"

Giving her a reassuring pat on the hand, Calder said, "All in good time, Victoria. All in good time." He turned, his gaze sweeping over the packed schoolroom. "Rather a large turnout for a council meeting, don't you think?"

Victoria did not answer. With a groan of despair she slumped backward in her seat.

It was at this point that there came a stirring from the rear of the room as the schoolroom's double doors swung open. "Aaaaah," said Calder, checking his watch. "Right on schedule."

Spectators made way as the frail form of lawyer Kratchet, a pair of gold-rimmed pince-nez resting on his snipe-thin nose, wove his way through the crowd.

"Begging the council's indulgence," Kratchet said, approaching the commissioners table. "But I have several documents I'd like to offer into evidence on the opposition's behalf."

The head commissioner frowned. It was clear he wasn't happy with the action of the lawyer or his unscheduled appearance. Leafing through the panel's agenda, he said, "I see no notation you were scheduled to appear before the board, counselor." He checked his watch against the long case clock on the far wall. "It's getting late and we were about to declare a recess."

Kratchet gave a slight bow. "A thousand pardons for my inexcusable tardiness."

Unmoved, the commissioner reached for his gavel, intent on putting an end to Kratchet's intrusion. "Any business you may have before this council can wait until-"

But the crafty old lawyer would not be dismissed so easily. "If I may be granted but a few minutes of the council's valuable time," he persisted, "I'm sure I could clear matters up to council's satisfaction." He paused, wiping the beads of sweat from his forehead with an overworked handkerchief. "Then perhaps we might adjourn to the veranda of the Viaduct Hotel for a cooling glass of Miss Julia's sweet tea."

The commissioner conferred with his colleagues.

Obviously tiring of Longfellow's apparent willingness to drone on and on, it didn't take long to reach a decision. "That would be a Godsend, counselor," he said, returning the gavel to its resting place. "The board recognizes Counselor Kratchet."

Kratchet held aloft a large packet of paper. "If it please the council I'll begin with a brief summation of the Battington/Longfellow petition."

Well aware of Kratchet's penchant for long-winded oratories, a collective groan rose from the villagers. They had come expecting to witness the undoing of Nora Battington at the hands of the inspector, or at the very least a spirited debate with Longfellow. So far they had seen neither.

Ignoring the rumblings, Kratchet continued, "In its purest form the petition states the owner of any animal found running free, or creating a public nuisance shall be charged under Art. 27 of the county code. Further, if said owner cannot be found, the animal is to be declared a stray and is to be put down." He looked to the commissioners for confirmation. "I assume, gentlemen, we are in agreement on those articles."

The three commissioners nodded in unison. "That is how the petition is so written," responded the chairman.

Kratchet whirled, pointed a boney finger at Longfellow. "Then gentlemen, I find it most ironic that under those very conditions Mr. Longfellow has so elegantly penned that he, as the petition's co-author, would be the first to be in direct violation."

"What!" Longfellow bellowed, springing from his seat.

"Oh, I can assure you it's quite true, Mr. Longfellow," smirked Kratchet. "And as an officer of the court, I would be remiss in my duty if I didn't call upon Sheriff Higgins to immediately, upon the bill's passage, place you under confinement."

There was a moment of stunned silence. Then, as

the weight of his words sunk in, the room erupted into a loud roar of laughter.

"That's utter poppycock," shouted Longfellow over the dim. "What kind of nonsense are you trying to pull, Kratchet? You know very well I'm not the owner of any animal." He shook an accusatory finger at the petitioner's table. "Especially one that is as vicious and vile as that animal."

Ignoring Longfellow for the moment Kratchet turned his attention to the commissioners. "It's interesting that the petitioner should use the term vicious animal," he said, "for that brings me to my second point." Withdrawing several copies of the county code from his briefcase, he handed each commissioner a copy. "I direct the panel's attention to page 145, Art. 27 of the county code, entitled Harboring of a vicious and Biting Animal, with special attention to subsection two, definitions. I quote verbatim:

Any individual/firm or establishment who knowingly gives, furnishes or permits its employees to provide food, shelter, or care to any animal domesticated or wild, or knowingly permits such acts to occur while under his/her control, shall be deemed by the court to be the legal owner/guardian of said animal. And further down the page, under the subsection Fines, we find. Upon conviction owner/guardian of said animal shall be guilty of a misdemeanor. Further each calendar day shall be considered to be a separate offense, punishable by the fine of not less than one, or more than two dollars, and/or one day in confinement in the county jail or both.

"Enough of this foolishness," retorted Longfellow. He thumped the desk with his fist. "This is some sort of legalized mares nest Kratchet has concocted. I have committed none of those acts."

Placing his briefcase on the table, Kratchet looked to the panel. "With the council's permission, I call Mr. Clem Simpson to the witness stand."

"I protest," shouted Longfellow. "This isn't a court

of law. I'm not on trial here."

The commissioner, thoroughly enjoying the sudden turn of events, banged his gavel. "Perhaps not, Mr. Longfellow, and since this is *not* a court of law, this panel is not bound by the laws of jurisprudence. However, as stewards of the village, we are duty bound to hear from all parties." He nodded to Lawyer Kratchet. You may proceed, counselor."

Someone nudged Clem, rousting him from his slumber. Clem rose, yawned, and giving a scratch to his unkempt hair, ambled to the front of the room.

"Now Mr. Simpson," Kratchet said, after Clem had seated himself in the hastily provided witness chair. "How long would you say have you known the defendant, Bounce?"

Longfellow again sprang from his chair. "Defendant? Really, I must protest. There is no such thing as a defendant in this hearing." He turned to glare at Bounce. "He's a dog, for God sake."

With a wave of the hand the commissioner dismissed Longfellow. "Protest noted. Answer the question, Clem."

"Well, sir..." Clem rubbed his chin. "Neigh on two years I'd say. If memory serves, it were during that bitter cold spell in of nineteen and ten, when old Bounce first came round." Clem, his lower lip pushed out, slowly shook his head. "He was a pitiable sight to behold. Chilled, nearly to the bone ye might say. Curled himself up next to the fireplace over at The Scarlet Lady, he did. Been there ever since."

"I see. And what about Mr. Longfellow? To the best of your knowledge, did Mr. Longfellow at that time, or anytime since, ever attempt to evict the defendant from his establishment?"

Clem shook his head. "No sir. Not that I knows of. Oh, they've had their differences from time to time like most folks do, but weren't nothing serious, not really."

The commissioner peered over his half glasses at

Longfellow, making several hastily scribbled notations in the process.

Happily launched and well away, Kratchet continued his questioning. "He looks well, wouldn't you say?"

"Mr. Longfellow?" Clem responded somewhat confused, once more sparking the room into laughter.

"No, no," chuckled Kratchet, motioning to Bounce. "I was referring to the dog."

"Oh," said Clem. "It's Old Bounce, you be speaking of. Why, I'd say he's as sound as a new dollar."

"And what do you contribute this remarkable health to?"

Clem didn't hesitate. "Oh Mr. Longfellow's cook, Ivy, for sure. Yes sir, she sees to it old Bounce gets his daily ration of kitchen scraps." Clem gave a wink and an all-knowing nod. "And many a times I've seen customers slip him a bite or two under the tablecloth."

"Under the table, you don't say. Well, well." Kratchet looked to the table where Longfellow sat, his head in his hands. "And was this done with Mr. Longfellow's full knowledge and consent?"

"Oh I don't know anything about knowledge and consent. But, if you be meaning, did Mr. Longfellow know about it?" Clem shrugged. "I'd say more than likely he did."

Longfellow slumped deeper in his chair.

"And what about his coat? This time Kratchet took the precaution of adding, "I'm referring of course to the defendant, Bounce. It certainly appears to be spotlessly clean. Is he always that well-groomed?"

"Naaaaa." Clem said, pausing to dig at the pesky fleas feasting on his sockless ankles. "If the truth be told, he's not always that clean. Why only last week that there agent feller-"

At this Kratchet broke in. By agent feller, you're referring to Federal Agent Percival, are you not?"

Clem nodded. "Yes sir, that's the one."

"Please continue," Kratchet urged.

"Like I was a-saying last week, I believe it were on a Tuesday, that agent feller was a-complaining about Old Bounce."

"About his cleanliness?"

"No." Clem shook his head. "Weren't that exactly. It were that god-awful smell. Most likely Old Bounce had gone and rolled in something dead, for he stunk powerfully strong."

"I see. And what did Mr. Longfellow do?"

"Well, Mr. Longfellow, he told me to take Bounce out back and give him a bath, and not to come back until he was good and clean."

Kratchet turned to the spectators. "Mr. Longfellow said that, did he?"

Clem nodded. "Yes sir he did."

"And don't come back until he is good and clean, those were the exact words he used?"

Clem's head bobbed. "The very same."

Asked what action he took in response to the directive, Clem replied, "Why, I gave him a good scrubbing with hot water and tar soap, of course. Even sprinkled a little lilac water on him when I finished." Clem hooked a thumb behind a suspender strap, gave a boastful tug. "If I have to say so myself, he smelled right proper after that."

"Lilac water," repeated Lawyer Kratchet, making sure its effect wasn't lost on the commissioners, or the villagers. "That's a rather expensive commodity, tonic water for an animal. I must say that was certainly a splendid gesture on your part, Clem."

"My part?" Clem chuckled. "Why, you've got hold of the wrong end of the stick, Mr. Kratchet. Weren't no gesture on my part. No, sir, it were the other way round." Clem looked across to the table where Longfellow sat slumped over, his head buried in his hands. Clem smiled. "It were all Mr. Longfellow's doings."

"The lilac water?" Kratchet said in mock surprise. "You're saying Mr. Longfellow supplied that commodity, along with the soap and water?"

Clem nodded affirmatively.

Kratchet turned to the spectators. "And what remuneration did you receive for your services?"

Clem twisted his brow into a mass of lines. "Re-re-remuneration?"

Turning back, Kratchet said, "That is to say, were you compensated... paid for your labors?"

"Oh," replied Clem. "You mean did I get pay. Why didn't you say so? Of course I got paid." Here Clem pulsed to smile in Longfellow's direction. "Mr. Longfellow's a right generous man when it comes to pay. He had Ivy fix me up with a right proper meal when I was done. Even gave me two bits to boot."

Longfellow leapt to his feet.

"If it pleases the council, upon further consideration my colleague and I would like to withdraw our petition."

This caught Nora by surprise. "You can't let them get away with this," she hissed. "Do something. Object!"

"Hush, woman!" Longfellow ordered.

"But the petition, you're not going to stand for-"

"The petition be damned! As it is, I'll be lucky if I don't wind up in the dock before old Judge Finnery. Everybody knows the man's got a soft spot for animals ... especially that dog." Longfellow looked across to where Bounce sat. "I've seem him shared his lunch with that damn dog on more than one occasion."

"But-"

"No more buts!" Longfellow held his hand up cutting off further conversation "The way I see it, it's my neck on the chopping block, not yours."

* * *

Later, at The Scarlet Lady Pub, Calder was attempting to console Longfellow.

"Oh, cheer up, Longfellow. Things aren't all that bleak."

Longfellow groaned as he continued wiping down the already spotless bar.

"Look at it this way," Calder continued. "You are now the proud owner of a wonder dog ... a genuine hero some might say. If you are clever enough, you can turn this to your advantage."

Longfellow looked up. "To my advantage? How?"

"It's plain enough a blind man could see it," replied Calder "Word will spread. People from miles around will come to your establishment and willingly lay their money down, just for the privilege of seeing the dog that foiled a bank robbery ... not to mention assisting in the eventual recovery of the Wright brother's aeroplane. Think of the money. There's bound to be newspaper articles, interviews with magazines complete with photographs, maybe even a dime novel or two. Damn Longfellow," he said, taking a sip of his beer, "You're sitting on a goldmine. I'm surprised a man of your business skills didn't work it out for yourself."

Longfellow paused in his duties, trying to envision the possible financial rewards the inspector hinted at. His eyes drifted to the fireplace, where Bounce laid peacefully dozing on the cool hearthstones. Bounce's legs gave several sharp twitches, as if he were in dreamily pursuit of a tasty rodent ... or, could it possibly be Longfellow's trouser cuff was his prey.

There was little doubt in Longfellow's mind where Bounce's sentiments lay.

His dream of riches gone, Longfellow picked up his cloth and renewed his polishing.

"Bah! Pesky, little beast," he grumbled.

The End

Other books by the author

All Aboard for Murder

A political thriller set in 1992 Baltimore

The Inspector Donahue Mysteries

… and Dance by the Light of the Moon

Murder at the Viaduct Hotel

IS WRITING A FORM OF TELEPATHY?

I think so. If done correctly we cannot only connect over distances, but also back in time. While I don't expect you to see Inspector Donahue, Victoria and the remainder of the zany inhabitants of Relay exactly as I do, I would hope that we are close. Are we?

Let's compare. Drop me a line at rt@rtraybooks.com and tell me what images you saw. How did the village of Relay appear in your mind's eye? Were you able to walk its cobbled stone streets or enjoy a Stoudt Lager in The Scarlet Lady pub?

What are your thoughts on the sadistic Fernell? If you by chance met someone with the same name, would the image of an ice pick spring to mind? If so, did it force you to double-latch your door before retiring?

While not a contest, I promise to read each response and should one catch my eye I'll send you your choice of one of my books.

Visit my web site **www.rtraybooks.com**

5720827R00132

Made in the USA
San Bernardino, CA
18 November 2013